TO:

A SMALL TOWN ROMANCE

If You GIVE A SINGLE Dad A NANNY

♡/ AE

ANN EINERSON

To: Nicole

Cover Design by Sarah, Okay Creations

Edited by Paula Dawn, LilyPad Lit; Nicole McCurdy, Emerald Edits; Tabitha, @probablyalovestory; Bryanna, @bryannareads

Proofread by Victoria Ellis, Cruel Ink Editing + Design

Formatting by Cathryn Carter, Format by CC

For those who have struggled to find their place. Family isn't defined by those who are biologically related to you. It's the people who love you unconditionally, support your dreams, and stand by you no matter what.

PLAYLIST

She's a Rainbow - The Rolling Stones
Colors - Stella Jang
Girls Just Want to Have Fun - Cyndi Lauper
Cover Me in Sunshine - Pink
Material Girl - Madonna
Rainbow - Meghan Trainor
How You Get the Girl - Taylor Swift
Pillowtalk - Zayn
I Want to Dance with Somebody - Whitney Houston
If You Let Me - Alina Baraz
Until I Found You - Stephan Sanchez & Em Beihold
Terminal - Echosmith
Paris - Taylor Swift
You Are The Best Thing - Ray LaMontagne
Home - Edward Sharpe & The Magnetic Zone

AUTHOR'S NOTE

Hey, Reader!

Thank you for picking up *If You Give a Single Dad a Nanny*. From the moment Dylan and Marlow made a cameo in *If You Give a Grump a Holiday Wishlist* they held a special place in my heart, and I knew I had to give them the happy ending they deserved. This is an interconnected standalone and was written to be read on its own.

If You Give a Single Dad a Nanny is a single dad/nanny, age gap, he's grumpy, she's sunshine, banter-filled, spicy small town romance. It'll tug at your heartstrings, and have you swooning over Dylan and Marlow's unexpected connection, and ultimately their all-encompassing love.

Marlow has neurodivergent tendencies. As I wrote her story it didn't feel right to give her a specific diagnosis, given the variability of neurodivergent symptom presentation.

If You Give a Single Dad a Nanny contains explicit sexual content, profanity, and mention of an absentee parent. Reading is meant to be your happy place—choose yourself, your needs, and your happiness first!

Xoxo,

Ann Einerson

If you give a single dad a neighbor, he may be tempted to ask her to be his daughter's nanny. And if he asks her to be his daughter's nanny, he'll start to have feelings for her. He'll want to invite her over for dinner and take care of her when she's sick, and then he'll kiss her in the hallway and call her a "good girl" in the back of an art gallery because she's all he's been able to think about…

CHAPTER ONE

DYLAN

"Daddy, I'm hungry and bored," Lola complains.

She flits into the kitchen, wearing a rainbow-colored tutu paired with a fuchsia shirt adorned with a unicorn on the front. Her long blonde hair, pulled back into a half ponytail and accessorized with a sparkly red bow, sways as she spins to the rhythm of the classical music playing in the background.

I chuckle at her dramatics. "I left a bowl of carrot sticks and blueberries on your craft table." I nod to the other side of the room. "You can eat those while you wait for dinner."

It's no easy feat keeping a highly energetic five-year-old entertained.

"I love blueberries," she declares.

"I know you do."

She goes off in search of her snacks, and I turn my focus back to preparing her lunch for school tomorrow. I carefully assemble her lunchbox, filling it with cherry tomatoes, carrot sticks, blueberries, cheddar cheese cubes, hummus, and pita bread cut into the shape of a unicorn. The final touch is a pink sticky note with *have a magical day* written on it.

After putting the packed lunch in the fridge, I gather the ingredients required to make chicken noodle soup for dinner.

The life of a single parent requires juggling a never-ending schedule and a list of to-dos, but I wouldn't trade my world for anything. I place the carrots and celery on the counter just as Lola's infectious laughter fills the air. I look up to find her with her face pressed against the sliding glass door, her eyes sparkling with excitement as she surveys the backyard.

"Ladybug, what are you doing? I thought you were hungry."

"I am, but there's a dog rolling around in the snow. He's so cute and fluffy," she exclaims. "Can I go play with him? Pretty please?" She clasps her hands together.

Aside from her unwavering love for unicorns and rainbows, Lola's newfound fixation is *Bluey*, a cartoon dog. While she's been asking for a dog for the past few months, the addition of an imaginary one in our backyard is a recent development.

"Maybe later." I take a knife out to chop the vegetables when I hear the unmistakable sound of barking from outside. I step over to the bay window overlooking our backyard, and lo and behold, there's a medium-sized dog rolling around in the snow with its tongue hanging out.

What the hell is a dog doing in our backyard?

"Isn't he the cutest dog in the whole wide world?" Lola squeals. "He really wants to play with me." She's practically bouncing on her feet with uncontainable anticipation.

"Ladybug, I need you to stay inside. It could be dangerous."

The dog could have rabies. Its erratic behavior definitely seems abnormal.

"He doesn't look dangerous," she states matter-of-factly.

"We're not taking any chances. Stay inside," I instruct in a gentle tone as I put on my shoes.

She folds her arms across her chest, pouting as I open the sliding glass door and step outside.

I stride across the deck, and the dog stops its playful antics, turning my way when it hears me. I note its unique combination of one brown and one blue eye and a distinctive tri-colored coat in white, black, and tan. Despite sharing several characteristics of an Australian Shepherd, this dog is smaller and has a long torso, short legs, and ears that are comically large for its body.

As I approach, a woman's voice grabs my attention.

"Waffles, get back here," the stranger whisper-shouts. "You can't go into other people's yards without an invitation. You're going to get us into trouble."

"What the…" I trail off as I spot a woman with long blonde hair in two fishtail braids, straddling the wooden fence running the perimeter of the left side of my property. I can see the top rung of a ladder on the other side that she must have used to climb over.

Her outfit is vibrant and colorful—a bright pink puffer coat, faded floral overalls, and silver sneakers with ribbon laces. She's most certainly not dressed for a winter in Maine.

"Hi there, new neighbor." She waves at me with a broad smile, losing her balance in the process.

Shit. She's going to fall.

I run down the steps of the deck and race toward her just as her hand slips. I open my arms to catch her, but the force of her falling sends me sprawling backward. The impact knocks the wind out of me, and I grunt when I make contact with the ground.

"Oh, no," the woman cries out as she falls awkwardly on my chest with a thud.

Once I've regained control of my breathing, I prop myself up on my elbow and give her a once-over to make sure she's okay. The last thing I need is for a stranger to complain that they got hurt in my backyard.

Relief washes over me when she finally lifts her head, and I draw in a deep breath as her gaze meets mine. I'm greeted with a captivating combination of one blue and one green eye. She has a pert nose, full, inviting lips and her cheeks are flushed as she looks down at me. I'm struck by the thought that I've never met someone this uniquely beautiful.

3

"Thanks for catching me." The woman lets out a melodic laugh as she pushes against my chest and stands up.

She has a smudge of yellow paint on her cheek, and I suppress the urge to wipe it off with my thumb. I'm so lost in my admiration that I'm caught off guard when the dog suddenly darts across the yard, heading for the house.

I scramble off the ground and sprint in the same direction. When I get to the backdoor, I find Lola on the ground, giggling uncontrollably while the dog playfully licks her face. I kick my shoes off before going inside and pulling the dog off Lola. She shoots me a disapproving scowl.

Feet slapping against the floor has me turning to find the woman from the backyard has followed me inside, trailing snow and dirt along with her. This is why I've stood my ground when Lola begs me to get a dog. They're messy, unpredictable, and high-maintenance—all things I like to avoid.

I prefer things to be organized and predictable, which is why I thrive when I have a routine and a structured environment. It's especially challenging to adjust to unexpected changes.

"Oh gosh, Waffles, what have you gotten yourself into now?" The woman puts her hands on her hips like she's scolding a child.

"Your dog scared my daughter," I say with concern, gesturing to the furry culprit.

"No, he didn't, Daddy," Lola chimes in. "Waffles was just giving me kisses, weren't you, boy?" She rewards the mutt with a good scratch behind the ear, and he thumps his tail, reveling in the attention.

I wince at the obscene amount of hair now on Lola's clothes. This is great. She's already calling the dog by its name. Next thing I know, she's going to invite him over for a playdate.

I pinch the bridge of my nose, praying for patience. Dealing with a pair of intruders before dinner wasn't on tonight's schedule.

"Waffles is completely harmless," the stranger says. "He was just eager to meet his new neighbors."

"Who are you?" I tilt my head at her.

This woman might be attractive, but her lack of manners and careless attitude are bothersome. She's making herself right at home, without considering the possible intrusion she's caused by coming into someone's house uninvited.

"Oh, sorry, I forgot to introduce myself. I'm Marlow Taylor," she says with a smile, her eyes bright. "We moved into the pink house next door a couple of days ago. It was a last-minute decision," she rambles, "but as soon as I saw it posted online, I knew we had to live there."

I stare at her outstretched hand, reluctant to accept the gesture. Despite my irritation, her presence sparks an unfamiliar fluttering in my stomach.

"Tell me, Marlow, is trespassing on other people's property and coming into their homes uninvited a regular pastime for you and Waffles?" My tone is mildly sarcastic as I glance back at her.

A flush of embarrassment spreads across her cheeks, and her eyes dim like a flickering candle as she pulls her hand back to her side. Something unpleasant gnaws at me, and a pang of regret creeps in, but I push it aside.

"You're absolutely right," she acknowledges. "I apologize for Waffles' unruly behavior. I let him out to play in the snow while I unpacked and when I went to check on him, he was gone. He must have escaped through a hole in the fence. I figured I could get him out before you noticed, but that didn't work out so well."

"I hadn't noticed." I deadpan. "How exactly did you plan on getting back to your yard? I saw that you used a ladder to climb over, so I'm assuming it would be tricky to get you and a dog back over the fence without it."

"Honestly, I hadn't thought that far ahead," she admits.

"That's what I thought," I mutter under my breath.

"It's just that Waffles can be quite the handful." She chews her lower lip. "I was worried what kind of trouble he might get into if I left him unsupervised for too long. He's not great at following directions."

That's the understatement of the century.

"He's a dog. He's literally trained to take orders."

"Um… not Waffles," Marlow corrects me hesitantly.

"What does that mean?"

"He's a rescue. I got him from a shelter in Los Angeles and haven't started training him yet." She looks down at the ground, shifting her feet side to side. "He's overly energetic, that's all."

As if he can sense that we're talking about him, Waffles yips while running around Lola. Unfortunately, she finds his antics thoroughly amusing.

"Well, I'd appreciate it if you'd make sure he stays in your yard from now on," I say through gritted teeth. "It's not safe to have an untrained dog around my daughter."

"Obviously," Marlow replies flatly as she watches Waffles and Lola play like they're the best of friends. "Come on Waffles. We've clearly overstayed our welcome."

He ignores her in favor of chasing his tail, while Lola claps her hands. Marlow is unfazed, taking a leash out of her coat pocket and clipping it to Waffles' collar.

I direct them to the front door as Marlow practically drags Waffles out, oblivious to the water, dirt, and dog hair being tracked through my house.

Before they can step outside, Lola darts past me, dropping to the floor to hug Waffles, her arms encircling his neck. "I'm going to miss you." She looks up at Marlow with pleading eyes. "Can I play with Waffles again soon?"

I'm stunned speechless when Marlow crouches down in front of Lola and tucks a piece of stray hair behind her ear. "Of course, you can." She shoots me a glare, daring me to say otherwise. "Besides, I don't think I could keep him away now that he's met you."

"Yay," Lola cheers, bouncing up and down in excitement. "Hey, Marlow?"

"Hey, Lola?"

"Why do you and Waffles have eyes that don't match?"

"Lola, remember our talk about not asking strangers personal questions?" I ask.

"Oh, it's fine." Marlow offers a friendly grin to my curious daughter, before her gaze darts to me. "We're not strangers, *neighbor*. It's called heterochromia," Marlow replies without missing a beat. "We were born with it. When I found Waffles at the shelter, I knew he was special, so I took him home with me."

"I think you're really pretty," Lola whispers.

My daughter's not wrong. Marlow *is* gorgeous, and despite her overly cheerful disposition and blatant disregard for other people's property I can't help but be drawn to her.

Marlow puts her hand over her heart in response to Lola's comment. "And I think you're beautiful." She lightly taps Lola on the nose. "I love your skirt. Rainbows are my favorite," she says in a low voice, like she's sharing a secret.

Lola's eyes widen in disbelief. "Mine too." She beams with pride. "Hey, Marlow, how come you have a flower sticking out of your shirt?"

Sure enough, a single daffodil is poking out of the front pocket of Marlow's overalls. How it survived her climb over the fence, I'll never know.

"I like to paint flowers, and I keep a fresh bouquet of them at home," she explains. "When a certain flower inspires me, I study it before I paint, and I tend to forget that I'm carrying it around." She plucks the flower from her pocket and hands it to Lola. "Would you like this one? It's a daffodil. It represents new beginnings, which I think is fitting for our situation."

"Yes, please." Lola carefully takes the flower from Marlow's hand.

"It might be thirsty, so make sure you keep it in water so it doesn't wilt."

Lola looks up at me. "Daddy, will you get my flower a drink?"

"Sure, ladybug, but let's see Marlow and Waffles out first."

The sooner our uninvited guests leave, the sooner I can get this mess cleaned up and finish getting dinner ready.

"It was such a pleasure to meet you, Lola," Marlow says.

When she stands up, she leans toward me so only I can hear. "I'm not sure I can say the same for you, but thanks for the tour, regardless." She winks. "You shouldn't frown so much or someday your face could get stuck that way." Her tone is teasing.

I raise a brow. "Did you consider I might have one less reason to frown if you and your dog didn't show up unannounced?"

The fluttering sensation is back in my stomach accompanied by a rush of remorse that proves more difficult to stifle than before.

She places her hands on her hips. "Did I not apologize for the intrusion, and promise you it won't happen again?"

"You did," I say, but I have a sneaking suspicion this won't be the last time Waffles and Marlow drop by for an unexpected visit.

Marlow tilts her head as she studies me, and an indecipherable expression crosses her face as if she's trying to read me. I school my expression, a carefully crafted wall firmly in place.

I clear my throat and pointedly glance at the door, hoping she'll take the hint and make her exit. I'm relieved when she finally steps onto the porch, leash in hand.

"Come on, Waffles. Let's go home and get you a treat." He barks with gusto, eagerly following her.

The unconventional duo strolls down the sidewalk as if they don't have a care in the world.

I glance over at the pink house next door and can't help but think that the color of the exterior matches the personality of the woman who now lives in it—obnoxious, quirky and eccentric, yet undeniably intriguing and charismatic.

Surveying the hallway, I notice the trail of melted snow and dirt left behind. It's a visible reminder of the disorder and chaos accompanying someone like Marlow wherever she goes. She leaves her mark, without recognizing the aftermath of her actions. What scares me most is the feeling that she could alter the carefully construed life I've built for Lola and me if I let my guard down.

"Daddy?" Lola tugs on my pant leg.

"Yes, ladybug?"

"My flower is really thirsty." She holds out her daffodil.

"We can fix that."

She follows me into the kitchen and climbs onto the closest barstool.

I fill a glass halfway with water and set it on the counter for Lola. She triumphantly gives her flower a drink.

"Thanks, Daddy. I hope Waffles comes to visit tomorrow. I miss him already." She sighs.

We'd be much better off if we steered clear of Marlow and her over energetic dog. Although something tells me Lola won't stop asking until she sees her four-legged friend again—and soon.

CHAPTER TWO

DYLAN

One Year Later

Guilt tightens my stomach into a knot, knowing that I'm two hours late to pick up Lola from my parents' house. I keep a strict schedule to make sure we get enough quality time together, and it bothers me when I have to deviate from my carefully planned regimen. My main priority is making sure she feels secure and never has to worry about where I am.

Unfortunately, it's unavoidable on occasion. My family owns Stafford Holdings, the largest real estate firm in the country. We have business holdings in every major city in the US, including hotels, office buildings, apartment complexes, and retail spaces. After my dad retired three years ago, my brothers and I assumed full control of the business. Harrison, my older brother, took the helm as CEO, Cash, my younger brother oversees operations, and I'm the CFO. Although I'm passionate about my career, it demands more time than I would prefer.

As soon as the helicopter touches down at the airfield near Aspen Grove and the pilot cuts the engine, I thank him for the ride and make a quick exit. I head for my SUV, parked in the nearby garage.

Because of the snow-covered streets, the drive to my parents' house takes longer than I'd like, and I'm relieved when I finally arrive at their modest two-story Cape-style home.

I'm not surprised when my mom opens the front door as I'm climbing the porch steps. She wraps me in a hug.

"Hi, sweetheart, how was work today?"

"It was long." I sigh. "After reviewing the financial report my team put together, Harrison gave the green light for the new Vanburen development in Brooklyn. There's a bunch of red tape for us to work through before we start building, so it's all hands on deck for the next few months." The mere thought of it leaves me anxious.

"Let's talk inside where it's warm," Mom suggests.

As she ushers me through the door, some of the stress leaves my shoulders.

My parents' house has always had a warm and inviting atmosphere. The space is filled with personal touches, from family photos to mementos collected from my parents' travels alongside a collection of Lola's art projects from school.

The open-concept floor plan makes the space feel roomy, but it's still a mid-sized home. My parents prefer to live well below their means even though they could afford a mega-mansion— several, if they wanted.

Despite my family's billionaire status, they prioritized providing their kids with a nurturing environment. Since we were young, they taught me and my siblings the importance of humility and hard work, regardless of the balance in our bank account. I want to do the same for Lola, and raising her in Aspen Grove is the best way to do that.

"How are your brothers?" Mom asks.

I raise a brow. "Didn't you call them both earlier today?"

"Yes, but that was this morning." She reminds me.

If she isn't able to talk to me and my siblings at least once a day, she gets worried.

"Harrison and Cash are fine. How was Lola this afternoon?"

11

"She was an angel, like always," Mom gushes. "Although she was disappointed that she didn't get to see Waffles tonight. She was looking forward to playing with him." She pats me on the shoulder when I tense up. "Don't worry, she cheered right up after she got a snack and watched a few episodes of *Bluey*."

"Thanks, Mom, I appreciate it."

To maintain a semblance of work-life balance, I commute to the city three days a week and work from home the other days. This arrangement makes it possible to be home in time for dinner most nights.

None of this would be possible without my parents' unwavering support. They've been with Lola and me every step of the way since she was a baby, and I couldn't be more grateful for their willingness to pick up the slack when I fall behind. It also helps that we have Kendra, Lola's nanny. She gets Lola off to school in the mornings, and occasionally watches her in the afternoons when my parents aren't available.

"It's my pleasure," she says with a smile. "I think it's so sweet that Marlow brings Waffles over to play with Lola. You're so lucky to have her as a neighbor."

"Sure," I say with a noncommittal shrug.

I'm so lucky that despite repairing the hole in my fence, Waffles still finds his way into my backyard and practically tackles Lola when he sees her. I can't count the number of times she's come inside covered in dog hair and slobber, thanks to the canine next door.

Evidently, Waffle's lack of training doesn't bother Marlow since she hasn't rectified the situation. Whenever I bring it up, she brushes me off, claiming that Waffles is perfect just the way he is. I beg to differ—that dog is a menace and needs proper training.

It doesn't help my case that Lola is smitten with our quirky neighbor. She's drawn to Marlow's eccentric wardrobe, bubbly personality, and infectious smile, which I find rather irritating. It's not natural for a person to be so damn happy all the time. It must be her age. At twenty-three, she still wears rose-colored glasses and thinks everything is made of sunshine and rainbows. Wait until she hits thirty-three when the responsibilities are piling up and life is an endless list of to-dos, appointments, and numbers, all weighing her down.

The demands of being a single parent are undeniably challenging, and I'm doing the best I can, considering the circumstances. But lately, I can't shake the feeling that I'm falling short of being a good father.

"Are you alright?" my mom asks, snapping me out of my thoughts.

"Do you think I'm a good dad?" I blurt out.

She flashes me a sympathetic smile. "Of course you are, sweetheart. I know things might seem impossibly difficult right now, but Lola is incredibly fortunate to have you as her father."

"Thanks, Mom. I needed to hear that. I just can't shake the guilt whenever I'm away from her; she deserves more."

She dismisses my concern with a wave. "Oh, hush. If you never left, she would get tired of you. It brings your dad and me so much joy when we get to spend time with our favorite grandchild."

"Lola's your *only* grandchild," I remind her.

"That won't be the case forever. I'm dreaming of the day when we're surrounded by grandkids." She lets out a wistful sigh. "I'm hoping Jack and your sister will start a family soon, and I'm still optimistic that you and your brothers will settle down. Until then, I'll happily soak up every second with Lola."

My younger sister Presley lives in New York. She got a job as the assistant to Jack Sinclair, the CEO of Sinclair Group, a large investment firm. After years of sidestepping their mutual attraction, a disastrous work trip to Aspen Grove led to them faking dating to hide Jack's identity from our family. One thing led to another, and they fell in love.

They're not in any hurry to have kids, and I know firsthand that my brothers have no intention of settling down anytime soon. But I don't want to be the one to break the news to my mom.

"Speaking of Dad, where is he?"

"He fell asleep in his recliner watching *Bluey* with Lola." Mom laughs. "He won't admit it, but I think he enjoys watching that show almost as much as she does."

I don't doubt it. Lola has her papa wrapped around her finger.

———

When I leave my parents' house, there's a fresh blanket of snow on the road.

As I pull down my street, I notice Marlow hasn't shoveled her driveway. I'm not surprised, given that she lacks a basic understanding that renting a house comes with certain responsibilities, including mowing the lawn in the summer and shoveling snow in the winter. She probably doesn't even own a snow shovel.

After parking in the garage, I carry a sleeping Lola up to her room. Luckily, she changed into her pajamas while she was at my parents' house, making it easy to settle her into bed and tuck her in.

I remember when I cradled my little girl in my arms for the first time and gazed into those captivating big blue eyes. She instantly captured my heart. I vowed she would always come first, no matter what. I just never expected that I'd be doing this whole parenting thing on my own.

Before Lola was born, I lived in the city with Maddie, my ex-girlfriend. She left when Lola was six weeks old, making it an easy decision to move back to Aspen Grove so Lola and I could be closer to my parents. Despite my mom wanting us to move in with her and my dad, I chose to buy a place down the street from the local elementary school.

"I love you, ladybug," I whisper into Lola's hair. "Nothing

will ever matter more to me than you." I press a kiss to her forehead before quietly leaving her room.

Once I've cleaned out her backpack and prepared her lunch for tomorrow, I step outside to shovel our driveway and sidewalk. With Lola and dozens of other kids walking to school, shoveling and putting salt down is important to prevent any potential accidents.

After finishing at my house, I go over to Marlow's. This routine started a week after she moved in. There was a massive snowstorm, and when she never came out to remove the snow, I ended up doing it for her. Now, whenever there's heavy snowfall, I shovel her driveway.

Like most nights, the lights are on in her loft. Whenever I have a late night in my home office, or Lola gets up in the middle of the night, Marlow is usually awake. It makes me think she must sleep during the day to make up for her nocturnal routine.

She's lived here for over a year, but I still don't know what she does for a living. Aside from taking Waffles on his daily walks and trips to town, she doesn't venture out much. I wonder what made her impulsively rent a pink house in a small town in Maine when she could live anywhere in the world.

I'm in a sour mood tonight as I toss snow off to the side. It's late, and I still have a financial report to finish before bed.

I glance up and spot Marlow standing at her window. Her golden blonde hair is tossed into a messy bun, and she's wearing her signature oversized overalls with a long-sleeved neon orange shirt underneath. Even from here, I can spot a smudge of paint splattered across her cheek, which can only mean one thing—she's been painting.

Like she does every time I come over, she gives me one of her infectious smiles and mouths the words *thank you*, pointing to the driveway.

Without thinking, I raise my hand to wave at her. Her mouth falls open in shock before waving back.

I quickly pull my hand to my side, frowning as I avert my gaze from the window. As I return to shoveling her driveway, I mentally scold myself for my unusual interaction. For a reason I can't explain, it's difficult to resist the captivating effect Marlow's smile has, momentarily changing my mood, and bringing a lightness to my step.

CHAPTER THREE

MARLOW

"Waffles, what are you doing?" I mumble, my voice hoarse from sleep.

I pry one eye open and am met with his nose pressed against my face, accompanied by the sound of his heavy panting.

"Can I help you?" I ask teasingly.

He barks gleefully when he realizes that I'm finally awake.

I glance at the clock on the nightstand and groan when I see that it's only 7:55 a.m.

"How come you're up so early, boy?"

I was up until 3:00 a.m. last night, finishing a commissioned hydrangea piece that was supposed to be shipped out a week ago. Inspiration strikes at the most inopportune times—like when I'm getting ready for bed. I planned to sleep in this morning, but it seems *someone* has other ideas.

Waffles barks louder, reminding me he's waiting.

"Okay, okay. You win."

He jumps from the bed and makes a mad dash into the hall, yipping with excitement.

I reluctantly climb out of bed, a shiver coursing through me when my feet touch the hardwood floor. To combat the cold, I put on a pair of fuzzy socks and slip on my cardigan, which was hanging on the colorful patchwork chair in the corner. One drawback to living in Maine is the long, bitter winters, but I couldn't turn down the opportunity to live in such a charming home.

Shortly after adopting Waffles, I was scrolling through a rental site and stumbled upon this adorable pink house in Aspen Grove, complete with a white picket fence and a porch swing. It felt like the perfect place for Waffles and me to start our new adventure together.

A little over a year later, and we're still here. This is the longest I've stayed anywhere since leaving my hometown.

I'm what my parents like to call a free spirit. I've always been easily distracted, impulsive, and constantly on the move. As college professors who ran their lives like clockwork, it was challenging to raise an exuberant child with a short attention span.

Throughout middle school, while they deliberated which extracurricular activities would look best on my transcript, I struggled to commit to a hobby for more than a week. I was always ready to explore something new. In high school, they invested countless hours reviewing my options for college while I daydreamed of taking a trip around the world.

Despite my parents' disappointment, I chose to travel after high school. Against their better judgment, they gave me a check for ten grand—a portion of my college fund. The rest was contingent on me pursuing a bachelor's degree, an opportunity I ultimately declined. Instead, I traveled the country, taking international trips when I wanted something more adventurous and chasing my artistic ambitions.

I'm standing in my kitchen waiting for Waffles to finish his business out back when my phone vibrates in my pocket.

I groan when I see Gavin's name light up the screen.

"Hey, Gav. Any particular reason you're calling me before noon?" I tease.

"Well, aren't you a ray of sunshine this morning?" he says in a playful tone. "You never answered the email I sent last week. I wasn't sure if you forgot or were ignoring me, so I figured I'd call you on my way to work."

"Honestly, it was a bit of both," I confess. I have an unhealthy habit of putting off responding to texts and emails when I can't think of a good response or if I don't have a definitive answer to a question. I tell myself I'll reply later, but I usually forget.

"Should I even ask how your new collection is coming along?"

Gavin's a curator for The Artist, a renowned gallery in New York City. He sent me a DM after he stumbled across my work on social media, and after a year of exchanging messages and phone calls, he convinced me to participate in my first art exhibition. We've been dear friends ever since he sent me that first message. This upcoming show will be my third at his gallery and could be my last if I don't get him these paintings ahead of schedule.

He's been so supportive, and I don't want to do anything to disappoint him. The idea of letting him down fills me with a sense of unease.

I chew on my lip, knowing he won't like my answer. "Um, it's coming?"

"Marlow, please tell me you've started," he says, desperation evident in his tone. "You told me last month it'd be a breeze to complete seven paintings in time for this exhibition."

"Relax, Gav. The show isn't for six weeks. I have plenty of time between now and then."

At least I hope so.

"That's what you said the last time."

"And you got my collection on time, did you not?"

"Sure. If you count overnighting the paintings the morning before your art exhibit." His tone is cynical.

"It wasn't *that* bad," I say, not sure if I'm trying to convince him or myself. "No, it was so much worse," he states. "Do I need to remind you that there was a delay with the delivery, and I had to bribe a coordinator at the shipping company to give me the contact info for the driver? I had to meet the guy in midtown to pick up the paintings in a rented U-Haul and get them back to the gallery with only an hour to spare before the show."

I admit I'm an unintentional expert at procrastination. With my short attention span and sudden bursts of inspiration, sticking to deadlines is like chasing a moving target. That's why I typically turn down invitations for gallery showings—I don't like committing to things I might not be able to deliver, especially when it could negatively affect someone I care about.

"Okay... yes, it was a disaster, but if I recall correctly, my collection sold out within an hour, did it not?"

"Yes," Gavin says reluctantly.

"And I'm pretty sure I gave you an incredibly generous commission to compensate for the trouble I put you through." I can't resist provoking him.

"Yeah, you did. But I'm quite sure chasing down those paintings shaved ten years off my life that I'll never get back," he exaggerates in a playful manner.

"I'm starting on the first piece today. I promise you'll have the full collection in the gallery the day ahead of the show."

Fingers crossed I can keep my promise.

"I'll believe it when I see it." His tone is skeptical, and I understand why. "Anything exciting happening in that small town of yours, or are you finally ready to move to New York?"

"I don't have any plans to leave yet. I've made a few friends, and Waffles would be devastated if I took him away from Lola."

I think she'd be equally as distraught, and the thought of making her sad sends an arrow through my heart.

"Marlow, don't forget that Waffles is your dog, which makes *you* the boss. Pets are adaptable, and he'll be content wherever you go next. Not to mention, you've told me that Lola's hot single dad is a total jerk and can't wait until you no longer have to be his neighbor."

Waffles takes that as his cue to whine at the door. I shiver as the cold breeze rushes in when I let him back in. He runs over to his dog bowl that I filled with food earlier and scarfs up his breakfast.

"In hindsight, Dylan had every right to be upset with me and Waffles," I admit. I was hopeful his icy demeanor would thaw quickly, but it's taken over a year to notice any signs of him warming up to me. "And to be clear, I've never called Dylan hot," I correct Gavin. "I said that the day we met when I was in the heat of the moment."

I think back to those intense, frosty eyes of his, glaring at me from behind a pair of thick-rimmed glasses. His short, black hair was ruffled and slightly unkempt, his hands running through it in agitation as if Waffles and I were the source of all his life's problems. But then I remember how those same brown eyes softened, his gruff tone leveling out, when he talked to his daughter.

"I looked Dylan Stafford up online. That man is a total DILF. Anyone who can pull off glasses like that deserves to be on the cover of GQ," Gavin says.

"I'm so telling Matthew you said that," I taunt.

"Go right ahead, babe," he says with a chuckle. "It's not anything he hasn't heard me say before." Gavin is an open book, never shying away from speaking his mind, regardless of what comes out. He pauses when someone shouts his name in the background. He must have stopped to grab his morning coffee on the way to the gallery. "When you're ready for your next adventure and want a break from that broody neighbor, Matthew and I would be delighted to have you and Waffles come to stay with us."

I raise a brow. "Does Matthew know you're offering?"

Gavin has a bad habit of doing things without consulting him first. "Matthew's the one who suggested it," he assures me. "You know how much he adores you."

"Tell him I appreciate the invite, but I'm going to stay in Aspen Grove for a while longer. I'll keep you both in the loop if anything changes."

"Sounds like a plan. I'm sorry to run, but I'm just walking

into the gallery and have a private showing with a client in ten minutes."

"Say no more. I'll talk to you later."

"You can count on it, babe. Now go get started on that collection."

"I will," I promise. "Bye, Gav."

After making myself a large cup of coffee, I head up to the loft that I've transformed into my art studio. One wall is lined with shelves that house all of my art supplies, including my vast collection of paints, texturing tools, and stacks of new canvases. The other wall has a wooden desk pushed up against it, covered with inspirational photos, invoices, and magazines. My filming equipment is in a haphazard pile in the corner where I keep it stashed when I'm not making videos.

To most, my studio would appear cluttered and disorganized, but for me, my creativity flourishes amid the chaos.

The floor-to-ceiling windows facing the front yard are my favorite feature of the room. There are two easels strategically placed nearby, where I do most of my painting.

I pull back the linen curtains and welcome in the morning light.

Fortunately, it didn't snow last night, leaving my driveway and sidewalk clear, courtesy of Dylan. For someone who doesn't seem to like me much, he consistently does nice things, like shoveling and mowing my front lawn in the summer.

Before moving to Aspen Grove, I always lived in an apartment complex, and have never had a yard before. When I rented this house, the owner assured me he'd find someone to do the yard work so I wouldn't have to worry about it.

When I saw Dylan Stafford shoveling my driveway for the first time, I figured the owner asked him to do it since he lives next door. I admit something is appealing about a man willing to look out for me, even when he maintains a distant demeanor.

I've made it my mission to bring a smile to his face, and last night marked the closest I've ever come to achieving my goal.

Aside from the trespassing incident when we met, I'm not sure why he dislikes me. It probably has to do with Waffles constantly finding new ways to get into his backyard and Lola often showing up on my porch asking if she can play with him. I think it's adorable how smitten those two are with each other, but it's apparent Dylan doesn't share the same sentiment. His frosty exterior extends to most everyone except his family and Lola.

I met his family last year when his mom, Johanna, invited me over for Christmas Eve. I didn't visit my parents during the holidays and my friends were out of town, so it was nice to spend time with the Staffords.

Dylan's entire world revolves around Lola and watching him treat her like a princess is heartwarming. The transformation is remarkable, considering the man acts like a grumbling grouch around everyone else.

I often wonder what happened to Lola's mom, but I don't dare ask Dylan about it. She hasn't been around since I've lived here, and Lola has never mentioned her. From what I can tell, Dylan is raising Lola by himself, and it's the two of them against the world.

I catch movement outside and see Lola and her nanny, Kendra, passing by my house on their way to school. Today, Lola's rocking fleece lined leggings paired with a rainbow skirt, a purple jacket, and a white pom-pom beanie. Like me, she prefers a vibrant and bold wardrobe, a choice that I can only imagine has faced protest from Dylan.

I hear paws on the stairs, and moments later, Waffles barrels into the room. He scrambles to the window, barking with glee when he sees Lola. She stops in the middle of the sidewalk, waving frantically in our direction, when she hears him.

"Good morning, Waffles. Hi, Marlow," she shouts, her voice carrying through the closed window.

I wave back with a smile.

On the days that I'm awake this early, it's routine for Waffles and me to greet her on her way to school.

Kendra appears to be in a rush today, tugging on Lola's backpack, nudging her along. Lola gives us one more wave before continuing down the sidewalk.

I step away from the window to mix acrylics for the first piece in my collection for The Artist.

Painting is the only thing that's ever been capable of holding my attention for extended periods. There's something peaceful about the rhythmic strokes of a paintbrush, the blending of colors, and the artistic freedom in expressing myself. It's exhilarating to transform a blank canvas into something beautiful and lifelike. The process has a way of holding me captive until I've finished a painting.

During an impromptu trip to Paris, I discovered a passion for the impasto technique. Combining my newfound interest with my fondness for flowers, I began creating textured floral pieces. My artwork is vibrant and bright, and every creation draws inspiration from those who've crossed my path.

On a whim, I posted my art on social media and quickly discovered that viewers had a fascination for painting tutorials and short clips illustrating how to create textures on a canvas. When a popular influencer shared one of my videos, all the paintings on my website sold out overnight. The rising popularity of my art has allowed me to maintain a comfortable lifestyle and continue to do what I love.

My dream is to participate in an art residency at the Paris Art Collective. Some of the best artists have trained there, and it would be a great way to improve my technique. However, the program is by invitation only so I may never get the chance, but if I ever do, I'd accept the opportunity in a heartbeat.

I'm relieved that the bouquet I picked up from Blooms, the local flower shop, yesterday is still in great shape. I always prefer to paint with real-life inspiration when possible, so I keep at least one flower arrangement in the studio.

I pluck a daffodil from the vase and examine it. They symbolize new beginnings, reminding me of the day Waffles and I met Lola. Her innocence and carefree spirit ignite my inner child, inspiring my first piece in this collection.

Before painting, I lift my arms into a power pose and take five deep, long breaths. I welcome the surge of confidence that courses through me.

Today is going to be the start of something wonderful.

CHAPTER FOUR

MARLOW

"Waffles, will you please slow down?"

Our afternoon walk around the neighborhood is cut short when he catches sight of Lola on her way home from school. He has a one-track mind where she's concerned. I tug on his leash, but it's useless. This dog is on a mission, and nothing will deter him, me included.

My steps falter when I see Dylan is with Lola. Most days, she spends the afternoon at her grandma's house until Dylan picks her up after work. On occasion, Kendra gets her from school and brings her back to the house.

Dylan is on the phone, his face twisted in a scowl. I don't envy whoever is on the other end of that call.

Lola skips over to meet Waffles and me in front of her house. Her oversized backpack bounces up and down with every step. Waffles jumps into her arms when she gets close enough, showering her with affectionate licks. Dylan looks on, his disapproval clear by the clench of his jaw.

"You're such a good boy, Waffles," Lola croons while scratching him behind the ear.

"He was very excited to see you," I say.

Lola glances up at me. "I made you something."

"You did?"

She bobs her head up and down with a toothy grin and sets her backpack on the sidewalk. While she sifts through a stack of papers, Waffles sticks his nose inside to investigate.

"Here," she exclaims, handing me a drawing of a rainbow covered with shimmering silver and pink glitter.

I crouch down on the sidewalk next to her, taking a closer look at the picture. "Lola, this is lovely. You're so talented." My heart swells with warmth at her sweet gesture. "How did you know I love rainbows and glitter?"

"Because you told me," she says with a hint of sass. "And you always wear those." She points to my silver sneakers.

My gaze darts to Dylan at the sound of his frustration. He paces the sidewalk a few feet away, as he huffs in annoyance. I stand. "Would you mind if I hang this picture on my fridge so Waffles and I can see it every day?" I ask Lola.

"I think Waffles would like that," she says.

"You're absolutely right about that. I have something for you too."

She watches intently as I take out a sunflower from the front pocket of my overalls.

"You remembered," she squeals.

"How could I forget?" I ask with a smile. Ever since I gave Lola a daffodil when we met, I always carry a flower with me whenever there's a possibility that I might run into her.

"Daddy, look what Marlow gave me." She lifts the flower to show him.

He quickly glances over, acknowledging her with a nod, before turning his attention back to his call.

"Hey, Lola," I whisper. "Your dad is on an important call. Why don't you play catch with Waffles until he's finished?"

She shifts her attention back to me, and I hand her Waffles' tennis ball that I had in my pocket. Lola tosses it into a patch of nearby snow, and Waffles chases after it, diving enthusiastically into the pile in search of his toy. When he retrieves it, he runs back to Lola, dropping the ball at her feet with an excited bark, eagerly waiting for her to throw it again.

Dylan shoots Waffles a stern look, covering his phone with his hand, attempting to muffle out the noise.

What has him in such a bad mood?

Curiosity gets the best of me, and I can't resist eavesdropping when he speaks again.

"No, I don't understand," he says with irritation. "Your website says that your team can handle last-minute requests. I'm willing to pay a premium for your services, so I fail to see the problem." He rakes his hand through his hair as he listens to the person's reply. "Yes, I know that Aspen Grove is a two-hour drive from the city, but I told you that cost isn't an issue. Like I said before, my nanny quit, and I need to find a suitable replacement as soon as possible." He lets out a heavy sigh. "Fine. As soon as you find a candidate willing to come to Aspen Grove, call me back." He disconnects the call and snaps his head in my direction, catching me staring.

"Um… is everything okay?" I ask cautiously.

"Yeah, it's fine," he says, glancing over at Lola and Waffles.

Worry etches itself on his face, and the words fly out of my mouth before I can stop them. "What happened to Kendra?"

I immediately regret asking when Dylan gives me an intense stare. "Do you make it a habit of listening in on people's private conversations?" he asks in a clipped tone.

"Only when the person is on the verge of spontaneous combustion." I backpedal when he purses his lips, clearly unamused by my joke. "You don't have to tell me if you'd rather not."

He studies me a beat before saying, "Kendra had a family emergency and is moving to Florida indefinitely to be with her parents."

"I'm so sorry to hear that. I hope you can find a replacement soon."

I've heard Dylan runs Stafford Holdings, a real estate

conglomerate, with his brothers. I can only imagine the stress that comes with that responsibility.

He relies on Kendra to take care of Lola in the mornings before school, due to his early work schedule. I know this because whenever I've pulled an all-nighter in the studio, I've seen him leaving the house while it's still dark outside. If he's not leaving at the crack of dawn, he's working from his home office that faces my studio.

The idea crosses my mind to offer to watch Lola until he finds a permanent replacement. I decide against it, though, assuming my unsolicited offer wouldn't be well received given his attitude toward me. Besides, Gavin wouldn't appreciate it if I did anything to cause additional delays in my painting schedule.

"I'll get it sorted out," Dylan says briskly.

"That's good. Lola is an exceptional girl, and whoever you hire should consider themselves lucky to spend time with her," I remark warmly.

The corner of his lips lift into a ghost of a smile. "Thanks for saying that."

He might not have given me a full-on smile, but it's more than I've gotten in the past, so I'm taking it as a win.

"Of course, she's my neighbor," I say fondly.

Dylan visibly relaxes, and I find it difficult to breathe when he moves closer. His typically serious and brooding demeanor momentarily fades, and I'm drawn to this glimpse of his gentler side, usually reserved for Lola.

An expression I can't decipher flickers across his features, and my heart rate speeds up when his gaze flits across my face, lingering on the spot just below my mouth.

"What is it?" I whisper.

"You have paint on your face," he says softly.

My breath hitches when he slowly reaches out and drags his thumb across my chin, grazing my lower lip, his fingers resting lightly on my jaw. A spark of electricity ripples through me at the unexpected warmth of his hand. I'm frozen in place, confused by my body's reaction. The intensity in his eyes mirrors how I feel.

Dylan snaps out of it first, blinking rapidly, and shaking his head. He jerks his arm back to his side, flexing his hand. Did he find it that repulsive, or could he be as equally stunned by the intensity of the moment we just shared?

"I shouldn't have touched you," he says in a serious tone. "It was a reflex, given how often I have to wipe things off Lola's face."

"That's alright." I give him a tentative smile and attempt to keep my voice steady. "If you hadn't, I probably would have spent the rest of the day with paint on my face."

He dips his chin in a firm nod and avoids my gaze. "It's time to go inside and wash up, ladybug," he calls out to Lola. "There are celery sticks and apple slices in the kitchen waiting for you." He glances down at his watch. "I have a call with your Uncle Harrison in fifteen minutes, so we need to hurry."

"But Waffles and I are still playing," Lola protests.

Oh boy.

Dylan won't be happy if my dog interferes with his meticulously planned schedule.

"You know what, Lola," I interject. "Waffles and I just got back from a long walk, and we need to get home so I can give him his afternoon treat."

Waffles halts in his tracks at the mention of his favorite word "treat." He ditches his tennis ball in the snow and sprints to our front door, barking at me to follow.

"Silly Waffles." Lola shakes her head and picks up the slobbery ball he left behind. Dylan visibly winces when she wipes it off on her leggings. Those will undoubtedly be tossed in the washer on the sanitize cycle as soon as they get inside.

"We have to hurry, ladybug." Dylan gestures to their house.

Lola hands me the ball. "Bye, Marlow," she calls out as she skips ahead and goes inside. I'm puzzled when Dylan doesn't follow her right away.

"I hope you both have a great night," I offer warmly.

I notice him flexing his hand again, a smear of red paint on his thumb. He opens his mouth like he wants to speak but doesn't say anything. After a few seconds, he nods curtly before turning around and going inside his house—the snick of the door closing loudly in the empty street.

CHAPTER FIVE

DYLAN

Today has been a disaster.

Kendra was running late this morning, so I had to get Lola ready for school. She wanted her hair done in fishtail braids, but it's the one hairstyle I've never mastered. When I broke the news she had to settle for pigtails, I distracted her with a set of pink, glittery bows that matched her outfit to avoid a complete meltdown.

Then, while preparing breakfast, I accidentally melted the plastic unicorn pancake mold, and Lola burst into tears when I served her a plate of banana oat pancakes shaped like circles instead of unicorns.

As if that wasn't enough, Kendra called me fifteen minutes before school was out for the day to tell me she wasn't able to pick up Lola and had to quit—immediately. She said her dad has been sick for a couple of months and has progressively gotten worse, so she decided to move home with her parents to help take care of him.

Kendra has been a part of our lives for over two years, and Lola will miss her. I sent her a year's salary to help with her father's medical expenses and encouraged her to reach out if she needs further support. Given everything she and her family are going through, it's the least I can do. Despite my irritable disposition, I make it a point to ensure my employees are well taken care of.

The nanny agency that helped me hire Kendra has been no help in finding a replacement. They don't have anyone else currently available to move to a small town for a part-time position, even though I'm willing to pay a full-time salary.

The one silver lining is that dinner and Lola's bedtime routine have gone off without a hitch tonight.

Once I finish reading her bedtime story, I rise from the bed and set the copy of *Madeline* on Lola's bedside table. It's her favorite book, and she constantly asks when I'm going to take her to Paris to see the Eiffel Tower so she can be like Madeline.

"Hey, Daddy?" Lola sits up in bed, pushing back her unicorn and rainbow comforter.

"Yes, ladybug?"

"I have an idea." Her face lights up in anticipation.

"What is it?"

"I want Marlow to be my new nanny," she declares.

Her unexpected request leaves me dumbfounded, because I'm not sure where this is coming from. When we ran into Marlow and Waffles on our way home from school today, I told her that Kendra quit, but the discussion ended there. It's not her problem to fix.

"Sweetheart, Marlow's not a nanny." I try to break the news as gently as I can. "Actually, I'm not really sure what her job is," I murmur to myself.

"She's a painter," Lola says, leaving no room for doubt.

"Yes, she paints as a hobby, but I don't think that's her job," I say.

"It is. She told me so."

"I'm sure you're right, ladybug," I offer to appease her.

"So, can Marlow be my nanny? Pretty please?" Lola gives her best puppy dog eyes.

I take a deep breath. "Like you said, Marlow already has a

job. But we'll find someone that you'll like just as much, I promise." I pull up the covers around her and tuck her in. "How does that sound?"

"I guess that's okay." Her voice carries a hint of disappointment as she frowns. "But they have to be able to do fishtail braids."

"I'll do my best, but fishtail braids are a complex hairstyle. Even I can't do that one," I say as I run a hand over her hair.

When Lola was a baby, my sister Presley was adamant that I learn how to do various hairstyles, so when the time came, Lola wouldn't go to school with a lopsided ponytail every day.

Mom and Presley were my guinea pigs, and when Lola finally had hair long enough to style, I was proficient in most hairstyles. Except fishtail braids, much to Lola's dismay. No matter how many times I've practiced that style, it always turns into a tangled mess.

She smirks. "Marlow can do them."

I chuckle at her attempt to redirect the conversation. "You're right, but I'm sure there are plenty of nannies who can too. We just have to find one."

Something tells me that it wouldn't be a good idea to be that close to Marlow every day, especially not after the incident earlier this afternoon. I glance down at the smudge of red paint still on my finger. I should have scrubbed it off while washing up for dinner, but I couldn't bring myself to do it.

Being around her has been messing with my head lately, solidifying my decision to avoid a situation where we'd see each other more than we already do.

———

"Daddy?"

Lola's muffled voice sounds like it's coming from a tunnel. The faint sound of an alarm goes off in the distance, and there's an odd pressure against my forehead.

"Daddy, are you awake?"

Lola's voice is louder this time. I slowly pry one eye open and find her standing next to me with her hand pressed against my forehead and her face scrunched into a serious expression.

"Ladybug, what are you doing?" I ask in a groggy tone.

"I'm checking your temperature."

I chuckle at her intense concentration. "Why?"

"I thought you might be sick since you're still in bed."

I jolt upright, the sound of my alarm finally registering. Panic sets in as I snatch my phone off the nightstand and see that it's already 8:00 a.m.

"Shi—crap on a cracker." One unexpected challenge of being a parent is that no one tells you how difficult it is not to swear in front of your kid. I usually catch myself, but occasionally, an accidental curse word slips out when I'm distracted.

Just last month, Lola's principal called me into her office and asked me to explain why my daughter shouted *dammit* when she bumped her knee on a table during playtime. Unfortunately, I didn't have a good excuse, but I assured her I'd talk with Lola about it and would do my best to make sure it didn't happen again.

I jump out of bed and sprint to my walk-in closet, grabbing the first pair of sweatpants within reach and throw on a black hoodie I find on a nearby shelf.

"Daddy, why aren't you wearing a suit today?" Lola asks when I come back into the bedroom.

I smile, amused at her observation, given that I rarely leave the house in anything other than a three-piece suit. "Since we're running late, I'm going to drop you off at school first, and then I'll come home and get ready for work."

"Oh, that's a good idea." She gives me a thumbs up. "Ms. Thornberry gets mad when we're late."

"We wouldn't want to upset Ms. Thornberry now, would we?"

"Nope." She rapidly shakes her head.

Thankfully, she's already dressed for school—a perk of raising a self-sufficient six-year-old who insists on choosing her own outfits.

I shoot my brothers a text, telling them I'll be late logging on this morning. Harrison won't be happy, considering we have an urgent matter to discuss related to the Vanburen project, but he knows Lola comes first.

"Let's do your hair, and then we'll head out. Sound like a plan?"

Lola nods in agreement, running to the bathroom, and I follow her.

I'm relieved she doesn't complain when I pull her long blonde hair into a high ponytail.

"Don't forget a bow," she reminds me. "I want my red one."

"Sure thing, ladybug."

I reach over and grab her favorite sparkly red bow from one of the ribbons attached to the woven rainbow hanging on the wall, holding dozens of other bows and hair clips. Lola's love for glittery and shiny things has no limits.

That must be why she's so captivated by Marlow. The woman lives in a pink house, wears glittery sneakers, and has a wardrobe full of colorful clothes. Add in her sunny disposition, and any little girl would be in love, particularly mine.

I'm concerned that Lola's fascination toward our eccentric neighbor might be contagious.

I secure the bow in Lola's hair, pleased with the final result.

"You're all set. Now, let's hurry and get you off to school." She's off like a shot. "No running," I call after her.

"I'm just hurrying like you told me to," she sasses back.

Considering the size of her attitude, it's a miracle I don't have a head full of gray hair yet. I can't imagine what life will be like living with a teenage Lola. God, give me patience when the time comes.

"Well, hurry a little slower," I shout after her.

Once I put away the hair supplies, I head to the kitchen, grab

Lola's lunch from the fridge, and slip it inside her backpack. When I get to the entryway, the front door is wide open, and she's waiting for me on the porch, impatiently tapping her foot.

"Come on, Daddy."

"I'll be right there." I quickly throw on a pair of tennis shoes and we head toward the school.

Until Lola stops in front of the pink house next door.

I glance up to find Marlow standing at her studio window. Even from this distance I notice spatters of blue paint on her face. Soon enough, Waffles appears by her side, barking enthusiastically.

"Hi, Waffles. Hi, Marlow," Lola shouts, waving with both hands.

Marlow waves back with a vibrant smile on her face.

God, why is she so damn pretty all the time? Even with paint on her face, she's stunning...

I dismiss the thought with a shake of my head. Happy. I meant, why is she so damn happy all the time?

I usher Lola along. "Come on, ladybug. We have to hurry or we're going to be late."

Against my better judgment, I turn back to give Marlow a second glance. She's still at her window, and when she catches my gaze, she gives me a wave of my own. Unsure what else to do, I wave back.

There I go again.

———

The one drawback to living in my neighborhood is the houses are uncomfortably close to each other, which means if your neighbors are loud, you'll hear it. Luckily, my house is at the end of the block, so I only have one next-door neighbor. The downside? That neighbor is Marlow Taylor, and she blasts '80s pop music at the most inconvenient times.

Both our houses have lofts—I've transformed mine into an

office and she uses hers for some sort of art studio. I have no idea what she does over there all day, aside from listening to loud music and painting flowers. Whatever that means.

I log into my conference call to find Harrison already waiting. His arms are folded across his chest, and his face remains in a permanent scowl. It's rare to see him smile these days. His black hair is styled in a tapered fade, and his muscular arms fill out the sleeves of his light gray dress shirt. He played professional hockey when he was younger and has maintained his athletic build. I clench my teeth in frustration as the chorus of "Material Girl" filters into my office. Every time I think Marlow's going to take a break, another song starts.

I lean back in my chair to get a better view through the window that faces her loft.

She's at it again.

Marlow is dancing around the room with a giant paintbrush in hand, belting out the lyrics to the second verse. She bends down to where Waffles is seated on his haunches, watching her impromptu performance. From this angle, I have the perfect view of her backside, and those tight mint green yoga pants do nothing to hide the toned shape of her ass. She usually paints in her overalls, but I much prefer the yoga pants. God, I sound like such a creep.

"Dylan, are you listening?"

I snap my attention to the computer screen and receive a disapproving glare from Harrison. Cash, who has since joined the call, covers his mouth in an attempt to suppress a snicker.

"Sorry, can you repeat that last part?" I ask Harrison.

He gives an irritated sigh. "What's up with you today? You're never this distracted."

"Sorry," I mumble. "My neighbor is having another one of her impromptu concerts for one in her loft, and it's very distracting."

In more ways than one.

38

"You're talking about the hot one that Mom invited over for Christmas Eve last year, Marlow, right?" Cash pipes up.

"Yeah."

For some reason, it bothers me that Cash called Marlow hot, despite it being true.

He's the fun-loving, carefree brother and the life of any party. When we were kids, he was in an accident that left him with a jagged scar on the left of his face, spanning from his ear to his chin. My mom was worried it would affect his confidence. Spoiler alert—it had the opposite effect. Turns out women have a thing for men with scars, and they flock to him in droves.

"It was nice of Mom to invite your neighbor over for the holidays last year," he says with a twinkle in his hazel eyes.

"Why did you have to remind me about that?" I groan.

My mom had the brilliant idea to invite Marlow over for our family Christmas Eve celebration. She knows Lola likes Marlow, and now Mom has gotten it into her head that Marlow and I would make a cute couple. The problem is that she's oblivious to the fact that Marlow and I are polar opposites. And that I'm far too busy juggling the roles of two parents to even consider dating right now.

Over the past five years, I've had a few dates and the occasional hookup, but I've made it clear I'm not interested in committing to a long-term relationship. I won't introduce someone new into our lives, knowing it could be temporary, and risk breaking Lola's heart, given how easily she gets attached.

That's one reason I'm glad Maddie hasn't come around since the day she left. I don't think I could handle explaining to Lola why someone who's supposed to love her unconditionally only visits when it suits them best. Her tender, loving heart wouldn't be able to accept that. It's much easier to avoid talking about an absentee parent altogether than to explain the behavior of a flaky one, who shows up sporadically.

Now, if only my mother would respect my decision not to date.

"If you two are done gossiping like a couple of schoolgirls, I'd appreciate it if we could get back to work," Harrison says tersely.

"Yes, boss," I taunt him.

He scowls at me, unimpressed by my jab.

A few years ago, he would have cracked a joke about our overly enthusiastic mom or my loud, quirky neighbor, but I rarely see that side of him anymore. His entire personality changed when he took on the role of CEO. He hardly smiles and spends most of his time at the office, reluctant to share his burdens with anyone.

With Stafford Holdings' recent expansion into Europe and the Vanburen project underway, I've shouldered more responsibilities to lighten his load. Still, he's as stubborn as they come, and it's like pulling teeth to get him to delegate anything of significance.

I have a natural inclination to take care of people. My mom calls me "the fixer" in our family. When there's a problem, I have to address it quickly and efficiently. It's not always the best solution, given the bind I'm in right now, taking on too many responsibilities at work while my personal life is imploding. Nevertheless, I'm doing the best I can, given the circumstances.

"Dylan, can you go over the cost-benefit analysis again for the Vanburen project?" Harrison asks.

"Yeah, sure thing." I bring up the presentation on my computer and share my screen.

Cash shuts his eyes, mimicking the sound of snoring. "Do I have to be here for this?"

My brothers might get a kick out of teasing me for being a nerd, but it's all in good fun. My knack for crunching numbers is one reason Stafford Holdings is growing so rapidly.

"If you want a paycheck, you do." Harrison's mouth curves up into a slight smile.

"Fine, but it's on you if I pass out from boredom," Cash mocks playfully.

I spend the rest of the meeting walking Harrison and Cash through the cost-benefit analysis while attempting to tune out Marlow's never-ending '80s pop hits playlist.

Not only is she distracting me with her loud music, now she's added those damn yoga pants into the equation, diverting me from work with her perfect ass.

Once I'm finally finished with my call, almost two hours later, my body is stiff from sitting so long, and I have a splitting headache. I stand up to stretch and take a moment to massage my temples to ease the tension. That's when I notice the silence.

She finally turned her music off.

The distant sound of a door catches my attention, and I rush to the window to find Marlow walking outside with Waffles in tow.

I jog down the stairs, not wanting to miss the chance to speak my mind without Lola around.

When I get outside, Marlow is standing in front of her mailbox, sifting through a handful of envelopes, while Waffles rolls around in the nearby snow. He tilts his head toward me as I approach and looks disappointed when he doesn't see Lola with me.

I march toward Marlow, preparing to unleash my frustrations. Not only was she playing her music too loud, but she was distracting me as she swayed to the beat in those goddamn yoga pants. My thinking is irrational considering she has no control over my wayward thoughts, but it doesn't prevent my annoyance that being near her causes my pulse to race.

I stop short when I glance up and am met with her unique blue and green gaze. She gives me a tentative smile and any inclination to reprimand her evaporates.

Damn, that smile of hers gets me every time.

How am I supposed to lecture her when she's being so damn nice without saying anything at all?

"Hi there, neighbor." Her tone is hesitant.

I clear my throat. "Hey, Marlow."

A look of astonishment crosses her face, seemingly confused by my uncharacteristic greeting.

"Someone's in a chipper mood today." She closes the mailbox. "Tell me, Dylan, do you make it a habit of dressing up when you check your mail?" She gestures to my three-piece charcoal-gray suit.

"This is what I wear to work," I say, feeling the need to defend my choice of clothing.

"Yeah, but you're home." The sunlight bounces off her golden hair. "Isn't the whole purpose of working remotely so you can wear comfy clothes, at least from the waist down?" A blush rises to her cheeks, and she laughs awkwardly when I don't respond. "Actually, never mind. I think that trend is more common with Gen Zers, not Millennials."

I'm not sure what she's talking about, but it occurs to me that until now, we've never had a normal conversation with just the two of us.

Waffles lets out a discontented bark, displeased that he's being left out. An idea pops into my head on how to best approach this awkward confrontation. I squat down so I'm on his level, and he runs over, practically jumping into my lap.

"Listen, Waffles, we need to have a little chat." I focus my attention on the slobbering canine, not daring to look at Marlow. "I don't want to cramp your style, but I use my loft as an office, and when I'm working from home, it's hard to concentrate when you play your music so loud. Is there any chance you could turn it down when I'm working from home?"

Bored with this conversation, Waffles plops down on the ground.

I click my tongue in disapproval. "I'm disappointed in you, Waffles. I thought you'd take this more seriously."

Marlow bursts out laughing, and when I glance up at her, she's quick to cover her mouth to stifle her reaction. And I find myself wishing she wouldn't.

That's a beautiful sound.

"Is something funny?" I maintain a serious tone.

She shakes her head, unable to speak in between another laughing fit.

"Honestly, Marlow? You shouldn't be encouraging his poor behavior."

She takes a moment to compose herself before crouching next to Waffles, cupping her hand against her ear, like he's sharing a secret. She glances in my direction a couple of times for effect, a grin threatening to pass her lips.

Unable to maintain my stern demeanor any longer, I crack a smile and play along. "Are you going to tell me what he said? The suspense is killing me."

When I glance at Marlow, her mouth is slightly agape.

Confused by her reaction, I furrow my brow, and a blush stealing over the apple of her cheeks when she notices me watching. She clears her throat as she rises to her feet. I follow suit, bringing us face-to-face.

"Waffles says he's sorry about his music being too loud. He zones out while he's working," she says as she tucks a piece of hair behind her ear. "From now on, he promises to wear headphones when you're home during the day."

My throat is suddenly dry. "Tell him I appreciate it. My schedule is all out of sorts since Kendra quit yesterday, and I'm working from home until I can find a new nanny." Marlow bites down on her plump lower lip like she's refraining from saying something she shouldn't, and I force myself not to stare at her mouth. "I hope using headphones doesn't mess with whatever project Waffles has going on up there." I nod to her loft.

"Painting."

"What?"

"Waffles is...I'm an artist," she corrects herself. "I paint textured flowers and sell them online. I figured you should know, just in case you assumed I spent my days hanging around my house with my dog and watching soap operas."

"I didn't think that."

Although I have been curious about what she does for a living.

"Well, I better get back inside; it's freezing out here." Marlow wraps her arms around herself.

I hadn't noticed until now that she wasn't wearing a coat.

"Yeah, I've got to get back to work," I rush out.

I grab a lone bill out of my mailbox before heading toward my house.

"Dylan?" Marlow calls out after me.

I pivot in her direction. "Yeah?"

"In the spirit of being honest, please tell me if you don't want to shovel my driveway anymore." She gives me a reassuring smile. "I'm sure Rick can find someone else."

I furrow my brow. "What does your landlord have to do with it?"

"When I moved in, he agreed to find someone to do the yard work. I'm sure he only asked you because you live next door. But I can tell him to get someone else to do it if you'd prefer not to anymore."

I've never met Rick in person, but I've heard about him. He lives out of state but owns several houses in Aspen Grove. From the stories I've heard from his tenants, he's a total flake and does a poor job of maintaining his properties. It turns out Marlow's been dealing with the same problem as the others, without even realizing it.

As soon as I get Rick's phone number, we're going to have a nice little chat about what it means to be a property owner and the responsibilities that come with it.

I'm flooded with a rush of guilt when I realize I've spent the past year judging Marlow, calling her irresponsible, because she didn't take care of her yard. In reality, she was under the assumption I had been asked to take care of it for her. That explains why she comes to the window to thank me when I'm shoveling outside.

"I don't mind doing it," I reassure her.

And for the first time, I mean it.

I've had all these preconceived notions about Marlow Taylor, and I'm beginning to wonder what others might be wrong.

CHAPTER SIX

MARLOW

I toss a box of limited-edition Lucky Charms with unicorn-shaped marshmallows in my shopping basket for Lola. Occasionally, I surprise her with a gift when I come across something she might like.

Even though she's obsessed with all things unicorn and rainbows, I doubt she's ever had this kind of cereal. From what she's told me, it sounds like Dylan has an aversion to junk food, which I assume includes sugary cereal. This further confirms my decision. You could say I have a thing for pushing his buttons—it makes me positively giddy.

If he saw the contents of my shopping basket, he'd probably develop an ulcer. It's filled with frozen corn dogs, Frosted Strawberry Pop-Tarts, Cheez-Its, creamy peanut butter, canned beef ravioli, and a loaf of bread—my essentials during a big painting project. They aren't the healthiest options, but I prefer quick and easy meals since I often forget to eat when I'm immersed in the creative process.

As I roam the aisles, my thoughts wander to my unusual interactions with Dylan in the last two days. First, there was the incident when he wiped the paint off my face. I'm weak at the knees remembering the touch of his thumb grazing along my lower lip, and his lingering gaze.

And yesterday, I would have figured he'd come pounding on my door, demanding I turn my music down. His approach of using Waffles as a mediator was surprisingly comical and endearing, and I nearly fainted from shock when he smiled at me. It's not like I've been trying to get that man to crack a smile for the past thirteen months or anything.

It's a drastic change from his typical responses, which include a glower, accompanied by sulking and grumbling, with the occasional curt nod tossed in when he's in a good mood.

Aside from his surly attitude, there is no denying that Dylan is attractive. He reminds me of a modern-day Clark Kent, with short black hair, chocolate brown eyes, a chiseled jawline, and his black-rimmed glasses. Not to mention he's positively mouthwatering in a three-piece suit, although I wouldn't admit that to anyone.

When I finish shopping, I take my grocery haul to the register at the front of the store.

Before I moved to Aspen Grove, I assumed small-town grocery stores like Doose's Market in *Gilmore Girls* didn't exist. That is until I visited Main Street Market for the first time and met the owner, Willis Moore. He's a stout man with a thick beard and calloused hands, a testament to being in business for forty years, and he often tells me he'll never retire. I hope he means it because I look forward to seeing him when I stop by.

"Good evening, Willis," I say as I place my basket on the counter and take out the contents for him to scan.

"Evening, Marlow," he greets me, his amber eyes sparkling with warmth. "Where's your little sidekick tonight? He's usually with you."

Despite his unruly behavior, Waffles has made more friends in Aspen Grove than I have.

Since he knocked down an entire display of oranges when he spotted a cat outside, Willis has him hang out behind the counter while I shop. He likes to give Waffles a homemade meatball while he waits.

"He was tuckered out from our afternoon walk, so I left him home to rest." I return the empty basket near the front entrance before coming back to stand at the counter.

Willis chuckles. "Those little legs can only carry him so far, I suppose."

He's right. Waffles might have the energy of a purebred Australian Shepherd, but his corgi genes get in the way of his aspirations.

"Bring him next time, will you? I'm trying a new meatball recipe that I want him to taste."

"You got it, Willis."

Once he's finished ringing everything up, I pay for my groceries and help him bag everything into the two reusable totes I brought with me.

"You're all set," he announces triumphantly when everything's loaded in the bags.

"Thanks so much. I hope you have a great night."

"You too." He pats me on the hand. "Be sure to give Waffles a treat when you get home. He deserves one after that long walk today." He pushes my groceries toward me.

"Don't worry, he'll be eating like a king tonight."

"Good, good," he says, nodding in approval. "See you soon, kid."

I take the bags off the counter and give Willis a parting smile. Another patron kindly opens the door for me on their way into the store.

Stepping outside, I inhale deeply before I begin my walk home, realizing just how much I've come to appreciate living in Aspen Grove. Everyone is friendly and always willing to help each other out.

For as long as I can remember, I've struggled with fitting in, driven by my constant urge for change and inability to stay in one place for very long. While I enjoy traveling and experiencing new cultures, I've felt like something has been missing. No matter how many countries I've visited, new people I meet, or adventures I pursue, I've never felt satisfied.

When I adopted Waffles, he filled a void that I never knew existed. We instantly became a family and moved to Aspen Grove shortly after. It's one of the only places I've lived where I feel like I can be myself without being judged or scrutinized for being different.

For the first time in my life, I think I've found a place I could settle down.

———

The glow of the streetlights illuminates my walk home. As I approach Dylan's house, Johanna's red 4Runner turns onto the street and pulls into his driveway. She steps out of the vehicle and waves at me as she circles the car to help Lola out of the backseat.

The front door of the house swings open, and Dylan steps onto the front porch, dressed in black slacks and a white dress shirt with the top button undone. With his shirtsleeves rolled up, his muscular forearms are on full display. His hair is tousled, as if he's run his hand through it all day. I focus my gaze forward and keep walking, not wanting him to lecture me for gawking, but I don't get far.

"What are you doing?" he shouts from the porch. A stern look crosses his face, his eyes darkened with concern.

When I turn back, he's marching down the driveway, heading straight for me.

Great, what have I done now?

I had hoped we'd be on better terms after yesterday.

He stops in front of me and gives me a disapproving stare. "You shouldn't be out this late by yourself."

"I had to go to the grocery store." A blush spreads across my cheeks while I rearrange the bags in my hand. I'm perplexed by the protective vibes rolling off of Dylan and how I'm finding him more attractive because of it.

"Why are *you* out so late?" I retort.

His brow shoots up in a challenge. "I'm not the one wandering around alone at night," he says incredulously.

"I wasn't *wandering*. I ran errands in town and got groceries on my way home."

"It doesn't matter. It's not safe for you to be out after dark, and there's no way that thing is keeping you warm in this weather." He motions to my puffer coat. "You're beautiful in whatever you wear, so a few extra layers won't do you any harm, if you're concerned about how you look."

I gaze up at him, blinking in confusion. Did Dylan Stafford just call me beautiful?

I refuse to admit that he's right however, about how cold I am, considering he's scolding me like a child.

"Yes, Dad," I mock loudly.

I startle when Lola erupts into a fit of giggles, and I catch Johanna out of the corner of my eye, attempting to contain her amusement. I forgot they were out here with us.

"I mean it, Marlow." Dylan keeps his voice low as he takes a step closer. "We might live in a small town, but that doesn't mean there aren't people who would take advantage of you walking alone at night. You need to be more cautious."

"Why, Dylan, it almost sounds like you're worried about me." I bat my eyelashes.

He opens his mouth to respond, but Lola runs over, tugging on my coat.

"Hey, Marlow." She beams up at me.

"Hi, Lola." I lean down to give her a side hug.

"What have I told you about interrupting?" Dylan asks her.

"Not to do it," she grumbles.

"Exactly. Marlow and I were in the middle of talking about something important."

"Are you asking her to be my new nanny?" Her eyes are filled with hope.

A lump forms in my throat.

Dylan runs his hand across his chiseled jaw and kneels in front of her. "Ladybug, we've talked about this," he says in a gentle tone. "Marlow already has a job."

She's asked him more than once if I could watch her? My heart warms from the sweetness.

"But Daddy, what if she wants two jobs? Why can't we ask her?" Lola pleads.

"Because I don't—"

"I think it's a wonderful idea," Johanna interjects, coming to stand next to me. "Marlow, I'm not sure if Dylan told you that Kendra quit or that he can't find a replacement." She ignores Dylan's glacial stare as she speaks. "Is there any chance you'd consider watching Lola on weekday mornings and occasionally in the afternoon? Dylan would be happy to pay you a premium wage," she says confidently. "I can't think of a better person for the job, and Lola is so fond of you. We both are."

I've already contemplated offering to help at least a dozen times since I found out that Kendra quit. It would mean I'd have to work longer hours to finish my collection for the art show on time, but it's a sacrifice I'd be willing to make for Lola's sake. The fact that Dylan is opposed to the idea is the cherry on top.

Dylan stands up. "Mom, I don't think—"

"I'd love to be Lola's nanny," I interrupt him. "I have a flexible schedule, and my mornings are free, so it works out perfectly. Besides, who could refuse when Dylan's willing to pay a premium?" I can't help taunting him.

I flash him a broad grin, my eyes bright with amusement, a stark contrast to his dark, brooding glare.

I'm not offering because of the money. I'll have to buy Lola a giant unicorn stuffed animal or hire a petting zoo in the summer with the money I earn. I'm sure Dylan would love that.

He arches a brow at my response. "You would?"

"Sure, I can't think of anyone who could say no to spending their mornings with the cutest six-year-old in Aspen Grove." I grin at Lola who's practically bouncing on the balls of her feet with excitement.

"Do you have any experience with kids?" Dylan asks and I go with the truth.

"Honestly, not really," I shrug. "I was an only child. There weren't many young families in our neighborhood, so I never babysat or anything like that." I hold my hand out before he can interrupt. "But I take care of Waffles, and I'd like to think I do a great job."

Dylan looks less than amused. "Did you just compare taking care of your dog to watching my kid? An undisciplined dog, might I add."

I huff in annoyance. "Is your opinion of me so low that you seriously doubt my ability to look after your daughter for a few hours each morning? Lola means a lot to me, and I would never do anything to jeopardize her safety. You should know that by now."

Evidently, I said something right because he visibly relaxes, even if only a little.

Johanna silently watches our exchange with a bemused expression.

"Daddy, please say Marlow can be my new nanny, pretty please?" Lola implores.

"Yeah, Dylan, pretty please," I add with a smirk.

"This is going to end in a disaster," he mutters under his breath. "Fine. But it's only temporary until the agency can find a long-term solution, got it?"

"Got it," Lola and I say in unison.

I'll just have to prove that I'm as capable as any professional nanny. Lola already likes me, so at least I have one thing going for me.

"And Waffles stays at your place. I don't want him destroying my house while I'm at work," Dylan says.

Lola frowns but doesn't argue.

"That's fine," I agree.

"Can you start in the morning?"

"Yeah, sure."

"Oh, thank you, Daddy." Lola throws her arms around Dylan's waist. "I'm so excited I could burst."

Her enthusiasm means everything.

Johanna leans in to whisper in my ear. "Don't worry, Marlow. Once Dylan sees how wonderful you are with Lola, he'll be begging you to stay."

I ignore the nagging suspicion that she's not talking about me being Lola's nanny.

CHAPTER SEVEN

DYLAN

I pace the length of the floral runner in my entryway, stopping at the edge before turning around and striding to the other end. It's 5:55 a.m., and I told Marlow to be here by 6:00 a.m.

This is a terrible idea.

I temporarily lost my sanity last night when I saw her walking by herself in that ridiculous pink puffer coat of hers. My protective instincts kicked in, prompting me to suggest she choose warmer outerwear and stress the importance of being more alert of her surroundings.

That should have been the end of it, but naturally, my mother misread the situation, assuming my actions had a different meaning. Which led her to agreeing with the silly notion that Marlow should be Lola's nanny. I'm sure she's hoping that our being in close proximity will lead to something more. She's going to be sorely disappointed when this doesn't work out how she envisioned.

While I might have misjudged Marlow, I have reservations about her watching Lola. She openly acknowledged her lack of experience with kids, and I can't get past the comparison she made between caring for my daughter and taking care of her dog.

Frankly, if the nanny agency hadn't reached out yesterday to tell me that it could be months before they can find a replacement for Kendra, I wouldn't have agreed to give her the position, even temporarily. However, given my current predicament, I'm not in a position to turn down her offer. It's just not feasible for me to work from home indefinitely right now.

Which brings me back to my original thought. *This is a terrible id—*

A light tap on the door brings my pacing to an abrupt stop. I open the door to find Marlow on the porch with a floral satchel slung over her shoulder. She's wearing a bold pink, purple, and white color-block sweatshirt, and matching pants paired with her silver sneakers. Her hair is pulled back into a high ponytail, secured with a shimmering red scrunchie.

She's gorgeous.

A thought that plays on an endless loop in my brain, overpowering any semblance of logic. And I am uncharacteristically nervous that this woman is now invading my personal space.

"Are you going to invite me in?" she questions.

"Oh, yeah, come in." I step aside, motioning for her to come inside. "We have a 'no shoes' policy in the house so if you'd leave yours on the rack"—I gesture to the shoe rack in the corner —"I'd appreciate it."

Marlow visibly winces, probably recalling the only other time she's been in my house.

"Of course," she says in a hushed tone. She tugs her sneakers off and puts them on the shoe rack like I asked.

"Why are you whispering?"

"I figure Lola is sleeping, and I don't want to wake her up."

Her expressed sentiment brings a wave of relief. At the very least, Marlow genuinely cares for Lola, and I firmly believe she wouldn't do anything to put her in harm's way.

"You don't have to worry about that. She's a deep sleeper and has a sound machine in her room. She rarely wakes up before her alarm goes off. Let's just say she's not an early morning person." That's putting it lightly. My child did not inherit my preference for starting the day early. However, since she started first grade, she's adapted to waking up in time for school.

Marlow lets out a melodic laugh. "She sounds like a girl after my own heart. I'm not a morning person either. I'm more of a night owl."

And yet she took a job that requires her to be here before sunrise?

"If that's the case, why did you take this position if you don't mind me asking?"

"Because Lola asked me to," Marlow states without skipping a beat.

Her answer catches me off guard. "You're telling me you agreed to be Lola's nanny because she asked you to? What about the money?"

She folds her arms across her chest, clearly offended by the insinuation.

"Believe it or not, Dylan, I do very well for myself," she shoots back. "I offered to help because it's the right thing to do. The only reason I'm not walking out that door"—she motions outside—"is because it would hurt Lola if I did."

I'm momentarily speechless. Despite not being a morning person, and having financial stability, she willingly agreed to this simply because my daughter wanted her to. It's becoming apparent that I should refrain from making assumptions about her altogether, although it's easier said than done.

"Fuck, you're right." I run my hand through my hair. "I apologize for jumping to conclusions. It was wrong of me."

"Did you just drop the f-bomb? I thought parents were supposed to avoid using expletives," Marlow quips.

"Yeah, well, I'm still a work in progress," I mutter. "I got in the habit of swearing as a teenager, and going cold turkey when Lola was born was impossible."

Marlow lets out a snicker. "You're older than I thought."

"I'm thirty-three, not sixty, thank you very much."

"That's ten years older than me," she says in disbelief. "I have to say I'm impressed you don't have any gray hairs yet... oh, wait, I found one."

Marlow moves closer, leaning in to graze her fingertips through the hair along my temple. Her brows furrow in concentration as she supposedly counts my gray hairs. She runs her hand along my scalp, and I briefly close my eyes, savoring her touch. Her hands are gentle and soft, and I'm aware of the faint scent of citrus and rose.

Wait... what am I doing?

My eyes snap open as I realize how inappropriate this is. Marlow is here to watch Lola, and my reaction to her touching me is anything but professional. She must be on the same wavelength because her eyes widen, and she jerks her hand away just as I instinctively step back.

"I uh—sorry. Is there anything I should know before you leave?" she asks.

"Yeah, follow me." I lead her past the living room, down the hallway, and into the kitchen. "Lola needs to be out of bed by 7:30 a.m., she eats breakfast at 7:45 a.m., and has to be out the door no later than 8:10 a.m. All the information you need is in here." I grab the binder from the kitchen island and pass it to Marlow. I woke up early to update several sections, including to add her contact info that she gave me last night.

She glances at the binder and back at me. "What is this?"

"Lola's binder. There's a detailed schedule of our daily routine, a list of her likes and dislikes, approved meal options, emergency contacts, our house rules—"

"Oh, is this all?" she teases.

"If you have something to say, just say it." I sigh.

"Dylan, this thing is two inches thick." She holds the binder up in her hand for emphasis. "Lola is six. All I need to know is if she has any food allergies and where to drop her off at school."

"It's all in the binder." I tap it for emphasis.

She lets out a heavy sigh. "Fine, I'll read through the binder. Now, don't you have a helicopter to catch or something?"

"Oh, shit." I check my watch to see that I'm running late.

I would prefer to work from home on Marlow's first day, but that's not an option since I have several in-person meetings scheduled today. I'll have to trust that she can handle things on her own this morning.

"I hope you watch your mouth in front of Lola. Or should I expect the principal to pull me aside during school drop-off and ask why Lola is swearing in class again?" She chuckles.

"Who told you about that? It only happened once, and that was over a month ago," I scoff.

This is one of the downsides of living in a small town. News spreads like wildfire, and it's all anyone can talk about for months.

"My friend Quinn owns Brush & Palette, the local art supply store. All the teachers and parents from the elementary school shop there, so she's well-formed about town gossip."

I cross my arms. "Did she also tell you that Henry Livingston's parents got a call from the principal because he was flipping off a classmate? He thought it was a gesture used when you like someone because his parents used it so much. Oh, and Judy Callister snuck in her phone to school last week and played her favorite song for her friends. Apparently, it drops the f-bomb every other sentence. Did I mention both kids are in Lola's first-grade class?"

Marlow shakes her head in amusement. "Yes, well, according to the gossip mill, Henry's parents have been in marriage counseling for years, and Judy's dad is a record producer who works with several famous musicians based in Los Angeles. In your case, it's quite the scandal that a chief financial officer can't control his language," she places the binder back on the counter.

My phone buzzes, alerting me to a message from the pilot asking me where I am.

"I have to go. Promise you'll read the binder before Lola wakes up?"

"Yeah, yeah," she waves me off. "Lola is going to be fine, I promise."

"I'll check in once I land in the city," I tell her before rushing out the door.

> How's everything going? Is Lola okay?

MARLOW

She's perfect. Just like the last thirty-six times you've asked.

> I left you alone with my kid. Of course, I'm going to check in.

MARLOW

But thirty-six times in an hour?

> Has she had breakfast yet?

MARLOW

I'm hurt by your lack of confidence.

Here's proof that we're doing fine without you

sent attachment

> What the hell, Marlow? Why is Lola eating Lucky Charms? Did you not read the binder? She needs a healthy and nutritious breakfast before school, not sugar cereal. Where did you find that anyway? And are those unicorn marshmallows???

MARLOW

Yup, aren't they adorable? Lola's obsessed.

And FYI... I brought the cereal with me 😊

I'm on the verge of going back to Aspen Grove until I look closer at the photo Marlow sent.

Fishtail braids.

She has woven Lola's hair into perfect fishtail braids, with sparkly red bows tied to the ends.

Lola's at the kitchen counter, perched on a bar stool, her mouth full of cereal. She's decked out in her favorite unicorn sweater, grinning from ear to ear. My heart swells with warmth at the sight of her. Regardless of my mixed feelings toward Marlow, Lola is thoroughly enjoying herself. And her fishtail braids.

Another text from Marlow pops up.

> MARLOW
>
> I better go. We have a schedule to keep, and I wouldn't want to get in trouble with the warden if we're late. 😊

> Text me when you drop Lola off at school.

> MARLOW
>
> Sure thing, boss. 🫡

Even in text messages, she's snarky, and her sunny disposition shines through. It's incredibly irritating so I'm not sure why I'm smiling at my phone.

I tuck it in my pocket as I exit the elevator on the top floor of the Stafford Holdings office building. With only five minutes before my first meeting, I have to hurry if I don't want to be late. My plan is thwarted when I get to my office to find Cash lounging in my chair, his hands interlaced behind his head.

"Do I need to remind you that breaking and entering is a crime?"

"Good morning to you, too," he says casually.

I place my briefcase on my desk and take out my laptop, but he doesn't make a move to leave.

"Any specific reason you're in my chair with a goofy grin on your face?" I ask skeptically.

"Yes, as a matter of fact, there is." He drops his arms and leans forward. He's always had a flair for theatrics.

"Well, are you going to tell me what it is?"

"Mom called Presley last night and told her that Marlow is Lola's new nanny." He pauses for effect. "The same Marlow you were complaining about a couple of days ago. Care to explain?"

"Why don't you tell me how you got this information first?"

Because I sure as hell didn't tell him.

"Naturally, Presley called me as soon as she finished talking with Mom so we could chat."

"Naturally." I deadpan.

Presley was born seven years after Cash, but despite their age difference, they've always been close. Since Presley moved to New York, Cash and her talk almost every day, which apparently include conversations about my new nanny.

"So, what gives?" he prods, drumming his fingers against the glossy black wood of my desk.

"There's nothing to tell." I tuck my laptop under my arm in preparation to head to the conference room. "I haven't been able to find a permanent replacement for Kendra yet. And when Lola practically begged Marlow to be her nanny, Mom intervened and said she thought it was a good idea. Marlow's only helping temporarily until I find a long-term solution."

"Uh-huh." Cash doesn't look convinced. "And what happens when Lola falls in love with Marlow?"

Unfortunately for me, she's probably already halfway there.

"I'll figure it out," I mutter.

"And what happens when *you* fall in love with Marlow?" His hazel eyes bore into me as he brushes his shaggy brown hair away from his face.

That's not going to happen.

"I think you've had enough fun for one day." I round the desk and grab him by the collar of his black shirt. "Get out."

He laughs as I practically shove him out of my office, not caring that a group of employees have stopped to watch our exchange.

"Have a wonderful day, Dylan. Don't think I didn't notice you avoided my question." Cash says with a smirk, whistling as he waltzes down the hall.

CHAPTER EIGHT

MARLOW

"I wish Waffles could have spent the morning with us." Lola sighs, glancing at my house as we pass by it on our way to school. "He looks so sad."

Waffles is standing in my art studio with his nose pressed against the window, gazing down at us. I can almost hear him whining from here.

"Does Kendra have a pet?" I ask.

"Yeah, her cat, Mr. Whiskers." Lola giggles at the mention of his name. "She showed me lots of pictures."

"Did she ever bring Mr. Whiskers with her to your house?"

Lola shakes her head. "Daddy doesn't allow pets in the house."

"Do you think he would have been happy if I brought Waffles over when he asked me not to?"

"No, he'd be mad."

"Exactly."

The last time Waffles was in Dylan's house, he was uninvited, resulting in a big mess, and I'd prefer to avoid a similar situation in the future. Dylan's already upset at me for giving Lola cereal for breakfast, and the last thing I need is another strike against me.

It took me a solid hour to read what I'm affectionately calling "The Manual." I did take a snack break and nodded off on the couch twice. In my defense, Dylan's sofa was exceptionally comfortable, and my reading material was more boring than a calculus textbook.

Did I mention the pages were single-spaced, and there weren't even any pictures? I deserve a reward for making it through the whole thing. Thank goodness I had a pack of markers in my bag, so I could highlight the important sections that I may want to reference later.

Once I finished my required reading, I explored while waiting for Lola to wake up, since I didn't have much of a chance to look around the first time I was there.

I discovered that Dylan's house is a utopia for organizational enthusiasts. A white monochromatic palette with gray accent pieces dominates the main floor. I assume he hired an interior decorator because the place has zero personality. Aside from Lola's pictures neatly hung on the fridge, there isn't any indication that a kid lives there.

The kitchen is impeccable—there's not a single junk drawer. Every drawer has a liner and dividers to keep everything in its proper place. The large pantry, with meticulously organized shelves filled with labeled containers, bins, and baskets, belongs in a home décor magazine. I couldn't help but notice almost every item was labeled as organic, and the snack choices were exclusively healthy options. There isn't a single Cheez-It or Pop-Tart in the place, which is a travesty.

The living room is just as impeccable. A massive media center with custom doors conceals the TV, and books arranged by size and color fill the gray bookshelf in the corner. It's worth noting that the white furniture doesn't have a single stain in sight— trust me, I checked.

When I went into Lola's room to wake her, I was relieved that it looked like a rainbow bomb had gone off. Her pink bedding is covered in unicorns, rainbows, and clouds. A hammock filled to the brim with colorful stuffed animals occupies one corner, and a massive shaggy rug is next to the bed. The one thing missing was color on the walls. I'm already plotting ways to convince Dylan to let me paint them.

Thankfully, we were out of the house by 8:08 a.m., or Dylan might have lost it.

When Lola and I get to the elementary school, I notice the other parents and staff are staring. I keep a low profile, but Aspen Grove is a small town, which means even the slightest deviation from the norm attracts attention. It's easy to predict the inevitable gossip circulating after everyone sees me dropping Lola off at school.

I disregard the curious glances as I follow Lola to the brick building's front entrance. When we reach the top step, she turns around to face me.

"Could you drop me off here?" she begs.

I hesitate for a moment, remembering the specific paragraph in The Manual—that I highlighted in purple—about having to escort Lola to her classroom.

"Your dad asked me to walk you to class, but I'm willing to compromise," I say.

She scrunches her nose in confusion. "What does that mean?"

"Compromise is when two people want different things and agree to meet in the middle. Make sense?"

"No." She scratches her head.

I drum my fingers against my mouth as I think of a better way to explain.

"Your dad asked me to walk you to your classroom, but you'd rather I drop you off here." I motion around us. "A compromise would be if I go inside the building but let you walk to your classroom alone. That way, I can watch you get there safely from a distance."

"Oh… okay." She smiles. "Can we do that?"

I nod. "Yeah, we can. Why don't we go inside now?"

She hurries to the door, attempting to open it on her own.

When it proves to be too heavy, she looks to me for help. I grab higher on the handle and provide the added force to open it.

Once we're inside, Lola points to the left side of the hall. "My classroom is door number three on that side."

"Thanks for showing me. I'll wait right here." I smile.

"Okay, thanks, Marlow." She wraps her arms around my waist, hugging me tightly. "I'm glad you're my new nanny."

"Me too, sweetheart."

She releases me and heads in the direction of her classroom. "See you later, alligator," she hollers over her shoulder.

"In a while, crocodile," I yell back, ignoring the irritated looks from several parents loitering in the hallway.

"I've never heard that one before. I like it," Lola exclaims as she skips down the hall. Her backpack bounces with every step.

Her teacher is standing by the door and welcomes her with a high five when she enters the classroom.

I send Dylan a text confirming that Lola has been dropped off at school.

I'd call this a successful first day on the job.

The bell's chime announces my arrival as I enter Brush & Palette.

The air is filled with some of my favorite scents—wood, paint, and cinnamon. There's an adorable string heart display near the front of the door, promoting an upcoming Valentine's Day craft night.

"I'll be right with you." Quinn's voice comes from the back of the shop. She must be knee-deep in restocking the new inventory from the big shipment she got in yesterday.

I browse the arts and crafts section and select a pack of washable paints. Johanna mentioned that I'll occasionally watch Lola in the afternoons and I figure it'll be fun for us to paint together. After I grab a bottle of mineral spirits from the aisle over, I pull out my phone and send an electronic payment for my purchases.

I know how much Quinn dislikes having to reconcile cash payments.

I find my friend at the back of the store, teetering precariously on a ladder, stacking a new style of wooden picture frames. Her shoulder-length black hair frames her face in unruly waves, and she's rocking her go-to work outfit: a blazer, dark-wash jeans, and a black smock over the top.

"One of these days you're going to fall and break your neck, if you're not careful," I say playfully.

She glances over at me. "You're late," she scolds. "I've been waiting for a half hour."

"I'm sorry, it's been a hectic morning." I move closer. "And I grabbed a couple of things when I came in." I hold up the pack of paints and mineral spirts. "I already transferred money to your account."

"That's great, thank you." She puts the last picture frame in place before climbing down the ladder to greet me.

Quinn Matthews was the first friend I made when I moved to Aspen Grove. We met while I was chasing Waffles down Main Street after he bolted after a squirrel during our morning walk. Quinn witnessed the entire spectacle and intercepted Waffles when he tried to run past her. I bought her coffee as a token of appreciation, and we've been friends since.

"So, when are you planning on telling me how your first morning as Lola Stafford's nanny was?" she asks with a raised brow.

"It was—Hold on. How did you know about that?" I haven't had the chance to update her about my new job since I only got the position last night.

"Sarah McCormick stopped by to grab some sketch pads for her daughter a few minutes ago. She mentioned that she saw you walking with Lola Stafford to school. According to her, you're the talk of the town."

"It seems everyone is interested in my whereabouts this morning."

While I've heard the saying that news travels fast in a small town, I never experienced it firsthand until moving to Aspen Grove.

"What do you expect? Dylan's one of the hottest commodities around. Ever since he started bringing Lola to the Mommy and Me craft class on Saturdays, attendance has tripled. I'm considering changing the name to Family Craft Corner because of him. Maybe more hot single dads will attend if I do." Quinn wiggles her eyebrows.

I frown. "You never told me he brought Lola to one of your classes."

"No, because Dylan Stafford is a topic of conversation you usually prefer to avoid."

"We're best friends. You're supposed to tell me everything, even if you don't think I want to hear it."

"Marlow, are you jealous that Dylan is spending his Saturday afternoons with a roomful of women who openly lust after him?" She gives me a teasing grin. "Don't worry, he doesn't pay them any mind. He only has eyes for Lola."

"Oh my gosh, will you stop?" I throw my hands over my face in embarrassment. "He's totally not my type."

That's a lie. He looks like Clark Kent—he's everyone's type.

Quinn shoots me a skeptical look, as if she has a direct line to my thoughts. "That's bullshit. He's a hot single dad, rich, and incredibly intelligent. He's the complete package, and dating him would be like winning the lottery," she says, like it's an undeniable truth.

"If he's so perfect, why don't you date him?"

"While I adore Lola, I'm not looking for that kind of responsibility. Dylan needs to be with someone who loves that little girl just as much as he does," Quinn says.

I let out a sigh of relief. The idea of Dylan with someone else makes me queasy, but I quickly shake it off.

"Are we going over to Brew Haven or what?" I ask, changing

the subject. "Andi texted me on the way over and said she can't get away from work, so it's just you and me today."

I put the paints and mineral spirits I bought in my floral satchel.

"That gives us plenty of time for you to give me all the dirty details on how this morning went." Quinn has a mischievous glint in her eye.

I roll my eyes. "Seriously, will you stop?"

My phone rings in my pocket.

When I check to see who it is, I don't recognize the number, but I need to answer in case it has to do with Lola.

"Hey, I have to get this," I tell Quinn.

"No problem." She picks up the box next to the ladder. "I'm going to put the rest of this inventory in the storage room, and then we can lock it up."

I give her a thumbs up and answer the call.

"Hello?"

"Hi, Marlow, this is Johanna Stafford, Dylan's mother. I'm so sorry to bother you, but is there any chance you could pick up Lola from school today?" I hear a car engine in the background. "Mike and I have dentist appointments this afternoon that I forgot about, and we won't be finished in time to pick up Lola."

"I'd be happy to," I say, moving to the front of the store.

"Oh, that's wonderful news. Thank you so much," she exclaims. "I can stop at your place once I'm finished with my appointment."

"Lola's welcome to hang out with me and Waffles until Dylan gets home tonight. As long as that's okay with you and Dylan, of course."

"Are you sure?"

"Definitely."

"Okay, Lola will be ecstatic. I'll call the school to tell them you're picking her up. Thanks again."

"Anytime."

I put my phone back in my pocket just as Quinn comes to the front of the store.

"Who was that?"

"Johanna Stafford. She asked if I could pick Lola up from school and watch her until Dylan gets home from work."

Quinn smirks. "And so it begins."

I give her a puzzled look. "What do you mean?"

She dismisses me with a wave of her hand. "It's nothing important. Let's go. I'm in desperate need of a caffeine fix." She flips the sign on the door to CLOSED.

As I follow her down the street toward the coffee shop, I'm left wondering what she was going to say.

CHAPTER NINE

DYLAN

It was a long day at the office, made longer when my mom called to tell me that Marlow was picking up Lola from school today. Supposedly, my parents had dentist appointments that Mom forgot about, but I don't buy it. She's even more organized than I am. So the idea that she forgot about an appointment until the day of doesn't add up.

Meetings consumed my entire afternoon, preventing me from checking in with Marlow as often as I'd have liked. She texted me when she picked up Lola from school and said they were going over to her house. I would have preferred they went back to my place, but I figured it was best not to push the issue.

When I pull into my driveway at 7:30 p.m., all the lights are off at my house. In stark contrast, Marlow's place is brightly lit, and the faint sound of music is coming from the loft. She's lucky the elderly lady who lives on the other side of her is hard of hearing, or she'd have a stack of noise complaints by now.

I head straight over to her place.

When my knock on the front door goes unanswered, I test the handle, a low growl escaping me when I find it unlocked.

Unbelievable.

First, Marlow strolls the streets of Aspen Grove late at night, and now this? It's absolutely unacceptable. She needs to be more careful. I doubt she was this careless when living in the city. At least I hope that's the case.

When I step inside, I nearly trip over a sneaker. The entryway is littered with dog toys, jackets, and shoes.

I peek inside the living room, not surprised that the space mirrors Marlow's vibrant and chaotic personality. The walls are painted a salmon pink, and a massive, multi-colored geometric rug covers the floor. Several pieces of furniture are strategically situated in the room—including a mustard yellow couch, two blue paisley print chairs, and a vintage wooden coffee table.

I follow the sound of "Girls Just Want to Have Fun" to the loft.

The door is wide open, giving me an unobstructed view of Lola, sprawled on the floor, finger painting. Waffles is sitting next to her, his head resting against her shoulder. Both are covered in splotches of purple and orange paint.

A smile tugs at my lips until I spot a plate nearby with the remnants of what look like corn dogs, Cheez-Its, and peanut butter.

Why is Marlow giving Lola junk food when I explicitly told her not to?

Marlow's on the other end of the room, her attention on a large canvas propped up on an easel. As I step closer, I see she's skillfully applying texture to a hydrangea. The flower is a mixture of white and various shades of purple. This isn't what I imagined when she told me she was an artist.

While art isn't my area of expertise, I still recognize an exceptional piece like Marlow's flower, which practically leaps off the canvas. Her artistic ability is unmatched, and her style is truly remarkable. If I weren't so wound up, I could stand here admiring her work all night and still find new elements to appreciate.

In typical Marlow fashion, she's decked in her faded floral

overalls, paired with a white long-sleeved shirt covered in pink hearts and red fuzzy socks.

"Daddy, you're back."

Lola's enthusiastic squeal has me turning to catch her as she runs into my arms. I disregard the sticky purple paint that's been transferred from her hands to my white shirt.

"I missed you, ladybug." I place a kiss on her head.

"I missed you too. Waffles and I painted you a picture," she says, holding out a piece of paper covered with dozens of orange and purple handprints, plus several orange paw prints.

"It's beautiful. I can't wait to put it on the fridge at home. Why don't you go down to the bathroom and wash the paint off your hands so we can go home? I'm just going to chat with Marlow for a minute."

"I can do that," she shouts over the music. "Come on, Waffles, let's go get cleaned up."

He follows her down the steps, leaving faded orange paw prints behind. It's a good thing this house has wood floors or that would be a nightmare to clean up later.

Marlow still hasn't acknowledged me, which frustrates me. She was supposed to be taking care of Lola, but apparently couldn't be bothered enough to play with her. Sitting her down with paints and letting her have free rein is unacceptable.

I stride over to the speaker on the cluttered desk and switch it off, sighing in relief when I can hear myself think.

Marlow finally sets her palette knife on the ledge of the easel and turns around with a grin on her face. "Hey, you're back. How was work?" she asks.

"Care to explain why you're working on a project instead of taking care of my daughter?" I perch on the edge of the desk.

Her smile instantly turns to a frown. "Excuse me?"

I wave to the mess Lola and Waffles left behind. "You can't leave a six-year-old unattended with paint. And in the future, I'd appreciate it if you'd keep your music down while my daughter

73

is in the room. You might not care about your eardrums, but I would prefer Lola not to have premature hearing loss."

She flinches at my insult, keeping her hands clenched at her sides. "Anything else you want to add to your list of grievances?" Her voice is noticeably icy.

"Actually, yeah, there is. Want to tell me why my daughter had corn dogs and Cheez-Its for dinner when there are ten pages of healthy meal options in the binder that you supposedly *read*?" I use air quotes for emphasis.

Marlow briefly closes her eyes and takes a deep breath before she replies. "For the record, the paint is washable. I picked it up from Brush & Palette earlier today. This studio is meant for creating, and the mess that comes with that doesn't bother me." She keeps her voice even and calm. "I read your stupid binder, and all the dinner options in there take at least an hour to make. When Lola told me she was hungry, she was on the verge of a meltdown, and I wasn't going to make her wait that long to eat. Plus, I'm not a good cook, so whatever I would have made probably wouldn't have been edible."

"What else were you complaining about?" She taps her finger against her mouth while she thinks. "Oh, yeah, the part where you think I neglected your daughter. Lola asked if she could paint you a surprise and didn't want me to see it. I pretended I wasn't paying attention, but I checked on her every few minutes. When you got here, I figured you'd want an uninterrupted moment alone with her." By this point, fumes are practically coming out of Marlow's ears. "I've told you; I'd never do anything to put Lola in harm's way. This arrangement won't work if you keep doubting my ability, temporary or not."

I stand up and close the distance between us. "You forgot to explain why the music was so loud." My throat is dry, making it difficult to get the words out. I try to ignore the tightening in my chest at Marlow's crestfallen expression, but there's something jarring about seeing her so subdued.

She shakes her head. "No, I just didn't want to admit that

you were right about that," she confesses with a downcast glance. "I'm sorry."

God, I'm such an asshole.

When I got here, Lola's excitement was palpable, and it's clear that she had an amazing time. Despite my concerns, she's safe and happier than I've ever seen her.

The reason for that is standing right in front of me. Marlow might be messy and chaotic, yet she has a way of connecting with my daughter like no one else can, and I took that for granted tonight.

"Look, I apo—"

I'm cut off when Waffles come running out of nowhere, tumbling into Marlow. I instinctively wrap my arms around her waist to keep her from falling, bringing her body flush with mine. She grabs hold of my shoulders to keep her balance, only a breath of air separating her breasts from pressing against my upper chest. Her scent tickles my nose—paint, citrus, rose, and something sweet.

A searing wave of warmth licks up my spine as her gaze moves from my Adams apple.. Her pupils are blown wide, and her breath catches, a clear sign she's affected by our close proximity too. The last time we were this close, I didn't take the chance to *really* look at her. I'm not making the same mistake again.

I take the moment to study her heart-shaped face. A rosy hue colors her cheeks, and she has a dusting of freckles along the bridge of her nose. Her mouth is slightly parted, and she tilts her head back as she observes me in return. My favorite feature is her unique mismatched eyes.

She's so goddamn beautiful.

My pulse quickens when I shift my focus to her pouty lips, and an unexpected notion crosses my mind, imagining what it would be like to kiss her. Without thinking, I wipe a smudge of purple paint off her cupid's bow, and she shivers at my touch.

"You and that dog of yours are a whole lot of trouble," I whisper.

"At least there's never a dull moment with us around," she murmurs.

I'm about to apologize for my outburst when we're interrupted again.

"Daddy, my hands are all clean, see?" Lola comes running into the room, holding out her hands.

I release my grip on Marlow and step back, creating some much-needed distance between us. I have no idea what came over me, touching her like that, but it won't be happening again.

At least that's what I'm telling myself.

I shift my focus to Lola, bending down to inspect her hands. Most of the paint is gone except for a couple of splotches between her fingers.

"You did a great job, ladybug." I affectionately tap her on the nose. "Why don't you say goodbye to Marlow and Waffles so we can go home? It's late, and you've got to get ready for bed."

"Will I get to see Marlow tomorrow?" she asks.

"Yeah, first thing in the morning."

"Oh, goodie," she exclaims, rushing over to drape her arms around Waffles. "I'll see you soon, boy."

Waffles licks her face, leaving a slobbery mark on her cheek. I wrinkle my nose as Lola wipes it off on her pant leg. Those clothes are going straight into the washer, and Lola is getting a bath as soon as we get home.

Lola hugs Marlow next. "See you in the morning."

"See you soon," Marlow says, avoiding looking at me.

"Come on, Lola, we have to go now." I scoop her up in my arms and hightail it out of the loft, locking Marlow's front door on our way out.

"Unicorns or rainbows tonight?" I hold out the two pairs of pajamas for Lola.

"Those." She points to the set with rainbows.

"Excellent choice." I hand them to her.

Once she's changed into her pj's, she jumps into bed, and climbs under the covers. I tuck her favorite stuffed animals around her and grab her copy of *Madeline* from the nightstand.

"Hey, Daddy?"

"Yeah, ladybug?" I sit on the side of her bed.

"Can we hang the picture Waffles and I made on the fridge like you promised?"

"Yeah, sure. I just need to get it from Marlow." I was in such a hurry to get out of there that I totally forgot about Lola's painting.

I shouldn't have said those things to Marlow earlier. She didn't deserve it.

She might not have done things the way I wanted her to, but Lola's happiness matters most, and it's obvious that spending time with Marlow makes her happy.

"Thanks, Daddy. You can leave now," Lola says quickly.

"Um, ladybug? We haven't read *Madeline* yet." I hold up the book to show I'm ready to start.

"I'd rather go to sleep." She lies down on her pillow, snuggling deeper into her blankets.

That's odd, because she usually rushes through her bedtime routine so we can read, and when I finish, she begs me to stay for *just five more minutes.*

I tilt my head. "What's the real reason you want me to leave?"

"Marlow's coming in the morning, and I hate waiting. If I go to sleep now, she'll be here sooner."

A lump forms in my throat. Lola never acted this way with Kendra, or anyone else for that matter.

"Makes sense." I stand up and put the book on the night-stand. "If you change your mind, you know where to find me."

"I won't," Lola assures me. "Goodnight, Daddy." She turns to her side and closes her eyes.

I turn off her unicorn lamp on my way out and close the door behind me.

I linger in the hallway, pondering my predicament. My daughter is more content than I've seen her in a long time, and I can't bear to be the one who takes that away.

———

There's a soft knock on my front door precisely at 6:00 a.m. I swing it open to find Marlow on my porch, nervously fidgeting with her hands and wearing an apprehensive expression—a noticeable contrast from her usual cheerful and bubbly personality. *I don't like it.*

"Is everything okay?" My voice is filled with concern.

She bites down on her lower lip. "Honestly, Dylan, I wasn't sure you'd want me back after what you said last night," she says softly. "I almost didn't come, but couldn't risk upsetting Lola.

Dammit, I should have called her after putting Lola to bed last night, but I wanted to apologize in person so she knew I was sincere.

"Can you come inside so we can talk?"

"Sure." She moves past me into the entryway, removes her shoes, and puts them on the shoe rack. When she's finished, she stands stiffly in the entryway.

"Listen, Marlow, I think I owe you an apology."

She raises a brow. "You think?"

I suppress a smile, glad to see her cheeky demeanor is back.

"As you've noticed, I have specific preferences, especially concerning Lola. I want the best for her, and it's hard for me not to have control over certain things." I rub my hand along the back of my neck as I think carefully about my next words. "It doesn't justify me taking out my frustrations on you last night. You did nothing wrong," I say with assurance. "I should have explained how I was feeling instead of losing my temper the way I did. Lola enjoyed her time with you, and that's all that matters."

The nannies I've hired previously adhered to the instructions I outlined in the binder, and my parents have always been willing to adapt to my way of doing things when it came to Lola. So, it was a shock when I came home yesterday to find that Marlow had done it differently.

She wasn't joking about reading the entire binder. She tabbed every section with the pink and yellow sticky notes I keep in the kitchen and highlighted important paragraphs in a rainbow of colors.

"Thank you for saying that," Marlow says, her gaze fixed on me. "I admit I was wrong to go against your wishes. Instead of giving Lola that junk food, I should have found an alternative dinner option." She nervously tucks her hair behind her ear. "When I dropped her off at school yesterday, she asked me what compromise meant. It got me thinking that you and I need to compromise on some things to make this arrangement work for Lola's sake."

She's right. I only wish I had come up with a similar conclusion sooner.

"I'm listening," I encourage her.

"It would be helpful if you made a list of quick and easy healthy dinner options for me to reference on the days I have Lola after school. While I agree Lola shouldn't have sugar cereal and Cheez-Its every day, I'd like to be able to give her a special treat on occasion as long as that's alright with you.

"You mentioned last night cooking isn't your forte. Why don't I make some premade options that can be kept in the fridge so all you have to do is warm them up? Would that work?"

Marlow smiles. "I'd appreciate it."

"I can live with Lola having the occasional sugary snack as long as you tell me about it," I say. "What else?"

"I shouldn't have played my music so loud with Lola in the room, but she rather enjoyed the songs, so I have every intention of playing them for her when we're together."

"That's fine. As long as the songs are age appropriate, and don't have profanity."

She lets out a throaty laugh. "I can assure you if Lola learns any more curse words, it'll be because of your bad habits, not mine."

"Touché." A subtle smile plays on my lips. I wish I knew why I enjoyed bantering with Marlow so much. "I don't mind the two of you spending time at your place in the afternoons. I only ask that if I'm running late, you bring Lola back here so her bedtime routine isn't disrupted."

"Yeah, okay. Look at us learning to compromise like adults," she says playfully.

"Compromising, yes. Like adults?" I gesture to her vintage T-shirt with a rainbow on the front, similar to one I bought for Lola when we went back-to-school shopping last year. "I'm not sure you qualify, since I'm pretty sure you bought that in the children's section."

I can't believe I said that.

I silently ridicule myself for putting my foot in my mouth, and I can't help but notice the way the T-shirt hugs her breasts.

Marlow looks at me with amusement shining in her eyes. "Lola told me that wearing her favorite rainbow shirt makes her feel extra happy, and I couldn't resist testing her theory when I found this one at the local thrift store." She points to her shirt. "I think she's right. It's giving me an extra dose of happiness this morning despite having to deal with your mood swings. Maybe we should get one for you too." She winks.

I'm about to tell her that's never going to happen when my phone buzzes in my pocket. A reminder that I have a meeting I can't be late for. "I have to go, but I'm working from home today, so text me if you need anything," I say.

She gives a thumbs up. "Will do. Oh, and Dylan?"

"Yeah?"

"For the record, Lola told me that she loves Cheez-Its." She smirks before disappearing into the living room.

CHAPTER TEN

DYLAN

I never should have put muffins in the oven before I got in the shower. I'm in the middle of rinsing my hair when the timer on my phone goes off.

"Fuck," I mutter under my breath.

I put my head under the running water one last time to make sure I've got all the conditioner out before shutting it off. I open the shower door and lean over to grab a clean towel from the rack.

The high-pitched alarm screams at me that the blueberry and bran muffins are on the verge of being burnt to a crisp. I stop the alarm before drying off as quickly as I can and tug on a clean pair of black boxers.

After my early morning workout, I decided to bake more muffins after noticing that the last two from the batch I made last week had disappeared. Lola doesn't like them much, which means Marlow must have eaten them. There's something oddly satisfying about her eating food that I've made for her.

In the past week since she started as Lola's nanny, she's crossed my mind far more times than I care to admit. When I'm at the office, I often wonder what she's doing at that particular moment. On the days I'm working from home, I have to stop myself from peeking out the window anytime I hear her front door open. And when she comes over to my house ever morning, I have to refrain from checking her out. Especially when she's wearing a pair of those tight yoga pants that hug her ass so well.

It's probably just a phase, and eventually I'll move on to thinking about something else. *At least I hope that's the case.*

As I jog down the stairs, Confusion grips me when I don't hear the other timer that was set on the microwave. I come to a standstill when I get to the kitchen and find Marlow hovering in front of the stove, pulling out the muffins using a thin dishtowel.

Why isn't she using an oven mitt?

"Ow," she cries as she yanks the pan from the oven. She grimaces but maintains her hold on the muffin tin until she gets to the counter and drops it like a hot potato. I watch as she frowns down at her finger, shaking off the discomfort. Unfortunately, I don't think that's going to make it feel any better.

"Here, let me help." I stalk toward her like a man on a mission.

Marlow whips her head around, her eyes widening as she watches me approach. I take hold of her finger and frown when I see that it's bright red. Knowing she's hurt doesn't sit well with me, and I have the urge to fix it immediately.

"That burn needs to be washed under cold water," I tell her, as I place my hand on her back, ushering her over to the kitchen sink. I turn on the faucet and make sure the temperature is cool before guiding her hand under the flow of the water.

I check the clock and see that it's only 5:50 a.m. She's earlier than usual, and always knocks, no matter how many times I tell her she can come inside without waiting for me to let her in.

"You're here early this morning," I observe.

"I'm sorry." Marlow bites down on her lower lip, directing her gaze anywhere but at me. "I couldn't sleep, so I came over a little early since you have to go into the office today. When I got here, I knocked, but you didn't answer. So, I let myself in using the key you gave me when I heard the alarm going off.

"There's no need to apologize," I say, quick to assure her. "I appreciate you saving the muffins, but why weren't you using an oven mitt?"

"I didn't know which drawer they were in. It must be the only thing you've left out of that binder of yours," she teases with a grin.

God, that smile of hers does me in every time.

I find her comment amusing and decide I'm going to add a section on where to find the oven mitts and other items that will help keep her safe when she's at my place.

Once Marlow's finger has been under the cold water for several minutes, I turn off the faucet and grab a kitchen towel.

"Does that feel better?" I ask, patting her hand dry.

She nods absentmindedly. "Uh-huh."

I knit my brows together when I realize she's staring at me, lost in thought. When her eyes lower to my chest I glance down, just now remembering that I came downstairs in a hurry, wearing nothing but a pair of boxers.

I'm on the verge of apologizing when I notice Marlow is looking at me with parted lips and that beautiful blue-green gaze of hers, like I'm an ice cream cone she's been craving on a hot summer's day.

My lips curve into a smile at seeing her reaction to my body. I can't explain why, but I like knowing that she's enjoying the view. Although my days are jam-packed, I make sure to block out time in the mornings for a workout in the basement, which I converted into a gym when I moved in.

"Are you checking me out?" I call Marlow out with a smirk.

A blush creeps up her neck at my insinuation. "Of course not," she rushes out as she looks away from me. "You're practically walking around naked so it's hard not to stare." She deadpans.

"I hope I'm not making you uncomfortable," I say as I take a step toward her.

What am I doing?

Marlow shakes her head. "You're not," she murmurs.

I keep my hands close to my side, shoving aside the notion of cupping her cheek and gently stroking her jaw. I don't move a muscle as her breathing become uneven, and she watches me intently, as if trying to anticipate my next move.

An intrusive thought crosses my mind of what it might be like to call her mine, and I will myself to snap out of it. But that doesn't stop me from imagining kissing her... again. Something I've been fantasizing about a lot lately.

That's enough.

I blink rapidly. "I better go upstairs and change or I'll be late for my first meeting," I say as I spin around, hightailing it out of the kitchen without giving Marlow a chance to reply.

If I don't get control of my runaway thoughts, they're going to get me in trouble one of these days. Marlow is my daughter's nanny, and I absolutely should not be thinking about being anything other than her employer. So why am I?

CHAPTER ELEVEN

MARLOW

After what turned out to be a disastrous first day, my second day as Lola's nanny was a breeze. Dylan apologized for how he reacted the night before and agreed to my suggested compromises related to Lola's care.

In the two weeks since, we've settled into a comfortable routine without further incidents. Dylan has reverted to his grumpy self, mostly avoiding me, aside from his countless messages to check on Lola when he has to go into the office.

There is one unexpected new development—he's started making breakfast for Lola and me before leaving for work or going to his home office. He prepares meals that can easily be reheated or served directly from the fridge. In addition, he leaves two sticky notes on the counter each morning—a pink one for Lola and a yellow one for me.

While Lola's notes include varying silly jokes or cheesy motivational quotes, mine is always the same.

Good Morning, Marlow,
I made you and Lola breakfast. Enjoy
-Dylan

I'm unsure how to interpret his unspoken, thoughtful gesture. Regardless, I appreciate it. The man might be a grouch, but he certainly knows his way around the kitchen.

We've steered clear of addressing the moment in my studio when Waffles ran into me and Dylan prevented me from falling. It was a brief lapse of judgment on both our parts.

But I can still recall the flurry of butterflies in my stomach as he wrapped his arms around my waist. And the current of energy flowing through me when I placed my hands on his broad shoulders in response. His eyes softened as he gazed at me with concern, and I had the urge to reach out and stroke his stubbled cheek. Thankfully, Lola interrupted before either of us did something we might regret.

Like I said, it was a temporary lapse in judgment and will absolutely not be happening again.

Apart from her dad's constant mood swings, nannying for Lola has been a dream, and I look forward to the time we get to spend together.

After I take her to school, I usually visit Brew Haven for my caffeine fix and drop off a cup of coffee for Quinn on my way home.

The rest of my days are dedicated to painting and dodging Gavin's constant check-ins. He's almost as bad as Dylan. I haven't told him about my new nannying gig because I'm afraid it'll send him over the edge, especially considering I've only completed two of the seven paintings for my upcoming gallery exhibition.

It's been difficult getting up early when I'm still staying up late most nights to paint. Plus, I've been dealing with a lack of motivation and inspiration. It doesn't help that I'm easily distracted, constantly finding ways to put off working in my studio.

For instance, I took a thirty-minute break to take Waffles on a walk this afternoon. What was supposed to be a quick break has turned into over two hours. First, I decided we should visit the dog park on the other side of town, and after that, I made an impromptu detour at Main Street Market to see Willis.

We're almost home now, and I'm already finding reasons to justify extending my break from painting in favor of ordering pizza and watching *Friends*. I'd call Quinn to come over, but she's visiting her grandmother in Florida.

"Marlow, hey there."

I look up to see Johanna stepping out of Dylan's house, waving at me with a big grin. I'm surprised to see her here, since she usually takes Lola back to her house after school. Her hair is styled in a shoulder-length bob, and she's wearing jeans, a cable knit sweater and a black knee-length coat.

"Hi, Johanna. Is everything okay with Lola?" I ask as she approaches me.

"Oh, she's fine," Johanna assures me. "She's inside watching a new episode of *Bluey*. Dylan's had a long week at work, so I told him we'd meet him here tonight so he could come straight home."

"Oh, that's nice of you."

Dylan has been working extra-long hours, and it doesn't end when he leaves the office. I've noticed that he's been putting in a lot of late-night hours in his home office lately.

"Do you have any plans tonight?" Johanna's question comes out of the blue.

"Not really." I give a noncommittal shrug. "I'll probably order a pizza and watch TV."

She looks utterly horrified at the idea and shakes her head. "An attractive woman like you can't stay home on a Friday night. You don't get out much as it is, and stopping for coffee at Brew Haven doesn't count." Before I can object and say it does count, she continues on, "Aspen Grove may be a small town, but there's plenty to do. My friend Stacy owns the Willow Creek Café and is hosting a get-together tonight for all the young folks in town. You should stop by."

"That's so sweet of you to invite me, but—"

"You have to go," Johanna insists, her blue eyes imploring me not to argue. "Trust me, you'll have such a great time. It starts at seven, and there's plenty of street parking."

"I'll keep that in mind. I'm not sure—"

"Excellent," she interrupts me again. "I'll let Stacy know you're coming." Johanna pulls out her phone and quickly taps away on the screen, glancing up when she's finished. "Stacy says she's looking forward to seeing you there. The meet-up will be in the events room, so you can head straight back when you get there tonight."

"Um, okay," I say awkwardly.

"Well, I better get back inside to check on Lola. I hope you have a wonderful evening, and I can't wait to hear all about it." Johanna leaves me standing on the sidewalk with my mouth gaping open.

"Bye," I say, even though she's already out of earshot.

What did I get myself into?

I glance down at Waffles, who's staring at me. "Don't look at me like that," I warn him with my hand on my hip. "What was I supposed to do? Johanna's not an easy person to say no to. How could I let her down when she looked so excited about the prospect of me getting out of the house?" I say with a heavy sigh.

So much for a quiet night at home.

CHAPTER TWELVE

DYLAN

"Mom, I've told you I'm not going out tonight." I maneuver around her, carrying a handful of dishes from her and Lola's earlier dinner. "I have to work on a hundred-page financial report for Harrison that he needs by Sunday." I don't mention that I may also have to go to New York this coming week to handle some in-person meetings.

"Harrison's report can wait," she says, following me to the sink. "If he complains, blame me. He can't be angry with his mother."

"Oh, I'm sure he'd love that." I deadpan. "Besides, I don't want to leave Lola." I rinse off the plates and utensils before loading them into the dishwasher.

"She's already in bed for the night, remember?" My mom places her hand on mine, forcing me to look at her. "Sweetheart, there's nothing wrong with having a life outside of Lola and your job. It's important that you do something for yourself on occasion." She's exceptionally pushy tonight.

"I appreciate your concern, but shouldn't you be getting home to Dad?" I utter with a hint of annoyance.

"No, he's at the Old Mill Brewery with some former colleagues, so I'm in no rush," she says cheerfully, propping her hip against the counter. "Now, will you please stop trying to change the subject? I was merely suggesting you go to the Willow Creek Café and socialize with people your age. Would that be so bad?"

Yes, it would.

Once I've finished loading the dishwasher, I start the cycle and dry my hands using the dish towel on the counter. My mom watches me like a hawk, impatiently waiting for me to answer.

"I know everyone in this town, and I can confidently say that I have no desire to spend time with any of them. Most people who go to these things live in their parents' basement, don't have a job, or are looking for a free ride—none of which I have in common."

"Oh shush, you're being dramatic. I guarantee there will be at least *one* person there whose company you'll enjoy. You just need to give it a chance."

"Mom, I don't want—"

"Honestly, Dylan, will you stop being so difficult?" She sighs in exasperation. "Please go for me?" She mirrors Lola's classic puppy dog eyes.

"Good grief," I mutter.

If persistence were an Olympic sport, my mom would have a gold medal. She has a gift for pushing until you give in to her wishes. While I appreciate my mother's caring nature, she goes overboard in her eagerness to help. You'd think I'd have mastered the art of saying no by now, but she makes it incredibly difficult to be the one to disappoint her.

"Fine, I'll go," I concede, throwing my hands up. "But only for an hour."

"If you say so," she says cryptically. "Are you planning to change first?"

"No." I head into the living room and she follows me.

"Sweetheart, suits are meant for the office, not a night out on the town."

"Would you rather I didn't go at all?"

"Don't be ridiculous," she dismisses with a wave. "Can you at least take off the suit jacket and tie?"

"Sure, Mom." I undo my cobalt tie and shrug off my jacket, draping them over the couch. "Happy now?"

"Yes, you look very handsome." She leans in to pat my face. "Now hurry along. You're running late."

I grab my keys from the basket on the entryway table and head to the front door.

"Have fun, sweetheart." She beams as waves goodbye.

"See you later, Mom."

If my mom's friend, Stacy, didn't own Willow Creek Café, I'd skip out and join my dad at Old Mill. But I know if I don't show up to this thing, I'll never hear the end of it.

On my way to my car, I notice that Marlow's Jeep isn't in her driveway, and her house is completely dark except for a lamp in her living room. That's odd since she's usually in her loft painting at this time of night, with every light in the house on.

Over the past couple of weeks, I've been distracted countless times, unable to resist watching her paint when I should be working. It's hypnotic watching her lose herself in the process of transforming a plain canvas into something extraordinary. The way her lips part in concentration, the world around her fading away. Every stroke of the palette knife is a testament to her dedication, as if she's pouring a piece of her soul into the masterpiece unfolding before her.

Without fail, she finishes every painting session with at least one paint smudge on her face. And every time I have the inclination to wipe it off—like I did that night in her studio a couple of weeks ago. I often take it a step further in my mind and imagine tracing the paint down her neck, over her collarbone, across the swells of her breasts.

I shake my head, attempting to clear all thoughts of Marlow from my mind, and get into my car. I need to remember she's my daughter's nanny, ten years my junior, and that her sunny disposition annoys me.

At least it used to.

There's a reason I've avoided her as much as possible since our encounter in my kitchen last week. She's messing with my head, and I don't know how to put an end to it.

Maybe my mom was onto something suggesting I go out tonight. It's better than staying home, watching Marlow's studio, wondering where she is, who she's with, and what she's doing. Tonight could offer a welcome distraction from her constantly occupying my thoughts.

It takes less than ten minutes to get to Willow Creek Café, one advantage of living in a small town. However, I have to park several blocks away, which is odd because this part of town is typically not busy.

When I enter the café, Stacy is standing at the hostess station. Her auburn hair is pulled back into a low bun, and she's wearing a teal button-up shirt and black slacks.

"Hey, Dylan." She greets me with a warm smile. "I would ask if you wanted a table, but I just got off the phone with your mom, so I know you're not here for dinner." She winks. "Why don't you head to the back? They've already started, but I'm sure they won't have any trouble finding you a seat. Good luck in there." She moves away to seat a couple, waiting for a table.

I venture to the back of the restaurant, shocked to find the events room packed. There must be other singles from the surrounding towns here tonight.

Tables are lined up in rows with women seated on one side, men on the other. It's then that I notice a chalkboard sign propped up against the door—Welcome to Aspen Grove's Speed Dating Mixer.

You've got to be kidding me.

My mom tricked me into coming to a speed dating event. I should have asked for more details before agreeing to come. We're going to have a conversation about boundaries when I get home, which is going to be much sooner than she expected because I'm not staying for this.

I'm ready to make a quick exit when I spot a familiar face across the room, framed with golden blonde hair and striking eyes—one blue, one green.

Marlow Taylor.

Her cherry red lips are turned up in a smile. She's styled her hair into an intricate halo braid, and she's wearing a vintage plum sweater dress with bell sleeves. She looks incredible, and I'm not the only one who's noticed.

She's seated across from Eric Schultz, the manager at the local bank, who's staring at her like she's going to be his next meal. Rumor has it he's in the middle of a messy divorce, so he has no business being here.

Marlow is worthy of a man who will treat her right and not use her as a rebound. She deserves someone willing to take care of her and who will be there when she needs them most. I highly doubt Eric fits the bill.

A sense of unease comes over me when Marlow touches Eric's arm, laughing at something he said. When Eric puts his hand over hers, all rational thoughts leave me and I'm storming straight for their table to save her from him because I—well, I don't know why. But he's not right for her.

Marlow's eyes widen when she sees me coming. "Dylan? Wh-what are you doing here?" she stutters.

I stop next to their table, my gaze locked on hers. "I saw you were here and thought I'd stop by and say hello."

Her brow furrows at my unusual behavior. "Don't you have your own speed dating partner you should be talking to?"

I glance down at Eric's smarmy face and can't imagine why Marlow would find him attractive.

"I'm much more interested in how yours is going."

She shifts in her seat. "I was having a nice conversation with my friend Eric here before you interrupted."

Eric seems less than enthusiastic about being labeled as her friend.

"Why do you care so much?" he demands in a whiny tone. God, this guy is grating on my nerves.

"Marlow is my daughter's nanny, and I'm looking out for her. Why don't you leave, or better yet, go find someone you're more compatible with." I glare at him.

Eric's chin jerks back to his thick neck. "Excuse me?"

Marlow lets out a nervous laugh as her gaze ping pongs between us. "Our time is almost up, so if you could—"

"Look, man," Eric interjects, which is another reason he's wrong for her. He won't even let her speak. "You'll get your chance with Marlow later. It's my turn now, so get lost." He jerks his head toward the exit.

I'm not sure why this situation is getting under my skin so much. Like I said, Marlow is Lola's nanny and I have no claim to her. Still, an intense blaze of jealousy sparked to life when I saw Eric touch her hand. The idea of her talking with him for another second creates an unexpected storm of emotions raging inside me.

Luck is on my side when a timer goes off, concluding this round of speed dating. The moderator instructs the men to move to the seat to their left so they can begin the next round.

"I think that's your cue to get lost." I practically shove Eric out of his seat.

He stands there gaping at me, but finally takes the hint to leave, moving on to his next victim at another table. Luckily, Marlow's next would-be date doesn't attempt to approach us after I shoot him a baleful glare.

I sit in the chair Eric vacated. "Hi, I'm Dylan." I feign an introduction as I extend my hand out to Marlow. "Why are you here, sunshine?" The nickname comes out unintentionally, but I rather like it.

"Don't call me that," she counters, ignoring my gesture.

"Why not? It suits you." I lean forward.

"Maybe you should leave." She motions to the exit.

I rest my elbows on the table, drawing closer. "I didn't know you were looking for a boyfriend," I say, ignoring her comment entirely.

"Who said I was looking for a boyfriend?" she retorts.

"The whole point of speed dating is to find someone you're compatible with. So, if you're not looking for a date, then why are you here?"

I can't help but wonder if she's interested in someone here. If it's Eric fucking Schultz, I can't be held accountable for decking him in the face for touching her.

I draw in a deep breath while tugging at the collar of my shirt.

"You okay, Dylan? You seem a little tense." Marlow's gaze searches my face, probably looking for the answer as to why I'm acting this way.

"I'm fine," I say as I flex my hands. "Now why don't you tell me why you're here if it's not to find a date."

She fixes me with a hard stare. "My personal life is none of your business. Besides, even if I were looking for someone to go out with, I hope you're not putting yourself in the running." A teasing smile passes her lips.

I raise a brow. "And why is that?"

More importantly, why does the idea of going out with Marlow sound so appealing? Typically, I'm quick to avoid the topic of dating altogether, but surprisingly the familiar sense of panic that accompanies the subject is notably absent.

"Because you're far too grumpy for my taste, you don't smile enough, and you're not a fan of '80s pop music. Plus, you don't like Cheez-Its which is an automatic disqualifier in my book." She rests back in her chair with a smirk.

"I'm not grumpy," I mumble.

Sure, I'm usually gruff when interacting with my employees and prefer to keep to myself aside from my family and Lola, but that doesn't mean I'm grumpy.

Marlow raises a brow, seemingly unconvinced by my response.

"Fine." I hold my hands up in surrender. "I admit that I'm a *little* grumpy, but you're forgetting my redeeming quality."

"What might that be?" She cocks her head to the side.

"I can braid hair. I'm told that makes every woman swoon."

"Ah, but you're forgetting one very important detail," she says with a twinkle in her eye.

"Which is?"

"You can't do fishtail braids." She teases.

Lola must have told her that.

God, I'm enjoying this playful conversation way too much.

"Well, at least—" I stop short when I notice the rest of the room has fallen silent.

Everyone in the room is far more interested in our conversation than their own.

"Why don't we talk outside?" I suggest in a hushed tone.

"There's no need," Marlow says as she pushes her chair back. "I was just leaving."

She strides out of the room, grabbing her coat from the rack on her way out. I chase after her, jogging to keep up with her brisk pace.

Marlow doesn't say a word until we reach her car that's parked a block down the street. She reaches for the door handle but pauses, spinning on her heel to fix me with a questioning glance. "What do you want Dylan?" She sighs.

"Will you please tell me why you came tonight?" I ask with sincere interest.

It's going to bother me until I have an answer. Despite denying my attraction, it's there, bubbling beneath the surface. The notion that she really did come here looking for someone to take her home makes my stomach turn.

"Did you forget that we were in the same room? What were *you* doing at a speed dating event?" She jabs her finger into my chest.

"I had no idea there was going to be speed dating." I don't miss Marlow's skeptical look. "My mom told me there was a get-together at Willow Creek Café and insisted that I stop by. I should have suspected something was up when she practically pushed me out the door."

In hindsight, I see that I was overly trusting. I didn't think pushing for more information was worth the effort.

Who am I kidding? This is my mother we're talking about.

Marlow stares at me, absorbing my answer, and then she laughs. "This is too funny. Your mom—" She covers her face with her hands, and every few seconds she tries to explain further, but bursts into another fit of laughter.

"Should I be concerned?" I give her a puzzled look.

She shakes her head as she takes a moment to collect herself.

"I ran into your mom earlier today, and she strongly suggested I come here tonight to get out of the house," Marlow explains. "She can be very persuasive when she wants to be."

I tilt my head in confusion. "Are you saying what I think you're saying?"

She nods. "I'm pretty sure your mom tried setting us up," she says, echoing my thoughts.

I wish I could say I was surprised.

"Why did you stay?" If I hadn't seen her, I would have left. I'm curious why she didn't do the same.

She shrugs. "I figured I might as well make some new friends while I was here."

When I get home, my mom and I'll be having a conversation about minding her business as far as Marlow is concerned.

"I hate to break it to you, sunshine"—I take a step toward her —"but none of those men wanted to be your friend. They were far more interested in taking you home." Just the idea of her spending the night with another man causes a burning sensation in my stomach.

Her mouth forms a perfect *O* at my assessment.

"It's not surprising… considering you were the most beautiful woman in that room."

"You can't say things like that," she whispers.

Maybe it's the full moon, or the romantic glow of the town square twinkling with golden lights. Maybe I'm lonely and she's just too tempting. Whatever the reason, I can't stop myself from rasping out, "Why not? It's the truth."

Marlow takes a step back, bumping into the side of her car. I pause for a beat, debating if I should walk away.

Fuck it.

I close the distance between us, placing my hands on the roof, caging her in. The tension is thick in the air as I lift my hand and trace her lips with the pad of my thumb. Her breathing picks up, and her eyes fill with desire. She's utterly irresistible.

"Dylan, what are you doing?" she murmurs.

"Thinking about what it would be like to kiss you," I say softly.

It's not the first time. I imagine she tastes like strawberries and pink lemonade, sparking my curiosity to test my theory.

She remains still as I cup her jaw, caressing her cheek. Her pupils grow wide as I lean in to brush my lips against hers in teasing strokes, refraining from outright kissing her. Her hands land on my hips, gripping me. The touch sparks a flicker of desire that ignites within me like a wildfire.

Her mouth is wickedly tempting, inviting me in for a proper taste. I'm seconds away from caving in when the sound of a door closing nearby shatters the bubble surrounding us.

"Shit, I'm sorry." I step back.

Marlow blinks rapidly, releasing a deep breath before turning and opening her car door, in a daze.

"It was a terrible error in judgment, that's all," she rushes out. "I got caught up in the moment when you called me beautiful. And then you looked at me with that ridiculous smoldering gaze of yours, and I fell under your spell." She holds her hand up to stop me when I try to get closer. "But I'm over it now, so you can stay right where you are."

God, she's adorable when she rambles.

More than anything, I want to tell her she's wrong, and

convince her to admit that she wanted that kiss as much as I did. But she's already nervous, and I can't risk losing her because of my selfish desires. Lola loves having her as a nanny, and I can't do anything else to put that in jeopardy.

"You're right. I got caught up in the moment, and I apologize if I made you uncomfortable," I say as I rake my hand through my hair.

She nervously chews on her lower lip. "Like I said, it was a lapse in judgment on both our parts," she reiterates. "Listen, it's getting late, so I better go." She hops into the driver's side of her Jeep.

"Yeah, okay, see you on Monday."

She gives me a small wave before driving off. I'm left standing alone on the curb, the scent of her strawberry lipstick lingering in the air.

Without a doubt, Marlow Taylor is a genuinely good person. She's thoughtful, kind, generous, and always willing to lend a helping hand to those in need.

I've spent so long avoiding emotional connections out of fear of getting hurt, and Marlow is the first person aside from Lola who's made me truly *feel* in the past six years.

She's slowly chipping away at my resolve without even trying, which might explain my impulsive reactions tonight. My physical attraction paired with the emotional pull toward her is an explosive combination, leaving me to question what would have happened if she hadn't stopped me from kissing her tonight.

CHAPTER THIRTEEN

MARLOW

My mind is still reeling from the fact that Dylan Stafford called me beautiful again last Friday. Not to mention that *almost* kiss lived rent free in my mind all weekend.

I can't explain the impulse, but a part of me longed for him to kiss me, curious about what it would feel like to have his lips pressed against mine. Images of him gazing at me with those chocolate brown eyes as he traces my jawline torment me. The scent of mint and cedar still lingers on my coat—a reminder that we really did almost kiss.

Seeing him at the speed dating event stirred a pang of jealousy within me. The prospect of him engaging in playful banter or meaningful conversation with someone else bothers me.

I was under the impression that he doesn't care for me, and it didn't cross my mind until recently that he could actually be attracted to me.

At first glance, we have little in common. He's a disciplined thirty-three-year-old billionaire, the dad to a darling little girl, and a literal genius. I'm a twenty-three-year-old free-spirited artist, the owner of an unruly dog, and I have a penchant for new adventures.

Our mutual love and concern for Lola is what's brought us together. That little girl has us both wrapped around her finger.

I was anxious about coming over to his house this morning, unsure how things would play out between us considering our last interaction. It turns out I was worried for nothing.

He called me last night and asked if I could watch Lola for three days while he was gone on a last-minute business trip. He asked his parents first, but they're visiting his aunt in Spring Haven this week.

I'm staying at his house overnight, and during the day I'll hang out with Waffles and work on my paintings at my place.

Dylan was running late when I got here this morning so our conversation was brief and used to review a few sections from The Manual related to Lola's bedtime routine. While we avoided making eye contact during our exchange I didn't miss him cracking a smile when he saw how many paragraphs I high-lighted in a rainbow of colors.

I let out a whistle when I open the fridge to grab something for breakfast while I wait for Lola to wake up. Dylan certainly outdid himself in the food department. There are enough healthy meals to last while he's gone, along with his signature sticky notes attached to each breakfast container. However, there's been a slight modification to the notes addressed to me.

Good morning, sunshine,
I hope you enjoy your breakfast. Have a great day.
-Dylan

I press my hand to my mouth, unable to suppress the grin that crosses my lips. I might have told him not to call me sunshine, but secretly I loved it, especially coming from him.

I take out my phone to send him a text:

> I just checked the fridge. You outdid yourself.

DYLAN

> Consider it insurance. It's one less chance you'll burn down my house while I'm gone. 😉

> Dylan Stafford, did you just use an emoji? I'm shocked. 🙀

DYLAN

> Did you check the guest bedroom yet?

I hustle out of the kitchen and hurry upstairs, tiptoeing past Lola's bedroom. When I step into the room Dylan prepared for me, I squeal like a little kid when I spot the giant box of Cheez-Its on the bed. His sweet gesture sends a flurry of butterflies dancing in my stomach. I'm touched that he went out of his way to do something so thoughtful, especially considering his aversion to junk food.

> Cheez-Its?!? Are you trying to butter me up??

DYLAN

> You're taking care of Lola while I'm gone. I figured it was best to stay on your good side.

> You're doing an excellent job. 🍻

> Btw, I'm also a big fan of Frosted Strawberry Pop-Tarts.

DYLAN

> I'll keep that in mind for next time.

> I'm stepping into a meeting. I'll check in with you later.

> Sounds good. Have a great day!

DYLAN

> You too, sunshine.

The past two days with Lola have gone off without a hitch. It's been a delight spending so much quality time with her. The only downside is I haven't had as much time to work on my paintings.

I groan in frustration as I stare at the blank canvas in front of me. I've been standing here for the past thirty minutes and still haven't decided what my next piece for the art gallery should be. I tap my finger against my lips, hoping inspiration will strike.

When another five minutes pass without a breakthrough, I leave my station and grab my phone from the windowsill. I scroll through my go-to playlist, selecting "Material Girl" by Madonna.

Since Dylan is out of town, I connect the music to my speakers and grin when the lively beat reverberates through the studio. I twirl around the room, using a paintbrush as a microphone, and sing along. In the middle of the third verse, an idea strikes me. I stop mid-spin and rush over to my desk, pushing aside piles of papers and magazines until I find my dog-eared copy of *Flowerpaedia:1000 Flowers and Their Meanings*. I flip through the pages until I find the entry I'm searching for.

With a renewed drive and sufficient inspiration, I return to my workstation, ready to create.

Several hours later, I step back, admiring the finished painting.

The piece draws inspiration from my recent experience as Lola's nanny and the moments I've shared with Dylan.

The two textured chrysanthemums give the illusion of a three-dimensional effect. Each one is a different color meant to represent its own emotion.

Red signifies the unwavering love Dylan has for Lola. To the rest of the world he's a grumpy CFO with fortified walls built around his heart. However, to Lola he's her steadfast protector who slays all her dragons, and fills her world with unicorns and rainbows.

Pink symbolizes the budding attraction I have for Dylan. Our exchanges have evolved from quippy remarks to a growing mutual respect combined with undeniable chemistry simmering at the surface.

My phone buzzes on the stool, and I immediately answer when I see it's a call from Lola's school.

"Hello, this is Marlow."

"This is Kate, the nurse at Willow Run Elementary. Lola was complaining of a stomachache, so her teacher sent her to my office. She has a fever and threw up while she was in the bathroom a few minutes ago. Can you come pick her up?" Before Kate has finished talking, I'm grabbing my keys and wallet, making a mad dash for my car.

"Absolutely. I'm on my way now."

"I appreciate it. See you soon."

I'm grateful the school is right down the street; otherwise, I'd be in full-blown panic mode already. I contemplate sending a text to Dylan but decide to wait until I get Lola home and can give him more information on her condition. I'm relieved he insisted on installing her booster seat in my car before he left, so I don't have to walk.

When I get to the school, I disregard the No Parking signs and pull up alongside the curb near the entrance. The front office administrator directs me to the nurse's office, where Lola is curled up in the fetal position on a couch in the corner. She's as white as a ghost, and her hair is messy from lying on it.

"Hey, lolabug." The new nickname slips out effortlessly.

"Marlow, you're here," she says hoarsely.

"Of course I am." I kneel beside her and gently stroke her forehead. She's hot to the touch.

"There's a stomach bug making the rounds," Kate informs me. "When you get home, I'd suggest giving her some children's Tylenol to bring down the fever, and touch base with her pediatrician. Also, make sure she gets plenty of fluids. A few good options are soup, popsicles, and Pedialyte."

"I will, thank you." I lift Lola into my arms, and she nuzzles her face into my neck. My heart squeezes at her innocent gesture, my hand stroking down her tangled hair, reassuring us both that everything is going to be okay.

"Can we go home now?" she groans out.

"Yeah, we're going back to your house right now."

"Can Waffles come over? I wanna cuddle with him."

"Sure, he can." I don't have the heart to tell her no while she's in this condition.

She gives me a weak thumbs up and is quiet on the way to my Jeep. By the time we pull into the driveway, she's fast asleep. I take her to her bedroom and try calling Dylan, leaving a panicked voicemail when he doesn't answer.

What am I going to do?

I've never taken care of a sick kid before, and I have no idea where Dylan keeps the medicine or how much Tylenol to give Lola. My anxiety intensifies when Dylan doesn't call me back. The one time I desperately need him to check in, and he isn't available.

I'm on the verge of a panic attack, when I recall highlighting a section in The Manual that outlines the steps of what to do if Lola's sick. I rush into the kitchen where the binder is and frantically flip through the pages.

Thank god for Dylan's need to meticulously plan everything. There are detailed instructions on medication and a complete list of emergency contacts, including Lola's pediatrician. Now, fingers crossed the Tylenol does the trick.

CHAPTER FOURTEEN

DYLAN

Today has been jam-packed with back-to-back meetings with no end in sight. I'm leaning back in my chair at the head of the table as Jared, one of my analysts, drones on about a revised cost-benefit analysis.

I check my watch to see that it's already 3:00 p.m. I had to disable notifications on my phone, and it's been bothering me that I haven't checked in with Marlow since before lunchtime.

I wasn't thrilled when Harrison told me I had to come to New York City this week for in-person meetings. But my team and I are entangled in extensive red tape to finalize the finances for the Vanburen project before the city approves the development, so there was no way around this trip.

While I'm taking the lead here in New York, Cash is in London, overseeing the training of a team for our new office. Although, judging from the photos he's posted on social media, it seems he's dedicating as much time to *extracurricular activities* as he has for work. He thrives on attention and is always the first to volunteer when a project requires extended travel. But that doesn't do me much good when we have multiple high-profile projects in different cities.

I've only been in New York for two days, but it feels like an eternity.

I asked my parents to watch Lola but they're in Spring Haven visiting my aunt. My mom said they've had these plans for months, but this past weekend was the first time I heard about it.

With my parents away, I asked Marlow to watch Lola. I was apprehensive at first since I haven't left Lola with her overnight before, but she's exceeding my expectations.

While I've been gone, Lola and I have a nightly video chat, and Marlow sends me hourly updates. My daughter seems to be thoroughly enjoying herself, although that doesn't take away the regret that I'm not home with her.

The truth is, Lola isn't the only one that's been on my mind while I've been away. Marlow has occupied my thoughts since last Friday. I've replayed our moment outside of Willow Creek Café countless times. The way her body was flush against me, the sweet scent of citrus and rose filling the air, and the look of lust in her eyes as she gazed up at me while I teased her mouth with mine.

I miss her infectious smile, the way she bites on her lower lip when she's nervous, and the way she makes me feel when I'm around her.

As soon as Jared wraps up his presentation, I'm out of my seat. "Let's take a break, and we'll reconvene in ten minutes." I'm out the door before anyone can respond.

I rush back to my office, anxious to check in with Marlow to see how she and Lola are doing this afternoon. Lola should be home from school by now.

My pulse quickens when I check my phone and see fifteen missed calls and texts from Marlow, asking me to call her back as soon as possible. A flood of concern sweeps over me as I listen to the last voicemail she left over two hours ago.

Hi, Dylan, it's me again. Lola's fever spiked, and her pediatrician wants me to bring her in as a precaution. I was hoping to talk to you

first, but I don't want to wait any longer. We're going to his office now.
Please call me back as soon as you get this. Thanks, bye.

Marlow's voice trembles like she's on the verge of tears. I kick myself for silencing my notifications earlier. Given her lack of experience with children, I doubt she's had to take care of a sick kid before.

I attempt to call her back repeatedly, letting out a string of curse words when she doesn't answer. The guilt hits me hard, knowing my little ladybug is sick, and I'm not there to take care of her. I'm grateful Marlow had the good sense to take Lola to the pediatrician, though. I have to trust that she'll hold down the fort until I can get home.

Unfortunately, Cash took the Stafford Holdings jet to London, and the helicopter is primarily used for the short-range commute to and from our headquarters in Maine, so I have no choice but to charter another flight home. I text my assistant, Max, to have him call a taxi and find me the earliest flight to Aspen Grove.

After a dozen more failed attempts to reach Marlow, I resort to calling Lola's pediatrician. Dr. Lassen's nurse informs me that Marlow brought Lola into the clinic a couple of hours ago. Lola was diagnosed with the flu, and Dr. Lassen said to give her Tylenol according to the instructions on the bottle, and make sure she gets plenty of fluids and rest.

By the time I touch down in Aspen Grove, my worry has morphed into frustration. I can't believe Marlow hasn't called back or texted an update.

I speed home from the airport and find her Jeep parked in my driveway. I pull in behind her, leaving my briefcase and luggage in the car as I rush inside to find my daughter.

"Marlow? Lola?" My voice echoes down the hall, but I'm met with silence.

I check the living room and kitchen, ignoring the messy state of the house. With no sign of them on the first floor, I go upstairs to check Lola's room, only to find it empty.

I'm seconds away from going over to check to see if they're at Marlow's house when I come to a standstill in my bedroom doorway.

Marlow and Lola are both asleep in my bed.

Lola is snuggled in against Marlow, one hand draped across her stomach and the other tucked against her chest. Waffles lies on Lola's other side, making himself at home on my memory foam pillow. He raises his head when I step further into the room, but quickly dismisses me, settling back against *my* pillow.

I quietly tiptoe over to the bed, leaning across Marlow to place my hand on Lola's forehead. I sigh in relief when it's cool to the touch. Thank god, her fever must have finally broken.

A warm feeling envelops me as I gaze down at Marlow and Lola together.

On my way home, I imagined every worst-case scenario. Nothing could have prepared me for the reality—finding my daughter snuggled safely in Marlow's arms.

Like she can sense someone is in the room, Marlow opens her eyes, giving me a sleepy smile when she sees me standing by the bed. But her expression quickly morphs into panic when she becomes more alert.

I press my finger to my lips, gesturing to Lola, who remains sound asleep. Marlow nods in understanding and slips out of the bed, tucking the blanket around Lola and Waffles. She follows me into the hall, closing the door behind her.

When she faces me, her chin is trembling. "Dylan, I'm so sorry," she utters.

I'm not sure she even knows why she's apologizing. She just assumes I'm upset with her.

"I was in meetings when you called earlier. I tried calling back, but you didn't answer," I say in a low voice so I don't wake Lola.

"I must have left my phone downstairs... Oh god, it's a disaster down there," she says with a mortified expression. "I swear I'll clean up before I leave."

"It's okay." I place my hand on her arm, rubbing gently to reassure her. "I called the doctor's office on my way home, and the nurse filled me in. How was Lola before she fell asleep?"

"We stopped to get soup, popsicles, and Pedialyte on our way home, and she was exhausted by the time we got back. She refused the soup, but I persuaded her to have a popsicle and sip on some Pedialyte while watching an episode of *Bluey*. After that, I took her upstairs for a nap. She wanted to sleep in your room and begged me to lie down with her." Marlow nervously tucks a piece of hair behind her ear. "I must have fallen asleep shortly after she did. I am sorry I missed your phone calls. You must have been worried sick."

"Waffles looked like he was rather enjoying my memory foam pillow," I say, half-kidding, nodding toward my bedroom.

Mental note: Wash my sheets and throw out my pillow.

Marlow gives me a guilty look. "Lola begged me to bring him over, and I didn't have the heart to tell her no." She drops her gaze to the floor, refusing to look at me.

Given my past reactions it's no wonder that she's concerned I'll be upset. I've been harsh with her in the past, getting upset over minor issues, and leading her to expect it as the norm. While I can't erase the past, I'm determined to treat her with the respect she deserves from now on.

She handled today's events admirably, and if the roles were reversed, I doubt I would have been as understanding, taking care of a sick child and unable to reach her dad.

I step forward and lift her chin with my hand. Her tear-filled eyes meet mine. "Please don't cry, sunshine." I wipe away a stray tear with my thumb.

To say I don't like seeing her sad is an understatement. I have an urgent need to fix the situation, but unlike Marlow, I don't have a manual handy with a section on "How to Console a Beautiful Crying Woman."

Acting on impulse, I pull her in for a hug with one arm wrapped around her shoulders, holding her tight, and the other cradling the back of her head. She tenses at the unexpected gesture but relaxes into my embrace, circling her arms around my waist and resting her head against my chest. It feels inherently right to have her so close, but I'm not prepared to unpack those emotions right now.

"I was so scared," Marlow whispers. "Lola was burning with fever, and I wasn't sure what to do. I couldn't reach you, and your mom's phone went straight to voicemail. Thank goodness for that ridiculous binder of yours, or I probably would have called an ambulance." She takes a slow, deliberate breath. "Are you sure you're not upset?" she asks in a strained voice.

"I'm sure," I say, as I rub small circles on her back.

The lingering unease I experienced on my way back from New York has dissipated entirely, allowing me to see things with a newfound clarity.

"Thank you." I lean back to meet her gaze. "I'm glad you were with Lola today. She's fortunate to have you in her life."

Marlow squints at me with suspicion. "Okay, who are you, and what have you done with Dylan Stafford?" she playfully demands.

"What if I said you make me want to be a better person?"

I rush to judgment more often than not, and Marlow doesn't deserve that kind of treatment. I'm a cynical son-of-a-bitch with exacting standards and view the world through a critical lens. Whereas she is sunshine personified. An eternal optimist who brightens any room she walks into. When I'm with her, my surroundings appear sunnier, inspiring me to see things in a more positive light.

A comfortable silence settles in as I wrap my arms tighter around her. She hasn't made a move to leave my embrace, and I take the moment to appreciate having her this close.

"I have a confession," I say softly.

"What is it?" Marlow looks up at me.

"Lola isn't the only one I missed while I was gone."

"She's not?" Her eyes widen at my admission.

I shake my head, not able to find the right words.

"Does this mean you're finally ready to confess your undying love for Waffles?" she asks with a gleam in her eye.

"I wouldn't bank on that happening anytime soon." I chuckle. "Not until he's learned to behave."

"Darn, he'll be crushed when I break the news." She flashes me a teasing smile.

Her smile is intoxicating, and the longer I hold her, the more difficult it is to not make a move. My resolve is on the verge of crumbling.

"In case it wasn't clear, I was talking about you." I slowly brush my hands down her arms, covering her skin with goosebumps. "Ever since that night at the café, I haven't stopped thinking about what it would be like to kiss you."

She takes a deep breath at my confession.

"Honestly, neither have I," she confesses in a whisper.

Her admission catches me off guard, considering she called our almost kiss a terrible error in judgment. It seems I'm not the only one affected by the tangible chemistry between us, despite our best efforts to ignore it.

Marlow's gaze shifts to my mouth, and she licks her lips. Even though I know I shouldn't tempt her, I can't help but lean in so our faces are mere inches apart. The sound of our intermingled breathing fills the hallway as her hooded gaze meets mine.

It demands every scrap of willpower I have not to close the remaining distance between us. The next move is Marlow's, and I focus on the steady rise and fall of her chest as I wait to see what she'll do next. A surge of excitement runs through me when she wraps her arms around my neck and lifts on her toes to place a chaste kiss on my lips.

Her touch sparks an inferno of desire that I've attempted to restrain. In this moment, I'm defenseless to her allure as I capture her mouth with mine, eliciting a soft moan from her throat. Lost in the moment's intensity, I entangle my fingers in her golden blonde hair, tugging her closer. She grips my shoulders in response, our bodies fused together.

"You taste sweeter than I imagined, sweetheart," I groan into her mouth.

Our kiss is electric, igniting a fire inside me that has me craving more. Our chemistry is all-consuming, leaving her gasping for air. She tastes like strawberries, pink lemonade, and all things sweet, and I never want this to end.

When I break the kiss, Marlow looks up at me with a dazed look on her face.

"Marlow, I—"

She places her hand against her lips. "I'm sorry I kissed you," she blurts out. "I'm not sure what came over me."

I chuckle. "In case you didn't notice, sunshine, I enjoyed it very much."

She chews on her lower lip. "That doesn't mean it was a good idea." I'm flooded with disappointment at her words, and her eyes widen when she sees my dejected expression. "I don't regret it if that's what you're thinking," she rushes out.

"Neither do I." My tone is resolute.

That was the single best kiss of my life, and I'd do it again… and again if she'd let me.

"It's just that we both have a lot going on right now and the last thing I want to do is complicate things. You and Lola are both important to me, and I don't want to do anything that could hurt you." She fidgets with her hands as she glances at the floor. "I'm not even sure how much longer I'll be in Aspen Grove."

I blink back at her, unsure how to respond. How am I supposed to remain unfazed when the very idea of her leaving is enough to make my stomach churn?

Her concerns have merit. My life is centered around Lola and my career, leaving little space for a romantic relationship. And like she said, she doesn't know how long she plans to stay in town. When she does leave, Lola will be crushed, and I'm not sure I can afford to introduce my complicated feelings into the equation. Although I'm beginning to think it's too late for that.

I run my hand through my hair, perplexed by my reaction. Hell, I'm usually the sound of reason and ready to run in the other direction at any sign of commitment, but as of late, when Marlow is around, all common sense is thrown out the window. It's like an invisible string draws me to her and it's all I can do to keep myself from getting tangled up in her beautiful chaos.

"It's late. I should probably get home," she says abruptly, pulling me out of my thoughts.

"Yeah, okay." I reluctantly let her go as she steps out of my embrace. I'm immediately left with a sense of longing to hold her again. "I'm going to keep Lola home from school tomorrow so you can take the day off. And don't worry about downstairs. I'll take care of it."

"Are you sure? I promise I had every intention of cleaning up before you got back."

"Yeah, I've got it."

I watch with disappointment as she slips into the bedroom to get Waffles, wishing more than anything she would stay.

A couple of months ago, I would have been bothered by the disarray left downstairs, but now that I know what it feels like to have Marlow wrapped in my arms—to kiss her—I'm not so bothered by the mess anymore.

CHAPTER FIFTEEN

MARLOW

Lola isn't the only one I missed while I was gone.

After days of Dylan dominating my thoughts while he was away, his confession invaded my consciousness, and caused me to momentarily lose all rational thought. As he leaned in, I felt the gentle whisper of his breath on my skin. The temptation to finally know what it felt like to kiss him was too strong to resist, and I closed the remaining distance between us.

When our mouths met, it sparked a wildfire of affection that I never wanted to end.

I got lost in the moment, but when Dylan pulled back, I panicked. It doesn't matter that he assured me he enjoyed kissing me. The very idea that he could reject me had me scrambling to find an excuse as to why it was a mistake.

For me, the fear of rejection is more distressing than the act of being rejected. Despite being illogical, the relentless reminders that I was inadequate when I was a kid linger in my subconscious. I've become an expert at avoiding scenarios where I could potentially face denial.

So naturally, I hightailed it out of Dylan's, like I did the night outside of Willow Creek Café. It's safe to say avoiding uncomfortable situations is my specialty.

Like the time I lived in Mesa, Arizona. I naively agreed to go on a date with my landlord, Stewart. To call it a disaster is an understatement. He droned on about his mother for a solid hour and picked at his teeth throughout the duration of our meal. As if things couldn't get worse, when the check arrived, he asked me to cover it since he left his wallet at home.

When I declined a second date, he sobbed and begged me to tell him what he did wrong. A pipe burst in my kitchen the week after, and I paid the repair costs myself so I could avoid another awkward encounter with him. Thankfully I had a lease with no fixed term and moved out the next month.

Dylan might not be losing his hair or have an obsession with his mom, but that doesn't make our situation any less awkward. If it weren't for Waffles and Lola, I'd probably be preparing to move somewhere warm year-round, and that doesn't include living next door to a hot single dad who I can't stop thinking about.

After getting home last night, I went straight to bed and slept for twelve hours. I hadn't realized how emotionally taxing taking care of a sick child could be, and I'm relieved that Dylan is back home with Lola. Watching her cry, unable to alleviate her pain, was heart-wrenching. A weight was lifted off my shoulders when her fever finally broke.

I want to check on her more than anything, but I don't want to interrupt her day with Dylan. And I remind myself that I'm avoiding him at the moment.

I'm feeling sluggish, so I'm curled up on the couch with a cup of coffee and my favorite cable-knit blanket.

I decide to call Quinn. We've texted a few times, but it's been a few days since we spoke on the phone.

"Hey, stranger," she answers in a singsong voice. "I was about to call in the search party. Is everything okay? How's Lola doing?"

"Thankfully, her fever broke last night, so I'm hoping she's back to her normal self soon. Dylan took the day off, so I haven't seen her today."

I texted Quinn while Lola and I were in the waiting room at the doctor's office yesterday. She didn't know until then that I'd been watching Lola while Dylan was out of town since she's been in Florida.

"I'm so glad to hear it," she says.

"How's everything going at the shop since you've been gone?"

I offered to take care of things at Brush & Palette while she's been visiting her grandmother, but she rightly pointed out that I have too much on my plate as it is. She's not wrong. I have a habit of spreading myself too thin, especially when it comes to helping people I care about.

"Martha's done a fantastic job managing the shop. She's also kept me in the loop on all the town gossip."

I don't like where she's going with this.

"According to her, Mr. Hot Single Dad got territorial when he saw you with Eric Schultz at the speed dating event last week." She lets out an excited squeal. "If I had known you were into that kind of thing, I would have invited you to the last one."

"I'm not." I let out a groan of embarrassment. "Dylan's mom convinced us both to go but conveniently left out that there would be speed dating. She got it in her head that Dylan and I should go together and decided to play matchmaker for two rather unenthusiastic participants."

At least we used to be unenthusiastic.

"You heard about what Johanna did to her daughter Presley and her boyfriend, Jack, right?" Quinn asks.

"No, what happened?" I saw them both when Johanna invited me over for Christmas Eve, but we didn't get to talk much.

"Presley was Jack's assistant for three years before they got together. The Christmas before last, he invited himself home with her for the holidays, and they pretended to be a couple when they got to Aspen Grove. And guess what?" She pauses for effect. "It turns out Johanna knew who Jack was the entire time but pretended she didn't, and she insisted Jack and Presley share a bedroom while they were in town. Now they're madly in love and living together in New York City."

Johanna's unconditional love for her kids is touching. She's willing to go to great lengths to ensure their happiness, regardless of their stand on her methods. While her interference can be frustrating, I also find it endearing. It's a refreshing take, given that my mom has never cared enough to be that involved in my life.

"I'm so glad things worked out for Presley and Jack, but my situation with Dylan is totally different."

"Sorry to break it to you, Marlow, but I think Johanna might be onto something," Quinn chirps.

"What now?"

"It makes perfect sense if you think about it," she starts passionately. "Dylan's whole life revolves around Lola, and she's completely smitten with you. Add to that the fact Waffles is infatuated with Lola, and you have one big happy family. You might as well explore your feelings."

She's far too happy about this for my liking. "Slow down, turbo. You're worse than Johanna." I rub my temples to ward off an oncoming headache. "You're forgetting one very important detail."

"What's that?"

"Dylan and I can't go more than five minutes of being in the same room without arguing."

"It's called playful banter," Quinn corrects me. "Which everybody knows is just another form of flirting."

If that were the case, then Dylan and I flirt *a lot*. We're constantly taunting each other and exchanging playful jabs, which I've grown to look forward to.

"You're awfully quiet," Quinn observes. "Anything you want to share?"

"I'm going to tell you something and you can't freak out, okay?

"Get on with it," she encourages.

"Dylan might have almost kissed me outside of Willow Creek Café last week and—" I pause when Quinn screeches on the other end of the line.

"Are you serious? Oh my gosh, why didn't you say so sooner? Wait, there's more, isn't there?" I have to move the phone away from my ear while she lets out another squeal. "Marlow Taylor, you better tell me this instant."

I roll my eyes at her theatrics. I forgot that she's the hopeless romantic in our friend group.

"We kissed after he got home last night," I confess.

I wasn't planning on telling anyone, but she would have kept prying until I did. Besides, it's a relief not to have to keep it bottled up any longer.

"Andi is totally going to flip when she hears about this," Quinn exclaims. "Tell me everything this instant."

"Will you please calm down? There's not much to tell." *Okay, that's a total lie.* "Lola and I took a nap after we got back from the doctor's office, and I didn't answer the phone when Dylan tried calling me back. When I woke up, he was back, and was unexpectedly understanding about the whole thing. He said that Lola was fortunate to have me, and one thing led to another and we kissed."

"And?" Quinn asks impatiently.

"And I went home."

"You've got to be joking." She doesn't sound pleased with my anticlimactic story. "Marlow, that *cannot* be the end of the story."

I leave out the part that I'm the one who initiated the kiss. I'm not ready to answer another round of her rapid-fire questions if I do.

"I'm sorry to disappoint," I chuckle. "I'm just not sure it's a good idea for Dylan and me to get any more involved than we already are. His focus should be on Lola, and I'm not sure how much longer I'll be in Aspen Grove. Clearly, neither of us are ready for a serious commitment right now." My throat is scratchy, so I take a long sip of coffee.

"Forget about serious," Quinn shrieks. "What's wrong with sleeping with the man a few times until he's out of your system?"

I nearly choke on my coffee, taken aback by her bluntness.

"Didn't you just tell me we should make it official and be, and I quote, *one big happy family*?" I use air quotes for emphasis even though she's not here to see.

"Come on, Marlow. When was the last time you got laid? You've lived in Aspen Grove for over a year, and I've never seen you with anyone."

"I've been focusing on my art," I say defensively.

"What better way to release those creative juices than with dirty, sweaty sex with a gorgeous single man."

"Please don't say sex and juices in the same sentence." My face betrays my inward cringe. "And that's why I have three battery-operated devices in my nightstand," I tease.

Before moving to Aspen Grove, I only engaged in casual flings since I never stayed in the same place for too long. Since living here, I haven't been with anyone romantically. My focus has been on my art, spending quality time with Waffles and my friends, and more recently my responsibilities as Lola's nanny.

"You wouldn't need those battery-operated devices if you hooked up with the hot, single dad next door instead of running out of there like your hair was on fire."

"Okay, that's it. I'm cutting off your phone privileges," I say with a small smile. "We'll talk more when you get back."

"You can count on it," she vows.

I'm not sure if it was from all of Quinn's high-pitched excitement, but my headache is now a migraine. Once she hangs up, I get up from the couch and go up to my bedroom. I'll take a quick nap before I start on my next painting and when I wake up, I'll feel as good as new.

CHAPTER SIXTEEN

DYLAN

Lola slept in yesterday, but by late afternoon, she was back to running around in her favorite unicorn dress, asking when she could play with Waffles. She wasn't happy when I wouldn't let her go to Marlow's.

The plan had been to give Marlow the day off, but it took every ounce of willpower not to go over and see her.

I regret not doing more to comfort her after we shared what was the best kiss I've ever had. Instead, I stood by and watched her leave. It's been a long time since I've dated, and it's clear, I'm out of practice where women are concerned.

I wish I had the courage to tell Marlow that I'm incredibly attracted to her, and if our situation was different, I wouldn't hesitate to take things further. As it stands, my life is overly complicated, with juggling being a single dad, working a high-pressure job, and wrestling with my feelings toward my daughter's nanny.

After having time to unpack my own emotions, I've come to the conclusion that my fear of being hurt is the underlying issue. The last time I put my heart on the line, I was left alone to mend the shattered fragments.

Honestly, I don't think I could survive that again.

What terrifies me the most is now that I know what it's like to kiss Marlow, I'm consumed by an insatiable longing to do it again. And whether or not I'm ready to admit it, she has the power to alter the course of my life. For better or worse.

It's Friday morning, and once again, I'm pacing the entryway. I have no idea what I'm going to say when she gets here, but I guess I'll come up with something when I see her.

I look at my watch, frowning when I see that it's already 6:10 a.m. Marlow's never been late. I text her and follow up with a call that goes straight to voicemail.

Now that I think about it, yesterday was abnormally quiet at her place, and she wasn't in her studio last night. *Yeah, I noticed.* A sense of unease takes hold of me, fueling the pressing need to make sure she's okay.

First, I check on Lola, who's fast asleep, snuggling with her plush unicorn. I turn on her old baby monitor that I haven't gotten around to getting rid of, just in case she wakes up while I'm gone.

It's freezing outside, and as I approach Marlow's house, I can hear Waffles barking inside. I knock on the door, and when there's no response, I check the handle, not surprised to find the house is unlocked. Marlow and I really need to have a serious chat about her safety.

I stick my head inside and all the lights are off.

"Marlow, it's Dylan. Are you home?" I call out.

I tentatively step inside when there's no answer. The second I cross the threshold, Waffles leaps into my arms, yipping with excitement. I try pushing him off, but I give him a good scratch behind the ear when that doesn't work.

"Where's Marlow, boy?"

He beelines for the stairs, and I follow him up to the second floor, to what I presume is Marlow's bedroom. He stands in the hallway, wagging his tail, waiting for me to make the next move.

The door is wide open, and the room is dark, with the curtains drawn.

"Hello?"

I step inside when there's no reply. *This is such a bad idea.* Marlow probably slept through her alarm and is going to be startled when she finds me in her bedroom.

I move cautiously across the room and find her curled up in her bed. There's a trashcan on the floor nearby and a box of tissues on her nightstand.

Shit, she's sick.

Leaning over, I switch on the bedside lamp to bring light into the room. She doesn't stir as I sit on the edge of the bed. Beads of sweat glisten on her forehead, and her features are contorted in a grimace. I gently caress her cheek, noticing that she's unusually warm.

"Sunshine, can you open your eyes for me?" I coax her.

She grumbles as she opens one eye, squinting up at me with confusion. "Dylan?" Her voice comes out hoarse. "What are you doing here? Am I dreaming?"

I chuckle. "No, I'm real." I brush a piece of stray hair away from her face. "I tried calling when you didn't come over this morning and got worried when you didn't answer."

Her eyes widen in disbelief. "Oh no, what time is it?" She jolts upright in bed, groaning in pain. "I'm so sorry I'm late. Let me get dressed, and I'll be right over." She scoots to the other side of the bed and attempts to stand up, nearly losing her balance.

"Whoa there. You're not going anywhere." I rush over to help her back into bed and adjust her bedding so she's more comfortable.

"What about Lola? You'll be late for work if you don't leave soon."

"Don't worry about that. You need to get some more rest. Is there anyone I can call to come take care of you?" I ask.

She leans back against the pillows, sighing in relief. "No, thanks. I'll be fine on my own. I'm sure after a few more hours of sleep, I'll be good as new." She reaches out, cupping my cheek with her hand, accompanied by a feeble smile. "I appreciate you checking on me, though. That was sweet of you."

Leave it to Marlow to maintain her cheerful disposition, even when she's under the weather. There's a tightness in my chest at the thought of her being home alone today.

"Of course," I say as I sit back down on the bed next to her, brushing her hair back from her flushed face. A soft moan escapes her lips as I run my hand along her brow.

"I have to make a phone call, but I'll be right back, okay?"

"You can go. I promise I'll be fine."

I rise from the bed. "I'll be back."

I go out into the hall to call Harrison, closing the door behind me. When I had to leave New York early, I called him in a panic. Even though he's in Las Vegas for meetings with the Stafford Holdings board, he was a sound of reason when I needed him most.

He answers on the second ring. "Hey, brother. How's Lola doing?"

"I'd say she's doing very well. Last night, she was dancing through the house in her rainbow tutu, singing 'Girls Just Want to Have Fun' at the top of her lungs."

"Interesting song choice for a six-year-old, don't you think?"

"Don't get me started," I mumble.

Lola has quickly fallen in love with Marlow's '80s pop hits playlist, and to say my daughter is now obsessed is an understatement.

"Are you going into the office today?"

"No, that's why I'm calling. I'm taking the day off," I inform him. "I've already texted Max to have him reschedule my meetings."

"You'll be out the whole day?" He sounds shocked. "You want to tell me what this is about? Because I can count on one hand the number of days you've had off in the past three years. And most of those, you ended up working from home."

That's accurate. Yesterday, I answered emails and worked on

a financial report while Lola slept in. I don't like sitting around and figured I might as well work, since something always needs my attention.

"Marlow caught whatever bug Lola had, and I don't want to leave her alone in this condition," I explain quickly.

"Wait, are you referring to Lola's nanny? The same Marlow, who is also your next-door neighbor?" he goads me. "Mom will be ecstatic when she hears about this."

"I thought you were above gossip?"

"Oh, I have no intention of telling her. But we both know once Cash catches wind of this, he'll call Presley, and she'll inevitably spill the beans to Mom. Haven't you heard? There are no secrets in this family," he says with a hint of sarcasm.

"Yeah, I know," I mutter. I'm grateful for my close-knit relationship with my family, but I wish they'd be a little less invested in my personal matters. At least I can count on my dad and Harrison to be voices of logic when everyone else gets carried away.

"I guess I should have seen this coming," Harrison says.

I rest my shoulder against the wall. "What's that supposed to mean?"

"You're a caregiver by nature, Dylan. You can't help but lend a hand when someone you care about could use support." He pauses briefly. "Wait a second, isn't Marlow younger than you? Weren't you the one who gave Jack a hard time for being too old to date Presley?"

"Presley is my kid sister; of course, I'm going to be protective." I don't mention the ten-year age gap between Marlow and me. It's not relevant. "And for the record, nothing is happening between Marlow and me. She's been incredibly helpful with Lola, and I'd like to return the favor."

It's nobody's business that we've kissed or that all I can think about is doing it again, even though I shouldn't.

"Mm-hmm. Sure." I roll my eyes at his playful skepticism.

"Listen, I'm walking into a board meeting, so I'll talk to you tomorrow."

"Yeah, sounds good," I say.

I hang up the phone and tuck it into my back pocket.

I'm glad we were able to chat. It was nice to catch a glimpse of his fun-loving side. Our conversations are usually strictly about work since he's too busy for anything else these days.

When I check on Marlow, she's fast asleep.

I head downstairs and spend a good five minutes scouring her kitchen for a pad of sticky notes and a pen. I leave her a note in case she wakes up before I get back from taking Lola to school.

Waffles follows me around the house and lets out a low whine when I'm about to leave.

"What is it, boy?"

He looks longingly at the front door, and it occurs to me that he most likely hasn't been let out since last night. He should probably go on a walk this morning, too, and Marlow's in no condition to take him.

I let out a heavy sigh. "Fine, you win. You can come over to see Lola, but just this once, and you're not allowed on the furniture, got it?"

He scratches at the door impatiently. I search for his leash, finding it wedged under a pair of Marlow's sneakers in the living room. I have no clue how she finds anything in this mess.

I make the mistake of opening the front door before putting Waffles' leash on, and he bolts outside.

"Waffles, wait," I shout.

He completely ignores me, hightailing it to my yard. At least I know where he's going, avoiding a high-speed chase. His behavior further proves my point that he needs to be trained. Starting today.

CHAPTER SEVENTEEN

MARLOW

I groan as I shift to my side. It feels like I've gone multiple rounds with a pro boxer. My body is achy, and the relentless pounding in my head won't stop. Exhaustion clings to me like a fog, zapping every ounce of energy I have left. I blink my eyes open and find my room is dark except for the soft glow of the bedside lamp.

I'm confused when I spot a humidifier on the nightstand, next to a bottle of water and two white pills sitting on top of a sticky note.

Good morning, sunshine,
Take these with water and call me so I can bring you
something to eat.
-Dylan

I'm either dreaming or woke up in an alternate reality because there's no way Dylan Stafford would willingly come to my house and take care of me... would he? I vaguely remember him being here earlier, but it's all hazy. It's possible he was a figment of my imagination brought on by the fever. I guess there's only one way to find out.

I fumble around until I find my phone tangled in the blankets. I'm shocked when I check the time and realize that I've been in bed for nearly twenty-four hours, aside from the occasional trip to the bathroom and letting Waffles out last night. There are dozens of missed calls and texts from Dylan—the last message saying he'll be back after he drops Lola off at school. That was over four hours ago.

When I stand, I wobble like a fawn taking its first steps and use the wall for support until I gain my bearings. I make my way downstairs, and my mouth falls open when I take in my surroundings.

The entryway is spotless—my shoes are arranged on a new shoe rack, Waffles' toys are piled neatly in a basket, and there's no trace of dog hair on the floor.

As I wander into the living room, my gaze lands on several stacks of laundry folded on the couch. This comes as a welcome surprise, since I usually skip folding and putting away my clothes, going straight from the laundry basket to wearing them. On closer inspection, I'm mortified to see that my panties are included, every pair folded neatly.

This isn't how I envisioned Dylan seeing my panties for the first time.

Whoa, where did that come from? It must be my fever talking.

I furrow my brow when I hear Waffles barking insistently and follow the sound to the kitchen.

Dylan is crouched in front of my dog, holding his jaw to keep him in place. He plucks a piece of chicken from a bowl on the floor and balances it on Waffles' snout. Waffles whines, not happy his treat is being held hostage.

"You got it this time," Dylan encourages.

He holds out a finger, signaling Waffles to stay still as he slowly releases his jaw. No sooner has he pulled back his hand,

Waffles drops the chicken to the floor, and scarfs it up, paying no mind to Dylan's irritation.

"This is hopeless," Dylan mumbles. "All you had to do was sit for a few seconds, and I would have given you two treats."

Waffles barks loudly and chases his tail at the mention of his favorite word.

"Unbelievable." Dylan throws his hands in the air. "You'd think after twenty tries, you'd have this—"

"Are you trying to train my dog?" I interrupt. "*Try* being the operative word."

Dylan turns in my direction, eyes wide when he sees me standing with my arms folded across my chest. He's on his feet in an instant, forgetting to grab the bowl of chicken off the ground. Waffles doesn't hesitate to seize the opportunity for an unexpected snack.

"What are you doing out of bed?" Dylan scolds, ignoring my question. "Didn't you see my note? I specifically told you to call me when you woke up."

"I'm fine." A sudden rush of dizziness hits me, and I lean against the counter for support.

"I'm taking you back to bed before you hurt yourself," he says, crossing over to me.

Without warning, he scoops me up, and I instinctively wrap my arms around his neck. I place my head on his chest, instantly surrounded by the smell of mint and cedar. As my gaze wanders to his face, the attraction is undeniable. He's downright sexy, particularly with his five o'clock shadow and glasses.

He smirks. "You think I'm sexy?"

Did I say that out loud?

"Yeah, you did."

That too?

He chuckles as he strides out of the kitchen. "For the time being, let's assume that whatever is going through your head is coming out of that beautiful mouth of yours."

"Will you stop being so nice? It's freaking me out."

He presses a kiss on my forehead. "You'll get used to it."

"I'm not so sure about that," I mutter. "Can we talk about how you cleaned my house, folded my underwear, and tried training my dog?"

"Maybe when you're feeling better." He doesn't explain further as he carries me up the stairs and puts me back into bed. "I'll be right back with some chicken soup," he tells me and hurries out of the room.

My stomach rumbles at the mention of food. I haven't had anything to eat since a piece of toast last night, and I couldn't even keep that down.

I wonder if I've entered the twilight zone when Dylan returns with a tray featuring chicken noodle soup, freshly cut strawberries, buttered toast, and a bottle of water. It looks like a gourmet meal compared to what I'm used to. He places the tray on the nightstand and settles on the bed beside me.

"That smells incredible." I nod at the soup.

"It tastes even better," he assures me as he pushes his glasses up on his nose.

Why is the fact that he wears glasses so appealing?

"What are you doing?" A look of confusion crosses my face when he picks up the steaming bowl of soup and a spoon.

"Feeding you?"

"I can do that myself." I reach for the bowl, but he moves it out of my reach.

"A few minutes ago, you almost fell over because you were so weak. I'm not chancing you losing your grip and spilling broth on your comforter."

"That's a bit dramatic, don't you think?" I challenge.

He shakes his head. "Would you rather keep arguing with me or eat something?

I'm tempted to counter with another comeback, but my stomach lets out a loud growl, silencing my protests.

Dylan chuckles, scooping some chicken noodle soup onto the spoon and bringing it to my lips. "Be careful, it's hot," he warns.

I blow on the soup before accepting the bite he's holding out for me. I moan softly when the mix of savory broth, carrots, celery, and shredded chicken hits my tongue.

"This is delicious." I greedily accept another spoonful. "Where did you get it? Canned chicken noodle soup doesn't taste this good."

"I made it," he says as he continues feeding me.

"With what ingredients?"

"Well, obviously, I couldn't use anything in your fridge," he quips. "Honestly, I have no idea how you've survived this long when all you have in the house are corn dogs, Cheez-Its, a jar of jelly, Pop-Tarts, and takeout leftovers. Even Waffles eats better than you."

This is true. I order him fresh, preservative-free dog food that's shipped to our door. It's an easier option than lugging a bag of dog food home every month, and he deserves the best.

"Cooking was never my strong suit. My mom tried to teach me, but her patience quickly wore thin." I pause to plop a slice of strawberry into my mouth. "After high school, I adopted a nomadic lifestyle, never settling in one place for too long. Ordering frozen meals and prepackaged snacks became my go-to solution. I tend to lose track of time when I'm working and often go an entire day without noticing that I haven't eaten. That's why I prefer quick and easy options."

"That's not healthy," Dylan says with disapproval.

"I'm well aware. I don't deliberately skip meals. When I'm in the middle of painting, eating slips my mind sometimes." My tone turns defensive. "I get it—I'm a hot mess, scatterbrained, and disorganized. A walking disaster. But I didn't choose to be this way; it's just how my brain works." My bottom lip trembles at my admission.

I've harbored a sense of inadequacy my whole life. I'm the quirky girl with strange eyes that no one could relate to. Even my parents found it challenging to understand me, and it felt like somewhere along the way, they gave up. It's exhausting to constantly justify or explain why I do things a certain way.

That's why I instantly fell in love with Waffles. When I overheard a volunteer at the animal shelter call him hyperactive, his fate was sealed. He deserved to be adopted by someone who gets what it's like to be judged for their personality, and lack of recognizing social cues, and who embraces his unique qualities. That's one reason I've been hesitant to train him—I'm worried that he'll lose what makes my sweet furball *him* if I do.

Dylan frowns as he sets the soup on the tray.

"I want you to listen carefully, sunshine." He cups my face with his hands and looks me directly in the eyes. "You might not be perfect, hell nobody is, but you are incredible just the way you are. You find the silver lining in any situation and have a gift for making people smile on their worst days." He caresses my cheek with the pad of his thumb. "And your artistic ability is unmatched. How you can turn a blank canvas into a masterpiece is a rare and remarkable talent. Your differences are what makes you so damn special."

"Let's not forget that Lola worships the ground you walk on, and it's your unique qualities that she loves most. She's obsessed with your colorful wardrobe, shares your taste in music, and most importantly, you treat her like she matters."

I fight back the tears threatening to spill. I've grown so accustomed to being reminded of my shortcomings that it's hard to believe when someone says otherwise. I've spent a lot of time in therapy unpacking my issues related to my self-worth, and there are still days that it feels like I'm back at square one. To hear Dylan speak from his heart and knowing it's sincere is priceless.

"Thank you." I place my hand over his. "It means more than I can adequately express. It's rare to hear someone say those things to me, particularly regarding my art."

Ignoring judgment has become second nature. In the past, I channeled all my energy into brushing the negativity aside. In doing so, I often lost sight of the importance of learning to appreciate and love the distinctive qualities that make me who I am.

"That's a damn shame." Dylan brushes his thumb across my cheek. "You should be reminded every day of how exceptional you are."

I draw in a deep breath, savoring his heartfelt words.

"I appreciate you saying that."

Dylan clears his throat and pulls his hand back.

"You should finish your soup now." He motions to the half-empty bowl on the nightstand.

"I will, but I'd like to take a shower first."

I hold out a section of my hair, noting how dirty it is. I haven't washed it in days, and it's damp with sweat. It'll be nice when it's clean and silky again.

It's a good thing I'm not trying to impress Dylan or anything.

He shakes his head. "There's no way I'm letting you take a shower when you were having a difficult time standing on your own earlier. What about taking a bath instead?"

"A bath sounds nice. You know, Dylan, you're very good at compromising," I say playfully.

"I've had lots of practice." He grins. "I'll be right back." He gets up and goes into the master bathroom. Moments later, I hear the water running.

He reappears and effortlessly carries me into the bathroom, placing me on the marble countertop.

"Thank you... aren't you going to leave?" I ask when he doesn't move.

"I thought you could use some help with getting into the bathtub."

I roll my lip between my teeth, overwhelmed by the flood of emotions crashing over me. While I could probably manage to wash my hair on my own, it would be much easier with help.

I'm embarrassed that my body is weak and shaky, and I'm not used to relying on someone to help with something so simple. It complicates things when the person is the hot single dad next door, and the man I shared a scorching hot kiss with the last time I saw him.

This situation is making it more difficult to ignore the brewing chemistry between us. Not to mention this would be the first time Dylan sees me naked.

Wait... The first time?

Evidently my subconscious hasn't got the memo that I'm sick and is scheming up additional scenarios where Dylan and I find ourselves in compromising positions that tempt our self-control.

My eyes dart between Dylan, who's patiently waiting for my reply, and the steam rising from the hot bathwater.

My mouth runs dry. "You can stay, but I'm keeping my bra and panties on. And I reserve the right to kick you out at any time," I warn him.

"I'll be on my best behavior," he says wryly. "You're in control here. Say the word and I'm gone," he adds after a beat.

We're playing with fire, but I can't bring myself to ask him to leave.

CHAPTER EIGHTEEN

DYLAN

This is a really bad idea.

Why the hell did I suggest I stay with Marlow while she took a bath?

Because she's sick and needs your help.

Tell that to my rock-hard cock straining against my boxer briefs while I watch her pull her shirt over her head, revealing a lilac lace bra. Her breasts spill out over the top, evoking an image of her straddling me while I worship her perfect tits. I force myself to avert my gaze before she catches me gawking.

You'd think that Marlow being both off-limits as the nanny and a decade younger than me would tamp down my attraction, but it seems to have the opposite effect.

The energy has shifted between us since that night at Willow Creek Café, and despite our best efforts to avoid the subject, the attraction between us is palpable. I can't shake the sense that it's only a matter of time before the dam breaks, unleashing the pent-up sexual tension between us.

"Could you help keep me steady while I step out of my shorts?" Marlow's question snaps me out of my thoughts, and I blink at her, unsure if I heard her right.

"Uh, yeah… sure." I stumble over my words.

"Thanks, I'm a little dizzy, so it'd be nice to have something to hold on to," she hurries out.

"There's no need to explain. I'm happy to help." *More than I should be.* "Put your hands on my shoulders," I direct her.

"Okay."

When she's in position, I grab hold of her hips and lift her to a standing position. She wobbles slightly, but I tighten my grip to keep her steady. She holds firmly to my shoulders as I bend to tug off her sleep shorts, and my pulse races at our close proximity. Despite my best attempts to avert my gaze, I catch a glimpse of her baby blue underwear, her sinful curves on display. It tests my self-control not to take another look.

I force myself to focus on the task at hand and toss Marlow's shorts out of the way. The smell of citrus and rose envelopes the room as I carry her over to the claw-foot bathtub and lower her down until she's seated in the water.

"This feels so nice," she moans.

My dick jerks in response, and I have to discreetly adjust my pants to hide my reaction to the sexy sounds coming from her mouth. I've got to get a grip.

"Would you mind getting my shampoo and conditioner for me?" Marlow asks.

"Yeah, no problem." I grab both bottles from the ledge below the window. and set them on the edge of the tub. "Want me to wash your hair?" I immediately cringe at my offer, remembering that it's not a normal question to ask a grown woman. "I'm sorry, I'm in the habit of asking Lola," I explain, hoping I didn't sound creepy.

It comes with the territory of being a girl dad with an independent six-year-old. Some days, she welcomes the help, and others, she's offended that I don't think she can do it herself.

Marlow peers up at me. "If it's not too much trouble."

"I wouldn't have offered if it was."

I kneel on the ground next to the tub and unbutton the cuffs of my dress shirt, rolling up my sleeves. It's a habit to avoid getting splashed on, but right now I couldn't care less about getting my shirt wet. I'm too focused on the fact that I'm about to help bathe my gorgeous next-door neighbor and have to pretend I'm unaffected.

"It's comical seeing you on the floor in slacks and a dress shirt." Marlow giggles.

I raise a brow. "I'm dressed like this every day."

"Sure, when you're going to or from the office. I just can't get over the image of you doing household chores in business attire."

"And tell me how you imagine me dressed when I'm doing chores?"

Her cheeks flush as she glances down at the water. "Uh... I'm not sure."

Before I say anything that'll get me in trouble, I lean down over Marlow as I rinse her hair, one arm easing her backward, using my other hand to scoop water over her hair. Her eyes fall shut and I take the moment to appreciate the view before me. Her lips are slightly parted, and she's not wearing a stitch of makeup, giving me an unobstructed view of the freckles scattered across the bridge of her nose.

My eyes wander to her wet lilac bra that is now see-through and I trace every bump and differentiating shade of her pebbled nipples. My gaze slowly moves back to Marlow's face, to find her watching me intently, her chest rising and falling more rapidly than before.

Our unspoken desires fill the charged air.

She's utterly captivating, and if our circumstances were different, I wouldn't think twice about taking her to bed, and worshiping her the way she deserves. As it is, the kiss we shared a couple of days ago could be the closest I'll ever get to a night with Marlow Taylor. Although I hope that's not the case.

"Sit up now."

She does as I ask, looking up at me with a tentative smile.

"Good girl," I praise.

Marlow's eyes widen and she drags her teeth across her lips. It seems I'm not the only one affected by calling her *good girl*. Although this isn't the setting in which I'd prefer to use the term. I might be reserved, but that doesn't mean I don't have a bossy streak in the bedroom.

Marlow pulls her knees to her chest as she watches me intently.

I grab the bottle of shampoo from the side of the tub and squeeze a generous dollop into my hand. She tips her head back as I run my fingers through her sun-kissed hair, massaging the soap into her scalp in slow, steady circles. Her body visibility relaxes at my touch, and I realize that I enjoy taking care of her. I think that's why I started making breakfast her each morning. It's something that I can do to make sure she's getting at least one healthy meal a day without crossing any boundaries.

"Mmm." Marlow hums her approval when I rub her templates. "God, you're so good at this," she says.

I can't help my thoughts straying as I imagine what it would be like to hear her say those words when we're both naked and she's lying on the bed. I'd kneel in front of her, my hands gripping her thighs as I gazed up to find a wanton expression on her face while I brought her unbridled pleasure. I'd lick her pussy with my tongue, her fingers tangled in my hair as I worked her clit hard, telling her to be my good girl and come for me.

What am I doing?

Marlow is sick. Now isn't the time to let my imagination run wild, no matter how much I wish I could do more with her at this moment.

I clear my throat. "I've had a lot of practice, remember?"

After I've rinsed out the shampoo using the shower attachment, conditioned her hair and rinsed it out a second time, I grab a towel and her robe from the back of the bathroom door.

She takes my hand as I help her out of the tub, but insists on drying herself off while I stand within arm's reach in case she needs me.

Her bra and panties are still damp, and I quickly help her into her robe when I notice the goosebumps covering her arm. I carry her to the bed, and get a pair of pajamas from her blue ombre dresser on the other side of the room.

The next two minutes are torture while she makes me face the wall, so she can change out of her wet underwear. When she's finished, I turn around to find her sitting on the edge of the bed, wearing the matching pink tank top and shorts I choose for her.

God, she's downright irresistible.

My hands are clammy, and my breathing is shallow knowing that she's not wearing panties under her sleep shorts right now. She didn't ask me to get her a pair when she asked for clothes, and it's taking all my resolve from letting my mind wander again.

"Do you want me to brush your hair?" I rasp out.

She nods, with a tired expression.

I grab a hairbrush from the bathroom and sit on the bed behind Marlow, with her back to my front. I run the brush through her hair in slow, steady strokes, careful not to tug too hard. Her waist-length hair cascades in golden waves down her back, and once I've got all the tangles out, I begin to plait a French braid.

"What are you doing?" She tilts her head back, curiosity shining in her eyes.

"Braiding your hair. I figured it'd be better to have it out of your face while you sleep."

"That's very thoughtful of you." She gives me a small smile before turning her head to face forward. "I've never met another man who's as skilled at styling hair as you are. I'm impressed."

"That's nice of you to say. I'm not sure if I've mentioned it before, but Maddie, Lola's mom, left when she was a baby. Back then, there were a lot of external factors controlling my life, but the one aspect I had power over was my reaction to the situation. Early on, I committed to do everything I could to guarantee Lola didn't miss out on a happy childhood because her mom wasn't around."

I pause, fastening a hair tie to the end of Marlow's braid. "That meant memorizing the *CoComelon* theme song when she was a toddler, learning to style her hair, and cutting sandwiches into the shape of unicorns and rainbows. I'd gladly do it all a hundred times over to make sure she knows that she's loved unconditionally."

"What happened to Maddie?" Marlow pauses as she turns to look at me. "If you don't mind me asking."

I usually don't like talking about it but with Marlow I feel inclined to open up and share more of my past with her.

"Maddie and I started dating in high school. In hindsight, I suspect part of her attraction was linked to my family's financial status. Unfortunately for her, I've never been interested in living an extravagant lifestyle, which became a source of conflict between us. We frequently argued, especially when I broached the topic of marriage or having kids." I draw in a deep breath as I rake my hand through my hair. "I was blindsided when Maddie left us when Lola was only six weeks old."

Marlow lets out a sharp gasp. "Where did she go?" Her tone is hushed.

"As far as I know she moved to Canada. I haven't heard from her since she left."

I was heartbroken when Maddie threw away ten years with me like it meant nothing and that she so easily left her daughter behind. I spent years resenting her for what she did, but eventually the anger and betrayal morphed into gratitude for giving me Lola in the first place.

When I look back at Marlow I'm alarmed when I see tears streaming down her face.

"What's the matter? Why are you crying?" I wipe away a stray tear with the pad of my thumb. "I didn't mean to make you sad." I start to pull my hand away, but Marlow reaches out to hold it in place against her cheek, pressing a kiss to my palm.

"I'm okay, I promise." She offers me a comforting smile. "You've been through so much, and yet you've put it all aside to make sure Lola has the best life can offer. I mean it when I say she couldn't have asked for a better father."

"Thank you." My chest tightens.

Marlow's observation resonates with me in a way she might not realize. I haven't told her I've been shouldering a load of guilt about not being enough for Lola lately, and her words strike a chord deep within me.

Even when she's feeling at her worst, she's quick to offer me comfort. Considering our past interactions, she has every reason to harbor resentment toward me, but she doesn't. Her kind-hearted and thoughtful nature is one of the reasons I'm finding it so damn difficult to keep my distance, even though it's better for both of us.

I caress her cheek, tracing her jaw with my fingertips as silence lingers between us, the crackling tension between us irrefutable. My gaze locks with Marlow's, and I'm having difficulty remembering why I shouldn't kiss her right now.

She shakes her head. "I've seen that look before."

"What look?" I feign innocence.

"The one you get when you're contemplating doing something you shouldn't."

"You think you know me so well, huh?" I ask with a playful grin.

She lifts a brow. "Am I wrong?"

"Honestly? No. I was convincing myself I shouldn't kiss you again," I say as I stare at her mouth.

Marlow covers my mouth with her palm. "You can't kiss me right now," she blurts out.

"Why not?"

"Because I'm sick, and the last thing Lola and I need is for you to catch it. I suspect that you'd be a challenging patient, and

I refuse to deal with your grumpiness when you're stuck in bed for days." She shivers at the thought.

I chuckle softly. She has a point. When I'm sick, I do have a tendency to be more irritable.

I lean in to press a kiss on her forehead. "I guess that will have to do for now. I want you to know that I do like you, sunshine."

"I like you too, Dylan," she murmurs.

The unspoken words linger in the air.

I'm not sure I'm in a place where I can commit to a relationship and Marlow can't guarantee that she'll still be in Aspen Grove six months from now. We're in different stages of our lives, and if we knew what was good for us, we'd dismiss our feelings for each other entirely and move on. However, I can't promise that if the opportunity presents itself to kiss Marlow again that I won't take it.

She gives me a sleepy smile, barely able to keep her eyes open.

"Why don't we get you back into bed?" I suggest. "I think you could use a nap."

"I think you're right," she agrees.

I get off the bed so she can get under the covers. Once she's settled, I tuck the blankets around her.

"I have to pick up Lola from school soon, but I'll stop by later this afternoon to check on you, okay? In the meantime, call me if you need anything else."

She places her hand on my forearm. "Thank you, Dylan, for everything—the soup, cleaning my house, washing my hair. I really appreciate it," she says in earnest. "But don't think for a second that you've got away with going all Cesar Millian on me by trying to train my dog." She holds her hand out when I open my mouth to say something. "We'll talk about it when I'm in a condition to win the argument."

I chuckle at her joke. "You got it, sunshine. Now get some sleep."

I lean down and give her another kiss on the forehead before turning off the bedside lamp.

As I leave her room, it strikes me that I haven't checked my work email a single time since I've been here. And surprisingly, I haven't wanted to.

CHAPTER NINETEEN

MARLOW

When I enter Brew Haven, I'm greeted with the aroma of freshly ground coffee beans and toasted pastries. They host a weekly Sunday brunch, so the place is buzzing with activity, packed with patrons eager for their caffeine fix and a hearty meal.

I spot Quinn and Andi waving at me from our usual booth in the back corner.

Since I moved to Aspen Grove, we regularly come here on the weekends, but it's been ages since we've all been together. I'm looking forward to catching up with Andi. Not so much to the interrogation I suspect Quinn has planned.

There's not much of an update since the last time we spoke, aside from Dylan coming over to my house on Friday. After getting Lola home from school, he stopped by a second time that afternoon. He brought me dinner and took Waffles for another walk. After my nap, I had enough strength to get to and from the bathroom, and I convinced him I was okay to be left alone.

Dylan and I have exchanged a few texts, but I've kept mine brief, not wanting to interfere with his weekend plans. Johanna and Mike are back in town, so he and Lola spent yesterday at their house.

That doesn't mean he hasn't been on my mind. Memories

flood my thoughts of his hands massaging my scalp as he looked down at me with a lust-filled gaze. I wanted nothing more than to ask him to join me in the tub, and the only thing that stopped me was being sick.

The logical side of my brain recognizes that there's much more at stake than the mutual attraction between two people. We have Lola to think about, and our lifestyles are totally different. However, the emotional side of my brain is a lustful bitch, who wants nothing more than to march over to his house and demand that he kiss me again.

It's difficult to justify the reservations I've had when he's been so good to me. I appreciate his ability to show he cares through actions and expects nothing in return.

When I finally got around to opening my fridge this weekend, I found a stack of precooked meals with a yellow sticky on the top container.

Morning, sunshine,
I hope you're feeling better. These are for you.
P.S. They take less time to heat up than a corn dog.
-Dylan

I reluctantly tried the vegetable lasagna, and he wasn't exaggerating; it was delicious. But that doesn't mean I'm willing to give up my precious frozen corn dogs quite yet.

Yesterday, I spent time locked in my studio, finishing another painting. My art exhibition is coming up soon, and I'm determined to prove to Gavin and myself that despite my poor procrastination habits and short attention span, I can finish this collection on time, even if it seems impossible.

"Look who finally showed up," Quinn says, giving me a teasing smirk as I approach our table.

"I'm only five minutes late," I say, leaning across the table to hug her.

"You look gorgeous. I'm obsessed with that jumper." She gestures to my outfit.

After being cooped up inside the last couple of days, I was excited to wear something other than yoga pants or sleep shorts. My corduroy jumper was a recent find at the local thrift store, and I paired it with a peach long-sleeve shirt and navy-blue tights.

"You look darling," Andi chimes in.

"Hey, stranger." I slide into her side of the booth and give her a hug. "Long time no see."

"Yeah, yeah," she acknowledges. "I've already gotten an earful from this one." She motions to Quinn. "Work has been busier than usual, and Charlie has a never-ending list of extracurriculars, so it's impossible to keep up."

Andi is a partner at the law firm in town and a badass aunt. When her sister passed away four years ago, she traded in her corporate job in New York City for family law in Aspen Grove to raise her nephew and his pet chickens. We became fast friends when Quinn introduced us. I'm a big fan of her willingness to speak her mind and her no-nonsense attitude.

"The important thing is we're all here now, which means Marlow can give us the scoop." Quinn fixes her focus on me.

"I can't do anything until I've had my coffee," I complain.

I've been to coffee shops all over the world and Brew Haven is one of my favorites. I may or may not be addicted, but I make no apologies.

"Here you go." Quinn beams, sliding a cup toward me. "It's a cappuccino with three pumps of coconut creamer, just the way you like it. I also ordered you avocado toast with eggs and a side of bacon, which will be out shortly."

"Bless you," I say, lifting the warm cup and savoring my first sip.

"Don't be fooled," Andi warns me. "It wasn't for your benefit. She figured that buying you brunch would butter you up, and cut down on the time she'd have to wait before she could interrogate you."

I take another sip of my coffee, waiting for Quinn's patience to wear out. It doesn't take long.

"For heaven's sake, Marlow, don't leave us hanging." She's practically on the edge of her seat. "While I was at the airport last night, Martha called me from the shop. She said there's a rumor going around that Dylan Stafford spent the day at your house on Friday. Is that true?"

I roll my eyes. "What is it with the people in this town? Don't they have anything better to do than gossip?"

"Not when the Stafford family is involved," Andi interjects. "Even I know that."

"Enough chitchat," Quinn says, leaning forward. "Tell us what happened."

Before I can say anything, Kelsey, one of the baristas, brings over our food, eliciting a glare from Quinn.

"Here you are, ladies." I practically salivate when she places my plate in front of me.

"Thanks, Kelsey. This looks amazing."

"My pleasure," she says before hurrying off.

When I reach for my fork, Quinn grabs my wrist. "Marlow, there will be plenty of time to eat later. Please don't make me wait any longer."

"Fine." I begrudgingly set my fork down. "Dylan came over on Friday morning to check on me when I didn't show up at his place. He found me sick in bed and took the day off to clean my house and cook me soup. He also washed my hair because I was too weak to stand in the shower. Oh, did I mention that he tried to train Waffles?"

"He. Washed. Your. Hair? Oh my god, I'm swooning." Quinn puts her hand to her forehead in a dramatic fashion. "Andi, please tell me you heard that."

"I heard." She laughs before taking a bite of her biscuits and gravy.

"That's what you got out of my story? Did you not hear the part where he tried training Waffles? My dog is perfect just the way he is," I declare.

"Except when he's terrorizing the town while chasing a squirrel down Main Street," Quinn pipes up between a bite of bacon.

"Or when he's trespassing into your neighbor's backyard," Andi adds.

Leave it to my friends to give me their unsolicited opinions.

"Okay, I guess Waffles could use some training, but is Dylan the right person for the job?"

Something tells me he probably is because he's good at everything else. I don't know any other men who can braid hair, cook gourmet meals, or who take a day off from work to care for his daughter's nanny when she's sick. Although I'd like to think I mean more to him than that.

"Girl, if a man willingly cleaned my house, made me a home cooked meal, and washed my hair, I would gladly let him train my dog," Quinn says with a mouthful of pancakes.

"Same," Andi agrees.

I suppose it wouldn't be the worst thing if Waffles learned to follow directions. I make a mental note to chat with Dylan about it when I see him in the morning.

"Does this mean you guys are an item now?" Quinn asks with an upbeat tone. "At least tell me you're planning to get some action. Clearly that man is into you."

"No. Right now, my focus is on Lola and my upcoming art exhibition." I avoid Quinn's gaze, staring down at my toast. I'd prefer not to hash out my overly complicated feelings for Dylan right now.

I pick up my fork, ready to dig in, only to be interrupted again.

"Enough about your non-relationship"—Andi uses air quotes for emphasis—"with Dylan. I want to know how your collection is coming along for The Artist. Gavin is doing a phenomenal job promoting it on social media, and I can't wait to see how it turns out. I wish I could be there in person."

Her nephew Charlie has a hockey game on the same day as my exhibition. While I would have liked for her to come, I would never ask her to choose me over her family obligations.

I groan as I throw my hands over my face. "It's been slow going. I have three more pieces to finish and only a few days to do it."

"Oh boy. Gavin won't be happy if he has to chase down another delivery truck around Manhattan," Quinn warns me.

"Yes, I'm very much aware." I shoot her a playful scowl. "I've blocked out my schedule this week, so aside from watching Lola, I'll be locked away in my studio until the collection is complete," I state confidently. "I'm feeling more inspired, so I'm hopeful these final pieces will be less challenging than the others."

Quinn smirks. "I wonder where your newfound inspiration came from."

"Will you stop it," I feel a blush rising to my cheeks.

"I didn't do anything," she says, feigning innocence.

"Uh-huh. In that case, I'm going to eat my breakfast now." I finally take a bite of the avocado toast drizzled with olive oil and groan in satisfaction.

We spend the next hour eating our breakfast and catching up. Quinn shares her plans to expand the classes she offers at Brush & Palette, and Andi updates us on the changes happening at her law firm. She also fills us in on the recent shenanigans Charlie has gotten into with his pet chickens.

"Oh shoot," Quinn mutters when she checks the time. "I've got to run. I canceled the Family Craft Corner class while I was out of town and rescheduled this week's session for today." She scrambles out of her side of the booth. "Should I tell Dylan hi for you?" she asks me with a smug expression.

I can't believe she actually changed the class name because of him.

"Don't even think about it," I warn her as she runs out of the coffee shop.

"I better go too," Andi says. "Charlie's hockey practice is ending soon, and he doesn't like it when he has to wait out in the cold."

"Oh yeah, sure," I scoot out of the booth so she can get out.

"For what it's worth, Quinn and I just want you to be happy," Andi says as she hugs me goodbye. "You're probably already planning your next big adventure, but who knows, maybe there's something or *someone* in Aspen Grove worth staying for." A muffled ring comes from her purse, and she rummages around until she finds her phone. "Shoot, it's Charlie. He's waiting for me. I have to go," she rushes out.

"That's okay. See you later."

She gives me a quick wave as she rushes out the door, leaving me alone to consider what it might be like if my next big adventure was letting two very special people into my heart.

———

I'm just stepping out of the coffee shop, debating if I should stop by Main Street Market on my way home, when Lola's singsong voice catches my attention.

"Marlow," she shouts, waving frantically with both hands.

She and Dylan are heading in my direction, and my stomach does a somersault when Dylan's face lights up with a grin.

I wish he'd do that more often.

"Hey, lolabug," I say as they get closer.

I take a moment to appreciate the view. I rarely see Dylan in anything but a suit, but today he's dressed down in dark-wash jeans, a long-sleeve thermal, and a beanie. He's the epitome of sex appeal, and I swear he somehow got more attractive since I saw him last.

"You're so pretty," Lola sighs dreamily. "Daddy, don't you think Marlow's pretty?" She tilts her head toward Dylan.

"Yes, she's *very* beautiful." His gaze is fixed on me as he speaks.

My heart skips a beat, and I offer him a shy smile. I'll never tire of hearing him call me beautiful, especially when his eyes light up with warmth, making me feel like I'm special.

I turn my attention to Lola when she tugs on my jumper. "Hey, Marlow, can you do my hair in a halo braid for school on Monday?"

"Absolutely," I promise. "Who did your hair today? It's lovely." It's styled in a side braid ponytail with a polka-dot bow.

"Daddy did it," she says proudly.

"He did an excellent job."

My heart melts now that I know the sentiment behind Dylan's ability to braid Lola's hair. His unconditional love for her has no bounds, and it's endearing that he's willing to do whatever it takes to guarantee her happiness.

"Where are you two headed?"

"Ms. Quinn's craft class," Lola exclaims. "Today we're making rainbow heart suncatchers. Can you go with us? Pretty please?" She clasps her hands together.

"Oh, I'm not sure—"

"You should come," Dylan interjects. "That is, if you're free."

His invitation catches me off guard. Everyone in town knows that his weekends are reserved for Lola and his family, but that doesn't mean I'm going to pass up the chance to spend time with them if he's sincere.

"Are you sure? I wouldn't want to intrude."

"We want you there, don't we?" he asks Lola.

She nods with a toothy grin.

"It's settled," Dylan announces, not giving me a chance to argue. "We better hurry, or we're going to be late."

Lola moves in between us, taking hold of both of our hands, leading us along. I pay no mind to the sidelong glances from passersby who are shocked at the sight of Dylan Stafford spending Sunday afternoon with his daughter and her nanny.

I have a hunch Quinn is going to have a heyday with this new development.

———

When we walk into the studio at the back of Brush & Palette, a hush falls over the room, everyone watching us with interest.

Quinn's eyes almost pop out of her head when she sees me with Dylan and Lola before she breaks into a smug grin. There's no chance she's going to let me live this down.

She comes right over to greet us. "Hey there, Ms. Lola. I'm so happy you're here," she says in a cheery tone. "Who's your friend?"

"This is Marlow. She's my nanny," Lola says proudly.

"I'm glad you brought her along. You want to know a secret?" Quinn leans in closer.

Lola's eyes shine with curiosity. "What is it?"

"Marlow is my friend too," Quinn whispers. "She comes by the shop to visit me after she drops you off at school."

"Does that mean Waffles is your friend too?" Lola asks.

Quinn chuckles. "Yeah, I guess we are."

Since Waffles almost plowed her down while chasing a squirrel, I've avoided bringing him to Brush & Palette. However, she spends plenty of time with him whenever she comes to my house. That dog has a talent for making friends, even when his first impression is less than stellar. Take Dylan, for instance. It's taken over a year, but he's warming up to Waffles, whether he'll admit it or not.

"Waffles is my *best* friend," Lola announces with gusto.

"He's one lucky pooch," Quinn says.

Lola giggles. "You're silly, Ms. Quinn. Waffles isn't a pooch. He's a dog,"

I steal a glance at Dylan, who's attempting to suppress a chuckle. I'm sure he'll educate her on the different names for a dog when they get home.

"You're absolutely right." Quinn puts her hands on her cheeks and shakes her head. "Why don't you and your dad show Marlow where your station is and you can start on your rainbow heart suncatcher."

"Oh, yes, please. Come on, Marlow. This is gonna be so much fun." Lola grabs my hand, tugging me across the room, Dylan trailing behind us.

Every station has a kid's apron, Mod Podge, foam paint brushes, a heart-shaped template, white card stock, two pairs of scissors, a pencil, and a selection of colored tissue paper cut into one-inch squares.

When we get to the station with Lola's name on it, she takes off her jacket and tosses it to Dylan. "Can you hold this, Daddy? I want to make my suncatcher now."

"Sure, ladybug." He tucks the coat under his arm. "But you have to get your apron on before you can start. You don't want to get your rainbow dress dirty, do you?"

"No."

Dylan grabs the pink apron from the counter and pulls it over Lola's head, securing it with a bow in the back. I look around to find that every other woman in the room, aside from Quinn, is swooning over him. I don't blame them, because I am too. There's something irresistible about a man who can braid his daughter's hair and takes her to a craft class, especially when he's the brooding type.

Lola grabs a piece of cardstock, and Dylan helps her fold it in half. He gives her a pencil and patiently guides her hand to trace the outline of a heart. After they've finished, Lola picks up a pair of scissors and furrows her brow in concentration as she does her best to cut along the shape of the heart.

"Excuse me?" Someone aggressively taps on my shoulder, and I spin around to see Sarah McCormick and her daughter standing behind me. We've never talked before, but I've seen her at morning drop-off.

"You're blocking our station." She sneers.

"Oh, I'm sorry." I step out of the way, but she doesn't move.

"I had no idea Quinn allowed guests to come to this class. It's already at max capacity as it is." She gives me a once over.

"Oh, I—"

"If you have a problem with Marlow being here, why don't you take it up with me since I'm the one who invited her," Dylan says loud enough for everyone to hear.

Oh dear.

Sarah's jaw drops in disbelief. Dylan is typically reserved in public, and it's not like him to cause a scene. Hopefully, no one will notice me grinning like an idiot, delighting in the fact that Dylan Stafford just stood up for me at his daughter's craft class.

"Th-there's no problem," Sarah stutters, blinking rapidly. "I just wanted to make sure there was enough room for the kids, that's all."

I squeak in surprise when Dylans pulls me toward him, turning me around so my back is against his chest, his hand possessively on my hip.

"There, now your daughter has plenty of room." He gives Sarah a terse smile.

"Dylan," I whisper. "You're making a scene."

"I'm only doing what Sarah asked."

Several moms are gaping in our direction, and Quinn is watching from the other side of the room, mouthing the words *so hot* as she fans herself.

Thankfully, the kids are too busy making their suncatchers to notice.

"Marlow, look at my pretty heart," Lola states proudly, holding it out for me to see.

I step away from Dylan and bend down to get a closer look. The uneven, heart-shaped cutout with jagged edges is one of the most beautiful things I've ever seen.

"You did such a good job," I coo.

She puffs out her chest with pride and returns to cutting out another paper heart.

"Thanks for that," Dylan whispers.

"I meant every word," I assure him. "She is an exceptional little girl who deserves the chance to shine. Who's to say that a crooked heart today won't be a world-famous art installation in a few years?"

He studies me closely like I'm a painting he's trying to decipher.

"Daddy, can you help me with the glue? It's all sticky?" Lola holds up her little hands, which are now covered in Mod Podge.

"Oh shi—shoot," Dylan mutters.

He rushes to her side and yanks out some wet wipes from a nearby dispenser. Once Lola's hands are clean, he picks up one of the foam brushes and dips it into the Mod Podge, lightly dabbing glue onto one of the paper hearts. He demonstrates how to place the tissue paper on the glued surface, beaming at Lola when she grabs a handful of pink tissue paper and follows his instructions.

"He's quite remarkable, isn't he?" Quinn remarks, coming to stand next to me.

"Yeah, he really is." I keep my gaze fixed on Dylan.

"No matter how complicated things are between you two, there's nothing wrong with letting yourself fall for him if that's what you want," she says.

The problem is, I think I'm already halfway there.

CHAPTER TWENTY

DYLAN

"Daddy, spaghetti is my new favorite food. Oh, except for Cheez-Its. I *love* Cheez-Its," Lola exclaims.

She takes a giant bite of a meatball, a splash of sauce getting on the napkin I insisted she tuck into her shirt to avoid getting any on her outfit.

"What about the broccoli?" I frown, gesturing to the three florets on her plate. "You love broccoli."

Lola's never been a picky eater, unless you count her food having to be cut into the shape of a unicorn or rainbow whenever possible. As a toddler, she was a huge fan of sweet potatoes, kale, and any other vegetable I put on her plate. If she's growing an aversion to healthy foods, I'm not above sneaking them into her meals.

"I like broccoli," Lola says with her mouth full, "but I *love* Cheez-Its and spaghetti."

I glance over at Marlow, who's twirling a forkful of spaghetti on her plate, pretending she's not listening to our conversation. I lean over and put my arm around her chair.

"Hear that, sunshine?" I whisper. "Lola's new favorite food is Cheez-Its. Any idea why that might be?"

She looks at me innocently. "Because they're delicious?"

I shake my head. "You're incorrigible."

"In my defense, you did leave me with a giant box of Cheez-Its when you were away on your business trip. Did you think Lola wouldn't find them and not ask me to share?" She raises her eyebrow.

"Touché."

She gives me a smirk, returning her attention to her plate.

I'm not used to having anyone over for dinner aside from my parents and siblings. I've never invited a woman over before. Kendra always left the second I got home from work, and anyone I've gone out with, I've met at a restaurant. Marlow is the exception. She's slowly breaking down my walls.

I was pleasantly surprised how things went at Brush & Palette. Marlow was nearby when Lola wanted her help with something, but let me take the lead, which I appreciated. My weekends with Lola are important and I'm grateful Marlow understands that.

After Lola's class, we stopped by Main Street Market. Willis had just put out a fresh batch of his famous meatballs. I got a dozen and figured I had to make spaghetti to go with them. Lola and I unanimously decided to invite Marlow over for dinner.

"Daddy, can I watch an episode of *Bluey*?" Lola asks after she's cleared her plate.

"You can watch one," I tell her. "It's a school night, so you need to go to bed on time."

"Yay," she shouts, racing into the living room.

Unfortunately, she's already a whiz with technology, which means she can access her favorite shows on her own. I had to set up parental controls last year after I found her watching *My Little Pony* on multiple occasions in the middle of the night. Now, she can only access the TV during certain hours.

"Should I put these in the dishwasher?" Marlow nods to the dirty dishes on the table.

"If you wouldn't mind putting them in the sink, that would

be great. I haven't gotten around to unloading the dishwasher." I carry the bowl of leftover spaghetti over to the counter.

"I can do that," Marlow says as she stands up. "It's the least I can do after you cooked such an incredible meal."

"Thank you."

As she collects the dirty dishes and carries them over to the sink, I get a container from the cupboard and fill it with the rest of the spaghetti. I'm sure Lola won't mind having it for leftovers this week, considering it's now one of her favorite foods.

"Ouch," Marlow yelps.

I spin around to see her standing by the dishwasher, clutching her left hand. I'm alarmed when I notice there's blood dripping from a cut on her finger. I grab a dish towel from the counter and rush to her side, wrapping the towel around her finger.

"What happened?"

"I cut myself on your vegetable slicer." She glares down at the offending object on the floor.

"Oh, I'm sorry. Come sit down." I usher her over to the table and pull out a chair for her to sit.

I grab the first aid kit and a bottle of rubbing alcohol that I keep under the sink. When I get back to the table, Marlow is holding the towel tightly against her finger, looking at me like I'm a puzzle she's trying to solve.

"What?"

"Nothing. You're just the most prepared person I've ever met."

"Unfortunately, having all the supplies doesn't equate to proper medical training. My expertise extends only to treating unicorn plushies and little girls who have a thing for wearing bandages like an accessory."

Marlow grins. "Healing a unicorn is impressive, so I'll take my chances."

I open the first aid kit and take out a couple of cotton balls, a bandage, and the antibiotic ointment before kneeling in front of her.

"Can I see your hand?" I ask as I apply alcohol to a cotton ball.

She nods, removing the towel, and holds out her finger for me.

Taking her hand in mine, I gently press the cotton ball against her wound. She winces, letting out a low hiss at the contact.

"I'm sorry that hurt," I say as I lean in and softly blow on the cut. The last thing I want is for her to be in any more pain than she already is.

"It's alright. Your touch makes it better." Her heated blue-green gaze meets mine, and I momentarily pause.

Taking care of Marlow brings me a sense of satisfaction that I've been missing. Now that I know what it's like, there's a part of me that yearns to be the one she trusts to heal all her wounds, the one to kiss away the pain.

I've tried and failed to maintain professional boundaries, and despite our best attempts at disregarding our feelings, an undeniable magnetic pull repeatedly draws us together.

I shift my focus back to her finger and tenderly pat the area dry with the towel before applying the antibiotic ointment and carefully wrapping a rainbow bandage around her finger.

"Thanks for saving me," Marlow teases, her eyes still fixed on mine. "This has to be the coolest bandage I've ever gotten." She nods to her finger.

"You have Lola to thank for that." I close the lid of the alcohol and set the used cotton ball on top of the towel. "If it's not from *Bluey*, a unicorn or rainbow, she wants nothing to do with it."

Marlow laughs. "She's just a girl who knows what she wants, and there's absolutely nothing wrong with that."

I place my hand over her uninjured one. "Lola is a spirited kid, and it can be challenging for people to relate to her. Kendra was her nanny for two years and was often at her wit's end because Lola had specific preferences for how she liked certain things done. But not you. From day one, you've accepted her for who she is, and I appreciate that more than you'll ever know." I idly draw circles on the back of her hand with my thumb, appreciating the warmth of her skin against mine.

"I know what it's like to be judged for doing things differently than others. As a kid, I wished more than anything that I had someone willing to be patient and see things from my perspective." Marlow tucks her hair behind her ear. "I want to be that person for Lola. She deserves nothing less."

I stare at her with awe. Marlow possesses a unique gift for recognizing the positive in people, and my daughter is no exception. She consistently showers Lola with sincere compliments and words of encouragement, and I couldn't be more appreciative.

I'm captivated by this confident woman who views the world through a kaleidoscope of colors. God, it's no wonder I'm falling for her when she's so caring, generous, and cheerful. I admire that she marches to the beat of her own drum, refusing to let the world tell her who she should be. Little by little, she is making her way into my heart, and she's completely unaware of it.

A blush rises to Marlow's cheeks as I reach out to caress her jaw, tracing her lips with my fingertips as silence lingers between us. Her eyes shimmer with the same longing echoing in mine.

"I wish I could kiss you right now," I whisper.

More than anything.

"But you can't because Lola's in the other room," Marlow says. "We're in way over our heads, aren't we?" She briefly shuts her eyes and inhales deeply.

"Hey." I press a kiss to her forehead, encouraging her to look at me. "We're just two people who know what we want, and there's absolutely nothing wrong with that," I say, quoting her words from earlier.

"And what is that you want?" she asks, her gaze filled with uncertainty. "We've tiptoed around this conversation for weeks, and I don't think you've ever said."

"For starters, I really want to kiss you, and if we're being blunt"—I glance down the hall to make sure Lola's still in the other room—"I want to strip you bare and fuck you."

Marlow's breath hitches at my admission. As I study her, the curves of her breast taunt me. Her plump lips are slightly parted, tempting me to kiss her and draw out an inhibited moan from that fucking sexy mouth of hers.

"I want that too," she admits as she places her hand over mine. "But I'm still not sure where that leaves us."

"Who says we have to define anything right now? We're two people drawn to each other and there's nothing wrong with wanting to explore that. I'm tired of fighting this, aren't you?"

Why can't I bring myself to ask Marlow to be in a committed relationship? The last thing I want is for her to see other people, yet a shadow of doubt hangs over me, warning that if this doesn't work out, I'll be left alone again.

Marlow nods. "I don't want whatever this is"—she motions between us—"to affect Lola negatively. She's your number one priority, and that's how it should be. Can you promise me that however this plays out, you won't use it against me? I'd like to be her nanny for as long as I'm in Aspen Grove… if you'll have me."

A heaviness settles in my chest at the thought of her moving away.

"Of course I want you to be Lola's nanny for as long as you'd like. Besides, Lola and Waffles would revolt if we tried separating them."

"I think you're right." She nervously bites her lower lip. "I wanted to ask, if you're open to it, I'd like you to continue training Waffles."

"Really?" My face freezes in disbelief. After my failed attempt last Friday, I wasn't sure she'd want me to try again.

"Yeah, you were right. It'll do him some good to learn to listen to commands."

"I'd be happy to help."

"Thank you, Dylan," she says, smiling. "Speaking of Waffles, I better get home and feed him. He won't be happy that I made him wait for his dinner tonight." She hesitates as her eyes trace my face, lingering just slightly on my lips.

Unable to help myself, I close the gap between us, allowing my lips to briefly graze hers.

"Mark my words, Marlow Taylor, when we finally get a moment to ourselves, I'm going to do much more than kiss you."

CHAPTER TWENTY-ONE

MARLOW

The past week and a half have gone by in a blur.

I stayed true to my word and locked myself in my studio to work on my art, only breaking to watch Lola in the mornings and take Waffles on his daily walks. I can't pinpoint if it was by sheer determination, my recent inspiration, or a combination of both, but I was ecstatic when I finished a day earlier than anticipated.

While riding high on my professional achievement, my personal life is in a dry spell.

The day after our talk in his kitchen, Dylan had a massive setback at work and has been putting in long hours at the office and spending his free time with Lola. I've only seen him when he's running out the door or up to his home office for a conference call.

I considered telling him about my art exhibition, but when he told me he had another last-minute business trip later this week, I decided not to bring it up. He didn't specify if he was going to New York again, but even if he were, I didn't mention my show, afraid that he would feel obligated to go. He said his parents are watching Lola while he's away, so my plans for the weekend never came up.

It's late afternoon, and I'm rifling through my fridge in search of something to eat. I polished off the last of Dylan's delicious homemade meals over a week ago, so I settle on a ham and cheese sandwich. I gather all the ingredients and put them on the counter, while I call Gavin. I forgot to give him the exciting news this morning about finishing the collection on time.

"Hello?" he says with hesitance.

"Hey, Gav. Are you with a client? I can call back later."

"No, now is fine. You're usually trying to avoid talking to me, so I'm a little nervous to hear why you're calling *me* three days before your exhibition. Is now a bad time to remind you that most galleries require artists to send their paintings weeks in advance?"

What I appreciate most about The Artist is their focus on promoting the artist rather than specific pieces of art. This means a collection isn't unveiled to the public until the night of the show.

"I'm very lucky to work with an exceptional curator who doesn't stifle my creative process." It doesn't hurt to butter him up when he's in one of his moods.

"Now you're sweet-talking me, which I don't usually mind, but it makes me think you have bad news to share."

"It was touch and go there for a while." I tuck my phone in the crook of my neck while I lather a piece of bread with mayo and mustard. "Dylan's nanny quit, so I've been watching Lola in the mornings, and I was down with the flu a week and a half ago. Oh, and I forgot to mention that I was in the worst creative slump—"

"Babe, you're rambling, and I'm going to develop an ulcer if you keep talking." His voice is panicked. "Hold on, did you say you've been nannying for the *GQ* hottie? How could you keep such a valuable piece of information from me?" Gavin gets easily distracted when gossip is involved.

"Would you rather talk about my next-door neighbor or get an update on the paintings?"

While I wait for his reply, I add a slice of cheese and several pieces of meat to my sandwich and fold it in half. I switch the phone to my other ear and hop onto the counter.

"Depends on if you have good or bad news," Gavin says. "I'm going to need a stiff drink if it's bad news. And before you answer, let me remind you that the demand was so high for this show that we had to make it a ticketed event." When I don't answer right away, his distress kicks in. "Marlow? For the love of god, please put me out of my misery. Were you able to finish the collection?"

"You can relax, Gav," I say in between bites of my sandwich. "The shipping company picked up the paintings today and they will be delivered to The Artist tomorrow morning. I also emailed over the photos for the programs a few minutes ago," I tell him proudly.

I omit the fact that it was a close call and I barely took so much as a coffee break to finish the last three pieces ahead of schedule. I had concerns about the last painting not drying in time to ship, but thankfully it did.

"I'm so damn proud of you, babe. I can't wait to see them in person. This calls for celebratory champagne. Matthew and I are taking you out when you get here," he declares.

"I'd like that," I say.

"Did you invite anyone to the show? Please tell me if I'm overstepping," he rushes out.

"Gav, you're one of my dearest friends. You can ask me anything," I reassure him. "I sent an invitation to my mom and dad, but they never got back to me. I'm going to check in with them after this."

I've invited my parents to every show in the past, but they always have an excuse for why they can't come. It would mean a lot if, just for a single night, they could pretend to be proud of my accomplishments. I guess that's too much to ask. Although I can anticipate their likely response, that won't stop me from checking in. As an eternal optimist, I find it hard to resist holding out hope, even though disappointment is inevitable.

"What about those friends of yours in Maine, or a certain *GQ* hottie?" Gavin asks with a renewed interest. "I wouldn't mind meeting him in person."

"Quinn can't leave her shop again so soon. Andi has a prior commitment with her nephew. And I didn't invite Dylan. Things between us are complicated, and he has a business trip this weekend, so he wouldn't be able to come anyway."

He lets out a low whistle. "You've been holding out on me, babe. That doesn't sound like you're talking about someone who's just your boss. You better dish out all the details when you get here."

"You and Quinn are relentless." I chuckle. "I promise I'll catch you up once I get to New York."

"I'll hold you to that. You better call your mom before you get cold feet."

"Yeah, you're right, I'll see you soon."

"Can't wait. Bye, babe."

I polish off the last of my sandwich and hop off the counter to pace the length of the kitchen, trying to find the courage to dial my mom. Gavin's right. If I don't do it now, I'll chicken out. I doubt this is the typical reaction most people have when they call their parents.

Drawing in a deep breath, I muster the strength to press the call button. As it rings, it takes every ounce of willpower not to end the call before she answers.

"Hello?"

"Hey, Mom."

"Oh, hi, dear." She sounds caught off guard by my call. "Is something wrong? Do you need your father to send you money?"

"No, Mom, that's not why I'm calling." I nibble my lower lip as I try to adequately articulate my thoughts. "I wanted to remind you about my gallery showing at The Artist this coming

Saturday. It would mean a lot if you and Dad could be there."
I'm shaking once I get the words out.

"What art show? You haven't mentioned it," she says,
sounding confused.

"I told you about it last month." I keep my tone steady. "You
asked if I could email you the details, which I did—twice."

There's a prolonged silence on her end before she finally
responds. "Oh, yes, I did see those. I must have forgotten to
email you back. Listen, honey, this coming weekend isn't good
for us. We have a dinner planned with a group of alumni at the
university on Friday night, and you know how your father feels
about New York City."

I sink down to the floor, struggling to hold back tears. I'm not
sure why I'm so emotional. It's not like I didn't expect this. My
parents haven't come to any of my shows and don't like traveling outside of California. I just wish the outcome would have
been different this time... but it never is.

"It's okay, Mom. I understand."

"I am sorry, dear. Why don't you come to visit us soon?" she
suggests. "But please don't bring that dog of yours. You know
that I'm allergic, and he's far too loud."

My parents haven't met Waffles in person, but we video
chatted shortly after I adopted him. My mom expressed concern
about how I could afford to feed him on an artist's salary, and
my dad questioned my ability to care for a dog when I could
barely take care of myself. As a result, I don't mention Waffles
much during our infrequent conversations.

"The next few months are going to be very busy for me, but
I'll see what I can do." It's been a while since I've visited my
parents, and I have no plans to change that.

"Listen, dear, I have a stack of papers to finish grading, so I
have to go," my mom says abruptly.

"Oh, okay. Please tell Dad I say hi."

"I will. Bye, Marlow."

"Bye, Mom."

My unshed tears stream down my face the moment I hang up.

Waffles comes racing over from his dog bed in the corner, jumping in my arms. He nuzzles into me, whining and licking my face. I've always appreciated his uncanny ability to be in tune with my emotions.

"I'm okay, boy. I promise." I hug him tightly. By dictionary standards, I had a perfect childhood. I was raised in a comfortable house in a nice neighborhood and provided with the best education.

My struggles stem from my parents' affection having conditions attached to it. They constantly encouraged me to fit into a mold because my thoughts and actions often differed from those around me. And they brushed me aside when they realized I would never be the person they wanted me to be.

I remind myself that I'm a strong, brave, and independent woman, not to mention a successful artist. My family might not get me, but I'm lucky to have the unwavering support of my friends.

During moments like these, I find myself wishing for the opportunity to build a family of my own. A family who will love me wholeheartedly, without conditions or stipulations.

Recently, I've been daydreaming about the possibility of being a part of Lola and Dylan's family. The day the three of us spent together gave me a glimpse of what it would be like to be part of something truly special, and I find myself wanting that more than anything.

CHAPTER TWENTY-TWO

DYLAN

"Can someone tell me why we're going to an art gallery on a Saturday night?" Cash grumbles. "We're in New York City; we should hit a club or something."

"Because mom got us tickets," Harrison chides him as we walk down the sidewalk toward The Artist, a local art gallery my mom told us about.

Cash lets out a heavy sigh. "Fine. I'll stay for an hour tops, then I'm out."

I wish I had a regular office job with fixed hours on days like today. Due to a setback with the Vanburen project, I had to take another last-minute trip to New York.

Cash and Harrison had to join me this time, so Mom seized the chance to organize a family trip to visit Presley and Jack since our meetings were earlier today and Monday morning. They must have been thrilled when my mom announced that the whole family was coming for a visit.

She insisted me and my siblings go out since it's Saturday night, and she and my dad stayed at Jack and Presley's place to watch Lola.

It's not like they're short on space. When they moved in together last year, Jack insisted on taking charge of finding a place. The result? A massive eight-thousand-square-foot apartment that spans the entire ninetieth floor of a skyscraper and offers a breathtaking view of Central Park.

The property was an off-market deal with multiple interested parties, so Jack made an offer without consulting Presley first. To say she was upset would be an understatement. When he broke the news, she told him off in front of the entire marketing department at Stafford Holdings. My mom was on the verge of a meltdown, thinking they would break up because of it.

The whole thing was quite comical because they made up the same night and didn't leave Jack's place for two days. Nothing could keep those two apart.

They ended up moving into the apartment, but Jack learned his lesson about making expensive purchases without consulting my sister. And springing news on her when they're at the office.

"Will you two stop bickering?" Presley complains to Cash and Harrison. "You've been going at it since we left the apartment." She leans into Jack, who's glued to her side, with his arm securely draped around her shoulders. "Don't worry, we don't have to stay at The Artist for long. I just want to see if the featured artist has anything that would go in my entryway." She turns to Jack, who clears his throat. "Sorry, *our* entryway."

"That's my girl," Jack commends her. "If you find a painting you like, let me know, and I'll make sure you get it."

"That's so sweet." Presley flashes him a smile.

"Don't worry, you'll be thanking me later." Jack smirks.

"Will you two get a room?" Cash grumbles.

"We have one at home, but it's more fun getting a rise out of you," Presley goads him, kissing Jack on the cheek.

Cash makes a gagging motion with his finger in response.

While I'm glad I get to spend time with my siblings, I'm less than enthusiastic that it fell on the weekend. I was hoping to invite Marlow to join Lola and me at another craft class at Brush & Palette—we had a blast the last time she came with us.

But that's not the only reason I wanted to see her this weekend.

I had hoped we'd finally have one-on-one time together. It's been a couple of weeks since our conversation in my kitchen when I promised we'd do more than just kiss the next time we were alone. Unfortunately, circumstances have made it so I haven't been able to make good on my promise yet.

I've been on the brink of insanity, not being able to touch her the way I want. It's absolute torture each night watching her from my home office while she works in her studio and not being able to go over there.

I have this fantasy of laying her out like a canvas and tracing every inch of her with paint. She would look stunning splayed on the floor with a rainbow of colors smudged across her body while I fucked her into oblivion. I may never get the chance to make my fantasy a reality if we're not able to find a moment alone.

As we round the corner leading to the gallery, we're met with a line of people stretching down the block. Jack bypasses the queue altogether, and we follow him to the entrance.

"Look," Presley exclaims with wide eyes. "The artist must paint flowers; how exciting." She points to a banner on the side of the building—In Bloom: A Textured Floral Journey by Marlow Taylor.

The world around me fades, and it's difficult to breathe. All the late nights Marlow's been in her studio flash in my mind like a movie. She mentioned once that she sells her paintings online, so I assumed that's what she's been working on.

"Dylan, isn't your neighbor's name Mar—" Realization dawns on Presley's face when she sees my expression. "Something tells me Mom didn't get us these tickets to check out an art exhibit."

I glare at Jack, who's stifling a laugh. "You knew about this?" I accuse him.

I swear I'm going to kick his ass if he did.

He shrugs. "Johanna might have mentioned she heard

173

Marlow had an exhibit in town, and I merely suggested she get tickets for us to come see it."

"Why wouldn't you tell me?" I demand.

If I had known sooner, I would have been here when the show started, and brought flowers for Marlow.

"Maybe this will teach you to think twice before you have someone arrested." He winks and takes Presley's hand, leading the way into the gallery, denying me the chance to reply.

When Presley brought Jack to Aspen Grove for the first time and pretended they were dating, Harrison was suspicious. After some recon, we found out that Jack was actually Presley's boss who had been tormenting her for years. We decided to prank him to teach him a lesson for messing with Presley.

It was the first time in a long time that Harrison, Cash, and I had played one of our famous pranks, and we might have gotten carried away. Jack wasn't thrilled when he had to spend a night in jail, and now, for some reason, he thinks I'm the only one who should pay the price for the stunt we pulled.

"Well, this night just took an interesting turn." Cash claps his hands together.

I ignore him as we step into the dimly lit gallery. The place is packed with people, but there's only one person I'm interested in finding.

I scan the room, coming to a standstill, when my eyes land on a painting of a daffodil illuminated by track lighting. It's white with a peach-colored center, like the one Marlow gave Lola the day we met.

My pulse races when I see the nameplate next to the piece—
The New Beginning.

There's a lump in my throat as I frantically scan the crowd. Why didn't she tell me about her art show? This has to be impor-tant based on the turnout and the SOLD sign next to almost every exhibition label, including the daffodil piece.

I don't have any right to be upset. We haven't exactly defined this thing between us, and I'm the one who suggested that we didn't have to.

Now I regret ever saying that.

I don't think I even told her where I was going on my business trip or that Lola ended up coming with me. Since Lola and my parents will go back to Aspen Grove on Sunday and I fly home after my Monday morning meeting.

It doesn't sit well with me that Marlow and I aren't open with each other. We've admitted our feelings, but until now, we've let the logistics and a million reasons why we shouldn't be together get in the way. That ends now.

I want to be the first person she shares her successes with and the one to hold her when she cries. Whether we have a day, a week, or a year together, I'm willing to take the chance. Because aside from Lola, she matters more to me than anyone else.

There she is.

Marlow stands on the other side of the gallery, wearing a black floral knee-length dress with sheer sleeves. The intricate mesh overlay of red, pink, and green flowers entwined with stems suits her perfectly. She's paired the ensemble with her favorite silver sneakers, and her flowing golden hair falls in waves down her back.

She's a goddamn vision and I want to make her mine. Only mine.

Just as I'm about to approach, another man sidles up next to her. He's tall and lanky, with curly black hair, and is dressed sharply in a navy-blue suit. The world spins around me as Marlow grins when he places a chaste kiss on her cheek. I reach my breaking point when he has the nerve to put his hand on her lower back.

I move across the gallery with determination, oblivious to the other patrons giving me a wide berth as I pass.

As I approach, I move in between her and the man, forcing him to drop his hand.

"Dylan?" Marlow's eyes widen in surprise, and her cheeks

turn red when she sees me. "What are you doing here?" she asks.

"I didn't know this was your show when I walked in, but thank god my mom decided to meddle again because I couldn't imagine missing this," I say as I place my hand on her back.

Marlow blinks up at me like she's not sure she heard me right. She deserves to have her accomplishments recognized, and I'm so damn grateful I'm here to help her celebrate.

If this weren't her art show, I would throw her over my shoulder and take her to the nearest hotel room.

"Babe, you said the *GQ* hottie wasn't going to be here," the man interjects with a raised brow.

The only word I pay attention to is *babe*.

I turn to face him, moving my hand to Marlow's lower back, and tug her closer to my side. "Who's your friend?" I ask as I pause briefly before extending my hand to the man.

"My name's Gavin." He gives me a firm handshake, unphased that I stepped in between them. "It's nice to meet you." That's when I notice his wedding ring.

"Gavin is one of my dearest friends and is a curator at The Artist. He set up my show," Marlow chimes in as she gives my chest a reassuring pat.

I grumble an acknowledgement. Friend or not, I don't like the way he touched Marlow or that he called her babe. I may be acting irrational but it's difficult not to let my emotions take over when Marlow's involved.

"Why didn't you tell me about this? It's incredible." I gesture around the gallery.

Regardless of the reason, I wish she would have extended an invitation so I could have been here for her from the start. I know it shouldn't, but it bothers me that another man is her primary source of support tonight when I wish it was me.

I'll do everything to make sure the next time it is.

"I didn't want to bother you when you had so much going

on. Besides, it's only a small gallery showing. It's not that big of a deal," she says, doing her best to downplay the situation.

"Not a big deal? You're joking, right?" Gavin scoffs. "Marlow, several patrons flew in from Europe to attend your show tonight. If that isn't proof enough that this *is* a big deal, we've sold all but one of the pieces in your collection, and the exhibition just started thirty minutes ago."

"I'm buying the last painting," I say to Gavin.

"Are you sure? It's the most expensive in the collection. It's ninety—"

"The cost doesn't matter. I want it," I state, leaving no room for argument.

"Consider it done." He glances between Marlow and me with a knowing look. "I'm going to mark that painting as sold. It was nice to meet you, Dylan." He strides away, leaving Marlow and me locked in an intense staring match.

"You have no idea what painting you bought. What if you hate it?" Marlow splutters as she steps out of my embrace.

"You made it. Of course I'll love it," I say with conviction.

She stares at me, stunned speechless by my declaration. After a few seconds, her eyes turn stormy, and she grabs my arm, tugging me toward the back of the gallery and away from the crowd. She doesn't stop until we're standing in a hidden alcove away from prying eyes. She releases my arm, turning to address me.

"I thought you were on a business trip," she says skeptically.

I anxiously run my hand through my hair. "I was… I am," I clarify. "I had business meetings this morning, and my mom suggested the whole family fly out for the weekend to stay with Jack and Presley. She's the one that suggested my siblings and I come here tonight."

Marlow lets out a humorless laugh. "Quinn mentioned your mom came into Brush & Palette last week. I wouldn't put it past Quinn to mention my show. Your mom will stop at nothing until we get together, huh?"

"I hope not," I admit.

Initially, I found her meddling in my romantic life far from amusing, especially when she was determined to set me up with Marlow. However, now I'm thankful for her interference because it's the only reason I'm here tonight.

"Dylan?" Marlow whispers.

"Yeah?"

"It doesn't matter how it happened. I'm glad you're here."

"Me too, sunshine." I walk us backward until she is pinned against the nearest wall, her eyes locked on me.

I'm tired of dancing around the inevitable truth that Marlow and I belong together, and I have every intention of giving her a taste of what it would be like to be mine.

"What are you doing?" she asks softly.

"Close your eyes," I order.

"Dyla—"

"Trust me?"

Despite her initial reluctance, she closes her eyes and leans her head against the wall, placing her hands at her side.

"Good girl," I say, kissing her forehead.

She lets out a shuddered breath in response.

"You like it when I call you my good girl, don't you?"

"Mm-hmm," she says with a nod.

With delicate precision, I trace her angelic face, trailing my fingers across her forehead, moving to her right cheek bone, then her left. My exploration continues, gliding across her pert nose, then outlining the shape of her mouth. I pause briefly, admiring her bright pink lipstick, before running the pad of my thumb across her lips.

I watch the rise and fall of Marlow's chest, noting the quickening of her breath when I trace the column of her neck. A surge of satisfaction courses through me, fully aware that I'm responsible for her heightened response.

"Have I told you how beautiful you are?" I murmur.

Her eyes flutter open, and I'm lost in her magnetic blue-green gaze. "You're not so bad yourself when you're not being a tyrant."

Marlow tilts her head back to look at me, and when she smiles, I'm a goner. She winds her arms around my neck, drawing me closer.

I cup her face with my hands, pressing kisses along her jawline. When I get to her mouth, I trace my tongue along her plump bottom lip in teasing strokes. She lets out a soft moan as her tongue meets mine and she tugs me closer. My eyes widen when she playfully tugs my lip between her teeth, and our connection transforms from a tentative exploration to wild and frenzied.

I crash my mouth to hers in a passionate kiss, leaving her gasping for air. I grind my cock against her core, and she pushes against me in response. Our mingled moans fill the air as I greedily explore her mouth with fervor.

It's a fucking turn-on to witness her uninhibited side first-hand, driving me to give her more than just a kiss, like I promised.

I bunch up the material of her dress, shoving it out of the way, and hike her leg around my waist, placing my other hand securely on her hip. When she grips my hair with her hands, it sparks a fuse inside me.

"No more waiting, sweetheart." I waste no time pushing her panties aside and sinking two fingers inside her. "Damn, you're soaked. Is this all for me?"

"Oh god, yes," she pants.

I lean forward, running my tongue along the column of her neck, peppering kisses along her collarbone. When I add a third finger, Marlow lets out a strangled sound of arousal, blending in with our vocalized pleasure. It's the most sensual sound I've ever heard, making me want her—want *this*—even more, if that's possible.

"Are you going to come on my hand with a room full of people only a few feet away?" I whisper.

She nods as she clenches tighter around me.

We're far enough away from the crowd that there's no chance of someone walking in on us, but I like watching her reaction at the notion we could get caught.

I give her another passionate kiss to muffle the sound of her pleasure. I refuse to risk anyone else hearing those sweet sounds.

"Oh… Oh my god, don't stop," she breathes out.

"Not until you come like my good girl," I promise.

I'm hard as a rock as I watch Marlow unravel before me. I can sense that she's close to the edge, her body coiling tighter with each plunge of my fingers. I thrum her clit with my thumb, and within seconds she shatters around my hand. She rests her head on my chest as she lets out a strangled cry of pleasure, plummeting off the precipice. She doesn't stop riding my hand until I've wrung every drop of desire from her core.

She is utterly captivating when she's on the verge of release but watching her come is something else entirely.

"That's my girl," I praise, with another kiss. "It's safe to say that listening to you come is now one of my favorite sounds."

I bring my fingers to my mouth, sucking them clean. Marlow bites her lip, watching me with rapture. I flash her a wicked grin as I groan, relishing the taste of her essence on my tongue. She doesn't take her eyes off me as she reaches down to massage my cock through my pants, but I shake my head.

"What about you?" she asks.

"This was about *you*." I gently stroke her jaw. "There will be plenty of time for that later." I carefully ease her down and smooth her dress into place. "We better get back out there."

"Do we have to?" Marlow asks as she adjusts my slightly crooked glasses, giving me an adorable grin as she rights them.

"Considering all those people are here for you, I'm afraid so." My gaze traces the flush on her cheeks. "My siblings were talking about going to a club or dinner after this, and I want you to come with us."

She tucks her lip between her teeth. "I don't want to intrude. We'll see each other when we get back to Aspen Grove."

I'm not waiting that long to spend more time with her.

"Your show sold out. You've got to celebrate, and I'd be honored if you'd let me and my family be a part of it."

Her expression softens, and a smile lights up her face. "I'd really like that."

I kiss her soft lips again. "Now let's get back out there. You've worked incredibly hard and deserve to enjoy every second of your success."

CHAPTER TWENTY-THREE

MARLOW

The moment I shared with Dylan at the gallery was *the* hottest sexual experience I've had thus far. I couldn't care less that only a few hundred feet separated us from a room full of people. I was done for the second Dylan called me his *good girl*.

He stayed by my side during the rest of the show, keeping his hand on my lower back as he guided me through the crowd. His family stayed too, and never complained about having to wait around.

I considered skipping my exhibition altogether tonight because it was difficult knowing my family, once again, wouldn't be there to show their support. Gavin picked me up from the hotel, afraid I wouldn't show up if he didn't. I was worried for nothing because the Staffords showed me more support tonight than I could have ever hoped for.

When we finally leave the gallery, Jack takes us to an upscale steakhouse, where we're ushered into a stylish backroom that doubles as a speakeasy.

Dylan pulls out my chair, tugging it closer to his before motioning for me to sit. Once we're both settled, he rests his hand on my knee under the table.

After our server takes our drink order, Harrison asks him a

work-related question. I try to keep up with their conversation, but I'm lost after the third time I hear the term "ROI." I'm relieved when Presley leans over, casually resting her elbow on the arm of my chair.

"I hear my mom's been playing matchmaker for you and Dylan. I'm sorry if she's overstepped. She means well, but as you've noticed, she gets carried away sometimes." She glances over at Jack with a knowing smile.

"It's okay. If it weren't for her persistence, I might not be Lola's nanny, and I wouldn't trade that for anything," I say, sidestepping her comment about Dylan and me.

"I'm happy to hear you say that." She beams at me. "Lola talks about you whenever we video chat, and she adores Waffles. I hope you don't mind me saying, but it's been a long time since I've seen my brother this happy." Presley takes a sip of her water before leaning in closer.

"Underneath that grumpy exterior is a thoughtful man, willing to face any storm for the people he cares about," she says in a hushed tone. "I understand that whatever is happening between the two of you is new, and you might not be ready to put a label on it yet. All I ask is that you be transparent with him about what you want... and what you don't." She looks over at Dylan who's still deep in conversation with Harrison. "Lola isn't the only person who easily gets attached."

I've considered the potential impact of our current situation on Lola, myself, and even Waffles. The thought that Dylan might get hurt if this goes south hadn't occurred to me until now. I figured he viewed our connection as fleeting, and it wouldn't affect him if it ended or if I decide to leave Aspen Grove. However, my assumption was wrong.

"I'm glad you're looking out for your brother," I tell Presley. "I have no issue being honest with him. In fact, he'd probably prefer I was less direct at times." I chuckle.

Presley bursts out laughing. "I can see why he likes you. You're such a breath of fresh air. After tonight, consider me a life-long supporter of your work. It's absolutely incredible," she gushes. "I fell in love with your sunflower piece and it devastated me when I saw someone had already bought it. I begged Jack not to, but he persuaded Gavin to cancel the original sale. Now I'm the proud owner of an original Marlow Taylor," she says with pride.

Her sincere compliment means so much.

I glance over at Dylan and he squeezes my thigh under the table when he notices me watching him, leaving me breathless.

"Oh, you should have told me," I turn back to Presley. "I would have been happy to make you a commissioned piece. I'm sure Gavin tacked on an obscene upcharge for the inconvenience."

"It's no problem. We want to support you. Especially after everything you've done for Lola and Dylan," she says with conviction. "The sunflower will go perfectly in our entryway. We moved in together last June, but Jack's idea of a comfy and cozy apartment is significantly different from mine." She shakes her head.

"At least you have the final say in the décor. It's obvious you have that man wrapped around your finger," I say, my eyes sparkling with amusement.

"I think you and I are going to be great friends." She grins.

———

My cheeks hurt from laughing so much. We spent several hours at the restaurant with Dylan's family. It was loud, boisterous, and absolutely perfect. The Stafford siblings tease each other endlessly, but that doesn't diminish the close bond they share. They're fortunate to have such a strong support system, and it makes me wish I were a part of something that special.

I mustered the courage to invite Dylan back to my hotel as we left the restaurant. I wasn't ready to say goodbye for the night, and it seems he wasn't either. Presley assured us that Lola would be in good hands until he got back to her place in the morning.

As we exit the elevator onto my floor, I can't help but nervously wring my hands. I've played out what our first time together might look like countless times. I never thought it would be in a run-of-the-mill hotel room in New York City. And now that we're here, I'm worried it won't live up to our expectations.

We stop outside my room, and I fumble with my keycard. After a brief struggle, I finally open the door, stepping inside and gesturing for Dylan to follow.

"It's not much," I say as I turn on the light. I look around the small space with a single queen-sized bed, a compact workspace in the corner, and a small en-suite bathroom. I'm sure it's a shoebox compared to his accommodations at Presley's apartment.

In the past, it didn't matter since I usually came back to my hotel room alone. But this time I have Dylan by my side and for once I don't feel the crippling sadness that I typically experience after one of my shows, knowing he's going to take care of me.

"I don't give a damn about the room," Dylan states softly from behind me.

The door clicks closed and he spins me around and pins me up against the closest wall. He presses his hands against either side of my head, trapping me in. It takes me back to the moment we shared outside of Willow Creek Café, but this time I intend to let him kiss me, among *other things*.

"I swear my siblings dragged out our dinner on purpose," he complains. "I've been waiting to get you to myself all night."

"Now that you have me, what are you going to do about it?" I ask in a sultry tone.

He rests his forehead against mine. "Marlow?"

"Mm-hmm?"

"Walking into that gallery tonight and seeing you with Gavin nearly drove me mad." There's a touch of anguish in his tone. "The idea of you with someone else messes with my head."

When I saw him walk in tonight, my heart practically leaped out of my chest. I didn't realize how much I needed him there until he came to stand next to me, wrapping his arm around me in a reassuring grip. I'll have to thank his mom for making it possible. Johanna might be pushy, but it was very much appreciated in this case.

I was moved by Dylan's gesture of purchasing one of my paintings. It showed he genuinely cares about me and my endeavors, which means more than he knows.

"What are you saying?" I ask tentatively.

"Be mine, sunshine? The only person I want to be with is you."

"Dylan, I can't promise—"

"I know." He presses a kiss to my temple. "All I'm asking is for tonight… and tomorrow. And the day after that. I'm fully aware that there's a chance you'll be leaving Aspen Grove soon," he says in a solemn tone.

The very thought makes me uneasy.

"I want to see where this takes us because I'd regret it for the rest of my life if I didn't." He clasps my hands in his.

"I don't want us to see other people either," I admit. "What about Lola? I don't think we should tell her anything for now."

The last thing I'd ever want to do is break her heart if things don't work out between her dad and me.

"That's a good idea, but…" Dylan sighs. "I don't want you to think you're my dirty little secret."

I erupt in laughter. "Oh, trust me, your siblings don't doubt that you have feelings for me. Not after the way you reacted to seeing me at the gallery tonight. And besides, what if I don't mind the idea?"

"What idea?"

"Being your dirty little secret." I let go of his hands, and gently remove his glasses, placing them on the chest of drawers beside me. Dylan watches me intently when I drop to my knees on the floor in front of him.

"Marlow, what are you doing?" His voice is strained.

"Something I've wanted to do since you fingered me in the back of the gallery tonight," I confess bluntly.

I unbuckle his belt and unfasten his slacks. He stands perfectly still as I pull down his zipper and tug down his pants. I gape at the sheer size of him straining behind his boxers before slowly dragging them down his legs.

I lift my hooded eyes to meet his smoldering gaze as I curl my fingers around his thick cock. He takes a sharp intake of breath as I move my hand up and down his shaft in slow, steady strokes. Pre-cum leaks from the tip, and I lean forward to lap it up with my tongue.

"Fuck, you're sexy as hell," he states.

Dylan winds his finger through my hair, urging me to take him in my mouth. I don't hesitate, sucking the crown with fervor, and when he tightens his grip, coaxing me to take him deeper, I hollow my cheeks until his head is at the back of my throat. He lets me set the pace as I adjust.

"Such a good girl," he croons as he strokes the column of my neck.

My panties are completely soaked through. His praise stirs a newfound desire within me, and I cup his balls, squeezing gently, as I suck him off. He loses all control, tugging my head forward, fucking my mouth with abandon as he lets out a low growl of approval. I'm drunk on the knowledge that I'm the reason for his unrestrained pleasure.

"Fuck, sweetheart, I'm going to come," he groans.

His cock jerks under my hand as his cum fills my mouth. His eyes widen as I lap up every drop, licking him clean. When I'm finished, his cock springs free from my mouth with a loud pop.

"Damn," he says with adoration, taking my hand to help me get up off the floor. "Let's get you out of those clothes. Turn around and put your hands on the wall," he orders.

I do as he asks, placing my palms against the faded wallpaper.

Every cell in my body is on fire as he pushes my hair over my shoulder, leaving my back exposed. He places one hand firmly on my hip and uses the other to slowly drag down the zipper of my dress—the suspense is unbearable. I exhale sharply as he grinds his rigid cock against my ass.

"You like that, sunshine?" he whispers in my ear. "Thinking about what it would feel like in that tight cunt of yours?"

"Oh god, yes," I mewl.

"That's my girl." He brushes my dress off my shoulders.

I feel his breath against my skin seconds before he presses kisses down my neck. He unclasps my bra, releasing my aching breasts from their confines, and reaches around to brush my nipples with his fingertip in teasing strokes. I whimper when he rolls my nipples between his fingers, pinching them roughly.

I'm burning with desire. If this is how Dylan Stafford does foreplay, I can't wait to experience what the sex will be like.

"God, I love that you're so responsive," Dylan states.

"Only for you," I murmur.

"I like hearing you saying that."

I whine in protest when he releases my nipples.

He pulls my dress down the rest of the way, letting it pool at my feet, before spinning me around to face him.

"Hold on tight, beautiful," he urges, scooping me into his arms. I wrap my arms around his neck as he carries me to the bed. He pulls down the comforter and top sheet, laying me in the middle of the mattress.

In a flash, he removes my shoes, and I lift my hips as he bends down to grab the top of my panties, dragging them down my legs. He tosses them onto the chair in the corner, standing in front of me fully clothed, while my body is laid out like a canvas before him—proof that he's in total control tonight. The contrast fuels the red-hot arousal racing through me, and I have the sudden urge to hear him call me his good girl again.

Dylan kneels on the bed, leaning down to brush his hands up my legs, leaving a trail of goosebumps in his wake. I wait with bated breath as he plants a kiss on my knee. His stubble rubs against my skin as he moves up my thigh inch by torturous inch. My legs quake with anticipation as he reaches the apex of my thighs.

He slowly licks along the seam of my pussy before plunging his tongue inside. I buck my hips, grinding against his face as I grip his hair in my fists. He eagerly explores, alternating between licking and sucking, and when he thrusts three thick fingers inside me, a tantalizing shiver courses through my veins. I gasp at the heat rippling through my core.

I'm already wound tight like a spring from having my mouth on his cock, and when I lift my head to see his head buried between my legs, I'm a goner.

"I need to come," I whimper.

"Come for me, sunshine." Dylan pinches my clit between his fingers, commanding my release, and I fall apart at his touch. My head drops back against the mattress as I call out his name while chasing euphoria, savoring every delicious moment.

"I don't want to wait another second to be inside you," he rasps. "Tell me I can go bare. I don't want anything between us. I haven't been with anyone since I was tested last year."

I nod in agreement. "I'm on the pill, and I was recently tested too."

He gets off the bed and strips out of his clothes in record time, leaving them in a pile on the floor. The Dylan I know would fold them neatly and set them on the dresser, but I'm rather enjoying witnessing his more relaxed side.

I lick my lips in anticipation as I get my first look at Dylan totally naked. I saw him with his shirt off the first week I nannied for Lola, but seeing him stripped bare is something else entirely.

"You've got to be kidding me," I dramatically sigh, gesturing to his bare chest. Every ripple and curvature of his well-defined abs is on display.

"What?" He frowns, glancing down at himself.

"Dylan, you're in your thirties and work at least eighty hours a week. Yet you've somehow maintained the body of a super-hero. It's so unfair." I sigh. It probably helps that he avoids junk food like the plague.

He furrows his brow. "Hold on, did you just call me old?"

"Compared to me you are," I quip.

"We'll see who has the better stamina, won't we?" He winks.

I can't wait.

Dylan climbs onto the bed and hovers over me. He grabs hold of his shaft, lining himself up with my entrance, pushing to the hilt in a single thrust. Our intermingled groans fill the room as I adjust to his size.

"You okay, sunshine?" He restrains himself, waiting for my answer.

I can feel every glorious inch of him and it has me craving more.

"Move, please move," I beg.

He intertwines our fingers, spreading my arms above me as he moves in a steady rhythm. I meet him thrust for thrust, basking in our connection. He has the ability to make me feel both cherished and seductive simultaneously.

"You're so fucking tight," he growls as he drives into me.

"Oh god, Dylan."

"I can feel you clenching around my cock," he pants out.

I can only whimper in reply, digging my heels into the mattress. He brushes his tongue against my lips before slipping it inside my mouth. I moan loudly as he picks up his pace, shifting the angle of his cock, pressing against my G-spot, and I gasp at the new sensation.

"I'm so close," I say.

"Play with your clit like my good girl." He drops his head

against my shoulder, putting all his energy into driving himself deeper.

I obey, reaching between my legs and strumming my clit eagerly. The added simulation has me shuddering as I unravel beneath him, and he roars in triumph as he finishes alongside me. There's no stopping the flood of emotions that washes over us as we come down from our heightened state of pleasure.

"You're perfect, sunshine," he croons, brushing a stray piece of hair from my face. "You okay?"

"Never been better," I assure him with a sated smile.

"Why don't we take a shower, and then I'll give you a massage?"

"That sounds nice," I say drowsily.

I'm grateful for Dylan's caregiving nature and his enthusiasm to look after me. Now I just need to convince him that includes another round in the shower.

CHAPTER TWENTY-FOUR

DYLAN

I wake to the faint scent of citrus and rose.

The first rays of sunlight filter through the window, signaling morning has arrived.

Marlow and I are entangled in a mess of limbs—she's draped across my chest, her legs intertwined with mine, and her head nestled in the crook of my neck.

We had sex in the shower last night—twice. Afterward, I gave her a massage like I promised. That led to fucking on the bed doggy style, with her hair gripped firmly in my fist, her head arched back to face me as I drove into her from behind. She drives me wild when I'm buried deep inside her perfect cunt.

When we both finally collapsed from exhaustion, I drew her to my side, falling asleep with her securely in my arms. One night with Marlow has left me greedy for more, which isn't like me.

After Maddie left, I blocked out the emotional side of intimacy. She shattered my trust, and I refused to give anyone else that kind of leverage over me.

During the past few years, sex has been strictly about the act. It required giving pleasure in exchange for receiving it, and I treated it like a transaction. Anyone I took to bed knew my terms —no strings attached, and no misconceptions of a commitment. Not because I didn't care for the women I've been with, but because I wasn't willing to risk getting hurt.

Marlow is different. We have an intense bond beyond physical attraction, and it feels like a magnetic force is drawing us together. She's brought with her a renewed sense of hope, an emotion that's long been absent in my life.

I push aside my looming worry for our future and focus on the here and now. If I don't, I risk jeopardizing the connection we share before we've had a real chance to explore it.

She stirs beside me, and when her eyes flutter open, I'm met with her striking gaze.

I lean over to grab my glasses from the nightstand and put them on to see her better.

"Good morning, sunshine," I say, showering her shoulder with kisses.

"Good morning," she replies, her voice husky from sleep. "What time is it?" She glances over at the clock on the nightstand to see that it's 7:05 a.m. "Do you have to get going?"

"No, not yet. I guarantee Lola is still asleep, and when she wakes up, she'll have a house full of people happy to spoil her rotten until I get back." I squeeze Marlow tighter into my chest.

I want to soak up every second we have together because there's no telling when we'll have another late morning alone like this.

"As long as you get me coffee before you leave, I'll be a happy camper," Marlow says.

"I'm not leaving until you've had coffee, breakfast, and *at least* one more orgasm," I promise.

"My hero." She grins, leaning in for a kiss.

Marlow is flying back to Aspen Grove tonight, but I have to stay in New York for additional meetings tomorrow morning.

I give her a hesitant look, and she furrows her brow.

"What is it?"

I found it unusual that she didn't have a single family member there to offer her support last night. If one of my siblings had an event like that, my whole family would be there, no matter what.

When Marlow was sick, she sidestepped my remark about calling someone else to come take care of her and now it has me wondering why that is.

"I was wondering why your family wasn't at your show last night?" Marlow stiffens in my arms. "I'm sorry if my question crossed a line," I backtrack. "You don't talk about them much, which I assume is for a reason."

"My parents aren't bad people, if that's what you're thinking." She lightly traces my chest as she speaks. "I'm an only child. They had me in their forties, and my grandparents passed away when I was a kid. My mom and dad are both professors and didn't accept my decision not to attend college. They were mortified when I told them I wanted to be an artist instead." A hint of sadness tinges her voice.

"Early on, I struggled to concentrate in school, and preparing for exams was challenging. I couldn't maintain focus for more than a few minutes, and often it was difficult to retain the material I did learn long enough to remember during a test." She nervously tucks a piece of hair behind her ear as she speaks. "Painting and travel became my escape, and I refused to compromise my happiness for my parents' or anyone else's expectations."

I press a tender kiss to the top of her head, needing to express my sympathy physically. "I'm sorry you had to go through that, sunshine," I utter. "Your parents should have found ways to make things more manageable for you, not given you the impression that something was wrong with you."

"My brain processed things differently than a lot of the kids I went to school with, and I was an easy target for teasing. My parents couldn't change the other kids' behavior, but they could attempt to adjust mine, which made me feel inadequate. I believe they did their best, given the circumstances." Her tone is defensive. "As I got older, they grew less interested in me, and I distanced myself until I could move out after high school. We don't talk often, but I invite them to all my exhibitions, which they decline to attend. But I'll never give up hope that someday they'll come around," she says with conviction.

I admire Marlow even more now that I've heard the difficulties she's faced. Even when dealing with challenges, she doesn't lose sight of the positive.

"You shouldn't have to wait. You deserve to be reminded of how exceptional you are every day."

I want to demand that she tell me the names of every single person who's ever mistreated her or made her feel inadequate, so I can confront them for hurting my girl. While that's highly unlikely, I can make sure that as long as she's a part of my life, I show her every day how extraordinary she truly is.

"That's why it meant so much to have you at my exhibition." Marlow strokes my stubbled cheek. "It doesn't matter that you showed up unintentionally. It was really nice to have the extra support since my friends couldn't be there."

"From now on you can count on the entire Stafford clan to support you, including my parents and Lola," I vow.

She smiles. "Thank you, Dylan."

Her hand trails down my stomach, and my cock springs to attention at her seductive touch.

"Sunshine, what are you doing?"

"I think you owe me for starting the morning on a sober note, don't you?" She gives me a wry smile.

This woman is insatiable, and I fucking love it.

Without warning, I flip Marlow onto her back, settling above her with my legs on either side, locking her arms in place over her head. "I'm going to fuck you nice and slow, and then take you to the best breakfast spot in New York."

"That's a start," she says, smirking.

I might not be able to change Marlow's past, but I'll damn well do everything in my power to shield her from being treated like that in the future.

CHAPTER TWENTY-FIVE

MARLOW

"Hey, Marlow?"

"Hey, lolabug?"

"Um… Why is Waffles jumping on Daddy?"

What?

I sprint to the window overlooking my backyard, and sure enough, Dylan's lying flat on his back on the deck. Waffles is standing over him, licking his face.

Dylan got back from New York an hour ago and was eager to have another training session with Waffles. He wanted to do it while the training videos he watched on the plane were fresh in his mind. From what I can see, they're not proving very helpful.

I open the back door and stick my head outside. "You guys okay back here?"

Dylan props himself up on his elbows to look at me. "Yeah." He glances at Waffles. "I think we've had enough for today, don't you, boy?"

Waffles barks loudly in response, sprinting toward me. I barely manage to step aside as he runs past me into the kitchen where Lola's standing with open arms.

"Hey, Waffles. I missed you," she exclaims.

Based on their reunion, you'd think they've been separated for decades, not a few days.

Quinn watched Waffles while I was in New York over the weekend. Thankfully, he was well-behaved, except for an unapproved visit to Main Street Market. He must have had a craving for meatballs.

"How'd it go?" I ask Dylan when he comes inside.

"We'll get there eventually," he says with determination.

I have no doubt he'll keep at it until Waffles learns to follow commands.

"Thanks for your help." I squeeze his arm in appreciation as he slides past, the desire to touch him—however innocent—is overwhelming. Judging by the banked heat in his eyes, he's feeling something similar.

"Daddy, Marlow, I have something to tell you," Lola says, impatiently waiting for us to listen.

"What is it, ladybug?" Dylan asks.

"At school today, Ms. Thornberry told our class that the older kids are doing a play called Allie in Wanderland."

"I think you mean Alice in Wonderland," I gently correct her.

Since Dylan had to stay in New York an extra day, Johanna and Mike flew home with Lola yesterday. She spent the night at their place, and Johanna dropped her off at school this morning. I offered to pick her up, giving me a chance to see her and Dylan this afternoon.

Ms. Thornberry sent me home with a newsletter with all the details for the upcoming play the fifth graders are putting on. Their teacher asked the first graders to take part in non-speaking roles.

"Yes!" Lola's eyes light up. "I'm going to be a daisy," she squeals with delight.

Her comment reminds me of the painting Dylan bought at my art exhibition. He still hasn't seen it, but it would be a wonderful surprise if it arrived in time for Lola's play.

The piece would be the perfect addition to his living room,

bringing a touch of color to the space. I don't miss the irony of shipping the painting to The Artist only for Gavin to have to ship it back to Aspen Grove.

"Daddy, can you help me practice being a daisy?" Lola asks Dylan.

"Absolutely, but considering Marlow's expertise in flowers, I think it would be a fantastic idea to involve her, don't you agree?"

"Yes," Lola shouts for joy. "I can't wait."

I offer Dylan a smile of appreciation for including me in this. Since our relationship is new, I'm letting him decide how much time I spend with him and Lola, especially since we're holding off on telling her we're seeing each other.

Dylan's phone buzzes in his pocket, and a serious look crosses his face when he checks the notification.

"Lola, it's time to go," he announces. "Nana and Gramps are waiting for you at our place."

Who are Nana and Gramps?

Lola calls Dylan's mom and dad Gigi and Papa, so I know he has to be referring to someone else.

"I can't wait to see them." Lola runs to the front door and races outside toward her house. Fortunately, I catch hold of Waffles before he can follow her.

"Wait for me, ladybug," Dylan hollers as he chases after Lola. "I'll be right back," he calls over his shoulder before shutting the door behind him.

I'm left standing alone in my kitchen, trying to make sense of what just happened. Dylan hadn't said he was expecting any visitors today, but then again, we haven't had a chance to catch up since he got back.

My curiosity gets the best of me, leading me to peek out the window in my living room.

A couple, who appear close to Dylan's parents' age, are standing in his driveway. They warmly embrace Lola, and as they talk with Dylan, his posture becomes noticeably rigid when the woman gives his arm a squeeze.

Lola hops into the backseat of the car, and Dylan buckles her in while the couple gets into the front seat. They must have had a booster seat installed already because Dylan wouldn't let her go without one. Once he's finished, he closes the car door and waves goodbye as they drive away. *I wonder where they're taking Lola.*

When Dylan heads back toward my house, I rush over to the couch and plop down. I don't want him to think I was intruding by watching his interaction with them.

He knocks once before coming inside.

"I'm in the living room," I call out.

He walks in and takes a seat on the couch next to me.

"I'm assuming you watched from the window?" he asks with a hint of amusement.

"Maybe." I shrug. "You ran out of here without an explanation, and I was curious about who those people were."

"They are Maddie's parents," he explains. "I forgot to tell you earlier that they were stopping by tonight to take Lola out for a few hours."

"Do they live around here?"

He shakes his head. "No. They moved to Michigan after she graduated from high school. They fly in every three months to visit friends and now to see Lola. They usually take her out to dinner and a movie."

I give him a puzzled look. "I didn't think Maddie was in Lola's life."

"She's not," he says quickly.

"I don't understand."

He scoots closer until our legs are touching and looks me in the eye. "Maddie was inconsolable when we found out she was pregnant with Lola. She said she wanted to have the baby, but when Lola was born, she withdrew completely." His voice lowers as he continues. "I came home from work one night to find Maddie waiting for me with her packed suitcases by the front door of our apartment. She said that after several conversations with her parents and therapist, she decided that she needed a fresh start that didn't include me or Lola. That's the last time we saw her."

I can't imagine what that must have been like for him. One day thinking they were a happy family, and the next, he was navigating the challenges of being a single dad.

"If Maddie's parents influenced her decision to leave Lola, why would you want them to spend time with her?" It doesn't make sense.

"It's not that simple," he states with deep-rooted frustration. "Her parents never explicitly suggested that Maddie leave us; they simply listened and acknowledged how she felt about the situation. They were just as shocked as I was when she left." He rakes his fingers through his hair. "As a parent, I can appreciate where they were coming from. They called shortly after and expressed an interest in spending time with Lola whenever they came into town."

"But aren't they still in touch with Maddie?" I ask with apprehension. "Aren't you worried about what they say to Lola when you're not around?" I could be overreacting, but the idea of anyone making that little girl feel unwanted or undervalued concerns me.

"They've agreed not to discuss Maddie with her. If, in the future, Maddie expresses a desire to reconnect with Lola, her parents will tell me, and we'll discuss the next steps. But I don't anticipate that happening anytime soon."

"Does Lola ever ask about Maddie?"

He shakes his head. "No, not often."

"Don't you think she'll ask more questions as she gets older?"

Like how I'm doing now.

"Probably, but I'll address it when the time comes." He heaves a sigh. "Marlow, I appreciate your concern, but I'm doing my best, given the circumstances. You might disagree, but I want Lola to have a normal childhood, including having relationships with both sets of her grandparents. It doesn't matter if it's challenging for me; it's what's best for her."

I nervously tuck my hair behind my ear. "You're right. I'm sorry. I didn't mean to make you think I was questioning your choices. You're an amazing father, and I know Lola will appreciate you giving her the chance to have a relationship with her grandparents as she gets older." I give him a tentative smile. "I get overprotective of the people I care about and should have expressed my concerns differently."

I often struggle with reading social cues. I get so caught up in my own emotions that I miss how others interrupt my words or actions. This often results in me unintentionally saying or doing the wrong thing.

"Hey." Dylan clasps my hands in his. "I'm not upset," he reassures me. "I'm just not used to explaining my decisions regarding Lola to anyone, but I value your concern. The fact you care so much means the world, and we're lucky to have you."

"*We*, huh?"

"Yeah, Lola isn't the only one grateful you're in our lives." He leans over to press a kiss against my lips. "You know, one advantage of having her spend time with her grandparents is that we have a few hours to ourselves."

"Is that so?" I smirk. "Whatever will we do?"

"I have a few ideas," he says with a mischievous grin.

CHAPTER TWENTY-SIX

DYLAN

Marlow shrieks when I sling her over my shoulder and carry her upstairs.

When we get to her bedroom, I lock the door behind us. Aside from Waffles, there's no one around to interrupt us, but it's a force of habit.

"Dylan Stafford, what has gotten into you?" she cries out.

She has. Marlow Taylor has become a fixture in my life, and I never want her to leave.

I always prioritize rational thinking, not my emotional impulses, but being with her has given me a fresh perspective. She's teaching me to find joy in the little things and how to live in the present. Her love for Lola is tangible, and it's a turn-on that she's as dedicated to my kid as I am.

On any other night when Lola is with her grandparents, I'd be reviewing spreadsheets or preparing financial reports for work—not tonight.

I stride across Marlow's room, stepping around clothes scattered on the floor. The comforter is gathered at the foot of the bed, and I toss it onto the chair in the corner.

I lower Marlow to a standing position by the bed, and she holds onto my elbows as she finds her balance. She's sexy as fuck in her skintight coral yoga pants, but I can't do what I want to when she's dressed.

"I need to get you out of these clothes, sunshine."

"What are you waiting for?" she urges.

"You better watch that mouth of yours, considering I'm in charge of your pleasure tonight," I caution her with a sly grin. "Now be a good girl and lift your arms."

She gives me a curious glance but complies.

I lift her sweater over her head and toss it to the floor. My hands are back on her within seconds, unclasping her bra. I have to suppress a groan when her pert breasts come into view. They're begging for my attention, but I restrain myself for now. There will be plenty of time to worship her perfect tits later.

I pull her yoga pants down until they pool at her ankles. She lets out a sharp exhale when I trace her thighs with my fingers in lazy circles. I can smell the scent of her arousal, and when I get to her panties, I slowly drag them down her legs. Marlow grabs hold of my shoulders and lifts one leg at a time, so I can discard her clothes.

Hot damn.

I'm captivated by her sinful curves, unable to look away. Her body is a work of art, and she's all mine.

"You're fucking perfect, sweetheart," I say as I notice her cheeks flush in response to my praise.

"I wish I could say the same for you, but you're still dressed," she playfully pouts.

"All in good time." I straighten to my full height and kiss her lips. "First, I want—"

I lose my train of thought when I spot something in her open nightstand drawer. When I look closer, I see the object is hot pink and shaped like a wand.

Well, this just got interesting.

"Marlow, what's this?" I ask coyly, retrieving the device and holding it up to show her.

"Um, my vibrator," she utters as her cheeks turn pink.

It's adorable that she's flustered, but she has no reason to be embarrassed. I'm turned on just imagining her getting herself off with the thing.

"You know, these are a lot more fun when you have someone to play with." I twirl the device around in my hand.

"Prove it," she challenges.

"Get on the bed, and I'll show you," I order.

Marlow scrambles to obey, crawling into the middle of the bed and lying down like I instructed.

I quickly undress, tossing my white button-up and dress pants on top of her clothes piled on the floor. Marlow watches me with a lust-filled gaze, and her eyes widen when I step out of my boxers, my cock proudly jutting out.

"Like what you see?"

She eagerly nods.

The mattress dips as I join her on the bed, hovering above her. I take hold of her wrists and cuff them above her head with my hands. With her at my mercy, I lean down and wrap my mouth around one of her nipples, gliding my tongue across the areola.

"Dylan," she breathes out, my name falling from her lips like a prayer.

"That's right, sunshine. I'm the one who owns your pleasure," I remind her.

She inhales sharply as I alternate between flicking her nipple with my tongue and tugging it taut with my teeth.

"Oh god," she cries out.

Marlow's unfiltered reaction is fucking captivating. I grin as I continue to ravish her tits with my mouth, my hand trailing down her chest until I get to her stomach, drawing patterns with the pad of my finger. When I reach her legs, they fall open, eager to accept whatever I have planned.

I groan with satisfaction when I find she's already dripping with desire, and I've barely touched her. I grab the vibrator and slowly push it inside her tight cunt. It's not nearly as thick as my cock, but she moans at the welcome intrusion, regardless. A soft hum buzzes through the air when I turn the device on.

When I increase the vibrator's setting, Marlow mewls, bucking her hips at the increased intensity, her hands clawing at the sheets. Watching her fly higher with each thrust of the device is mesmerizing.

"Dylan, I'm going to come," she whimpers.

"No, you're not," I challenge. "You're going to be a good girl and wait until I give you permission." I give her an encouraging kiss on the lips.

She quivers as I continue my punishing assault, biting down on her breasts as I plunge the vibrator inside her in rapid succession. She's hanging on by sheer determination, sweat dripping from her brow, and it's euphoric, knowing I'm in control of her pleasure. When I turn the vibrator onto the max setting, she screams out my name.

"Please, Dylan. Please let me come," she begs.

"Have you been a good girl?"

"Yes," she mumbles as she averts her gaze.

I grip her chin with my hand so she's forced to look at me. "Look at me when you come."

I give her clit a pinch, sending her careening into her release.

While she's high off euphoric bliss, I toss the vibrator on the bed and remove my glasses, setting them on the nightstand. Within seconds, I'm back on top of her, taking hold of my shaft, guiding it inside her perfect pussy inch by glorious inch. Her cunt clenches around me, and she winds her hands through my hair to pull me closer.

"Oh," Marlow gasps.

"That's it. Take it, take the whole damn thing." Once I'm fully seated, I pause to give her a moment to adjust. "You're so fucking tight," I grit out, my voice strained.

I grip her waist as I move in a steady rhythm, and she eagerly meets me, thrust for thrust. God, this woman has me completely under her spell, and I'm basking in the gratification of being claimed by her.

"Oh, yes," she cries out.

I look down to where our bodies join. "Damn, look at you taking my cock like such a good girl."

I lean down and kiss along the edge of her jaw. Her breathing picks up as I seal my mouth over hers in a possessive kiss. My tongue dances along the seam of her lips, groaning when she opens her mouth, letting me in.

She moans as I pick up my pace, bucking her hips in time with mine.

"Holy shit," I call out as she clings to me. "You almost there, sunshine?"

"Yes," she mewls.

I reach down and roll her clit with my thumb and forefinger, and soon we're both barreling toward release. I roar as uninhibited pleasure surges through me at the beautiful sight of Marlow unraveling. I hold her tight as we ride out our orgasms together.

"Fuck, that was incredible." I nuzzle my nose into her neck, inhaling her scent—a combination of citrus and rose—as I ease out of her, not wanting to cause her any pain. I stifle another groan as I watch our mixed cum drip onto her thigh.

I collapse onto the bed next to her and draw her into my embrace. Silence lingers between us as we lie wrapped in each other's arms.

For the first time in a long time, I'm truly content. The internal noise inside my head is quiet, and I'm not concerned about sticking to a schedule, cleaning my house, or checking my work email. Marlow is teaching me by example how to live in the moment, and I'm grateful for it.

I'm falling hard for this woman, and I push back the nagging worry that if she leaves, Lola won't be the only one who's heartbroken.

Marlow's stomach rumbles, and I laugh.

"Someone must be hungry. How do you feel about street tacos?"

"I'm a fan," Marlow says.

"Excellent. Let's get cleaned up, and then we'll go over to my place. I'll make you dinner." I pause briefly. "Waffles can come over too."

"Really?" Her eyes widen in surprise.

"Yeah. Lola will want to see him when she gets back. This way, we can save ourselves a trip back here to come get him."

I want Marlow to spend more time at my place, and the easiest way to make that happen is to let Waffles come over too. It's a compromise I'm willing to make for Marlow's sake, but that doesn't mean he's allowed on the furniture, especially my memory foam pillow.

CHAPTER TWENTY-SEVEN

MARLOW

I look up at the Stafford's charming two-story Cape-style house. It has a wraparound porch with a swing, similar to mine, and a bright red door. The sidewalk has been cleared of snow from the storm we had last night, and ice crystals are clinging to the trees surrounding the property.

Lola sprints up the porch steps, with Dylan and I trailing behind her. She swings open the front door, leaving it wide open as she races down the hall, shouting for her Gigi and Papa.

Before Dylan can follow her inside, I grab his arm. "Are you sure about this? What if your parents are upset that you invited me?"

He raises a brow. "Have you forgotten my mom's multiple attempts at setting us up? Trust me, she'll be over the moon when she sees you're here."

We've fallen into a new normal in the weeks following my art show. Our morning routine is the same, but our afternoons look much different than before. Waffles and I pick up Lola from school now, and we hang out in my art studio until Dylan gets home from work.

I was worried that Johanna might be disappointed since she usually watches Lola after school. However, Dylan assured me she was genuinely happy about the change. We haven't told her we're dating yet, but she must suspect it since Dylan spent the night with me in New York and because of the changes we've made to our schedules.

Most nights I have dinner at Dylan's, then wait downstairs for him while he puts Lola to bed. With his demanding work schedule, I want to make sure they get quality daddy-daughter time whenever possible.

These last three weeks have been the best of my life. After Lola goes to bed, Dylan and I cuddle on the couch while he reviews financial reports, followed by mind-blowing sex. We've agreed to not have sleepovers, and it's getting more difficult to say goodbye to him each night.

Dylan leans in to kiss along the edge of my jaw. "Everything is going to be okay. I promise."

"I believe you." I look up at him with an appreciative gaze.

Now that I've had a glimpse of what it would be like to be a real family, I can't shake the feeling that this is where I belong.

Dylan tucks a piece of hair behind my ear as he gently cups my cheek. I lean into his touch, and he seals my mouth with a possessive kiss. Without thinking, I grip the collar of his jacket, tugging him closer, a moan escaping my lips as he slips his tongue inside my mouth.

"Lola, I told you not to leave the door op—"

Dylan and I freeze, spinning around to find Johanna standing in the doorway. Her eyes dart between us, a broad smile lighting up her face.

There's no doubt in her mind that we're dating now.

My cheeks turn red as I release my grip on Dylan. I'm mortified that Johanna caught me kissing her son. I expect her to make a dramatic response about what she just saw, but she ignores it entirely.

"Marlow, what a pleasant surprise," she says, pulling me in for a bear hug. "Dylan didn't tell me you were coming." She gives him a disapproving look.

"I hope you don't mind." I nervously bite on my lower lip.

"Of course not." She waves off my concern. "You're always welcome. Why don't we go inside? Dinner's almost ready."

I follow her into the foyer, taking in the inviting atmosphere I remember from the last time I was here last Christmas Eve. A living room is on the right, and on the left, a stairway leads to the second floor. Like Dylan's house, whites and grays dominate the space. What sets it apart are the personal touches—photos of the Stafford siblings, a stack of quilted blankets, and various knickknacks.

"Are Cash and Harrison here yet?" Dylan asks.

"Harrison called earlier and said he has a meeting he can't miss, so he won't be able to join us tonight." Johanna frowns. "Cash got here half an hour ago. He's in the kitchen with your dad and Lola."

She guides us down the hall to a farmhouse-style open-concept kitchen, featuring exposed ceiling beams, butcher-block countertops, and sage-green cabinets. A massive wooden dining table, with seating for ten, is on the opposite side of the room.

Dylan's dad is at the kitchen island tossing a salad. He's wearing tortoiseshell glasses, and with his short black hair and brown eyes, he bears a striking resemblance to Dylan.

"Honey, look who's here," Johanna says in a singsong voice.

Mike sets the tongs on the counter and comes over to greet us.

"Hey, son." He smiles and gives Dylan a pat on the back. "Marlow, what a pleasant surprise. It's good to see you again."

"Thank you, Mr. Stafford."

He chuckles. "Please, call me Mike."

I hear giggling in the corner and turn around to find Cash and Lola at a craft table near the bay windows overlooking the backyard. As I step closer, I see they're coloring pictures of unicorns. Lola's tongue is poking out in concentration as she tries to stay within the lines.

Cash is next to her, hunched over in a chair that is far too small. It's so sweet that he's willing to play with Lola. His shaggy brown hair covers most of the scar spanning from his ear to his chin, and I wonder if that's intentional. Dylan mentioned he was in some kind of accident growing up but hasn't elaborated.

"Guess what, Uncle Cash?" Lola chirps.

"What's up, ladybug?" Cash pauses from drawing to give her his undivided attention.

"I'm going to be a daisy in Alice in Wonderland," she says slowly.

I beam with pride when she gets the name right. We've been practicing.

Cash lets out a low whistle. "A daisy, huh? That's an important role."

"Uh-huh." Lola bobs her head up and down. "Daddy and Marlow have been helping me practice every night."

"Is that so?" He glances over at Dylan with a knowing look. "That's very nice of them."

Before either of us can respond, Johanna claps her hands to get our attention. "It's time to eat," she announces.

The table has been set with dishes and silverware, and there's a pan of lasagna along with a salad and homemade breadsticks in the middle. Everything looks mouthwatering. Now I know where Dylan got his culinary skills.

My heart melts as Dylan helps Lola onto her chair and tucks a napkin into her shirt so she doesn't get her clothes dirty. He comes over to me next, pulling out my chair.

"Thank you," I say as I scoot in. "Don't I get a napkin too?" I wink.

"How could I forget?" he teases as he grabs another napkin from the table and places it in my lap.

"You've outdone yourself, Mom," Cash says as he dishes up a large serving of lasagna. "It's a welcome break from eating out three times a day."

Dylan told me Cash is overseeing the training of a team for

Stafford Holding's new office in London and has been spending a considerable amount of time there.

"I'm always happy to make you a home cooked meal, sweetheart," Johanna says enthusiastically. "Oh, that reminds me. I ran into Everly's mom at Main Street Market the other day, and she told me Everly is living in London, running the Townstead's European division. Why didn't you tell me? Have you seen her yet?" Johanna peppers Cash with questions in between bites of her salad.

"Theo mentioned it," Cash shrugs. "But I haven't seen her."

"Oh, that's too bad," Johanna pouts. "She's a nice girl."

"Yeah, I guess," Cash says, averting his gaze.

Dylan leans over to whisper in my ear. "The Townsteads live on the other side of town, and we grew up together. Theo and Cash have been best friends since elementary school. Everly is Theo's twin sister."

I nod as I take a sip of my water.

"Marlow." Johanna turns to me. "I almost forgot to tell you that you should bring Waffles next week. We have a big backyard that he'd enjoy."

I blink at her in shock, not sure if I heard her right. "Oh, I don't think that's a good idea. He's quite the handful, just ask Dylan." I nod to him.

"Daddy's teaching Waffles how to sit," Lola blurts out as she shovels a forkful of food into her mouth.

"Dylan? Training a dog? Now this I gotta see." Cash flashes a mischievous grin. "How's it going, big brother?" he taunts, as if he already knows the answer.

Dylan glares at Cash over his glass of water. He's had several more unsuccessful training sessions with Waffles. He's given up on the online videos and contacted a local training facility for advice. I suggested we hire a professional trainer, but he is determined to do this on his own.

"Trained or not, we'd love to have Waffles over," Johanna says sincerely. "Don't you agree, Mike?"

"Absolutely. He's welcome anytime," Mike assures me from his spot on the other end of the table.

"Thank you."

Dylan gives my leg a reassuring squeeze. He must know that his parent's gesture means a lot to me.

Being here gives me a comforting sense of belonging, a stark contrast to feeling like an outsider in my family while growing up. The Staffords have welcomed me with open arms, flaws and all, and a part of me never wants to leave.

CHAPTER TWENTY-EIGHT

DYLAN

I'm running late for my next conference call, and when I join, Harrison and Cash are already online.

"You should have seen Mom at dinner last night. I haven't seen her this excited since she found out Jack and Presley got together," Cash informs Harrison.

"Tell me about it," Harrison grumbles. "She called this morning and lectured me about *making* him work so much. I may be the CEO, but it's not like I have any control over you two." He throws his hands up in the air. "Plus, with the Vanburen project underway, it's all hands on deck right now."

My mom has been bugging me nonstop today as well. I've explained that Marlow and I are taking things slow, but that word isn't in her vocabulary.

She does make a good point about me working too much. I've already decided that once this project is wrapped up, I'm going to scale back and hire another senior analyst, so I have more time with Lola and Marlow. They're my top priority, and it's time that I gave them both the attention they deserve.

Marlow fits right in with my family and I have every intention of having her join us for dinner every week—Waffles too.

"You guys know I'm on the call now, right?" I ask with a raised brow.

"Oh, Dylan, we didn't see you there," Cash says, feigning innocence.

"Did you also tell Harrison that Mom asked if you've met up with Everly yet?" I question coyly. "If she knew you had a crush on Everly when we were kids, she'd already have a date lined up for you two."

My mom has always had a soft spot for Everly and was overjoyed whenever she came over to play at our house when we were younger. Without a doubt, she's held out hope that Everly would someday become a permanent part of our family.

"Shut up," Cash mumbles with a sheepish grin.

"You're right, Dylan." Harrison's eyes light up with recognition. "Didn't he get suspended for punching Jacob Barlow in the face when he stood up Everly at senior prom?"

"Yeah," I exclaim. "And he carried her books to class every day."

"Will you guys stop?" Cash complains. "Don't we have business to discuss?"

"You're the one who started it." I shrug. "Besides, if things go well with Marlow, eventually Mom's going to lose interest. And if she finds out about your little crush on Everly, she's coming for you next," I warn playfully.

"That's not going to happen," he mutters.

I keep my self-satisfied smirk contained.

Yeah, I thought the same thing and now look at me.

———

It's late once I've finally finished work for the day. I texted Marlow earlier, asking her to get Lola ready for bed, something I've never asked her to do when I'm home. In the past, I've handled it on my own, as Lola's bedtime routine is something special that we've always shared. However, I quite like the idea of Marlow being a part of it. *And not only for tonight.*

When I leave my home office, I follow the sound of "I Want to Dance with Somebody" by Whitney Houston coming from Lola's room.

"Yes, just like that," I hear Marlow say.

Lola giggles. "I love being a daisy."

"You're a natural," Marlow declares.

I peek into the room to see them swaying with their hands at their side. Lola has already changed into her unicorn PJs, and her hair is plated into French braids.

She has taken her role as a daisy seriously and has insisted that we practice every night. The only difference is the song choice—she prefers Marlow's '80s playlist.

She might not have any lines in the play, but she's certainly going to be the best daisy on that stage.

Once the song has ended, Marlow pauses the music and tucks her phone into the pocket of the overalls she's wearing.

"Okay, lolabug, it's time for you to get into bed."

Lola leaps onto the mattress without complaint and climbs under the covers. Marlow helps her arranges her stuffed animals and then grabs her copy of *Madeline* from the nightstand.

I'm tempted to go in and take over, but I stop myself, more curious to see how this plays out.

"This is *Madeline*," Lola tells Marlow as she clutches the book tightly to her chest. "Daddy reads it to me every night. Someday, I'm going to Paris to see the Eiffel Tower just like Madeline," she grins.

"I love *Madeline* too. It's one of my favorites," Marlow says. "Would you like me to read it while we wait for your dad?"

Lola nods. "Yes, please."

Marlow joins her on the bed, and Lola snuggles in next to her, eagerly handing her the book.

"Thanks," Marlow murmurs as she opens to the first page.

She's just started reading when Lola interrupts her. "Hey, Marlow."

"Yeah, lolabug?"

"I love you," Lola whispers as she wraps her arm around Marlow's waist.

I'm rooted to the spot at my daughter's declaration. I've never heard her say those three words to anyone except my parents and me, not even my siblings. Marlow is misty-eyed as she looks down at my daughter with adoration and devotion.

We could be a real family someday.

The thought doesn't cause me panic or confusion. In fact, I'm thinking of ways I could make it a reality.

"I love you too," Marlow says reverently as she strokes Lola's hair.

She glances in my direction, her eyes widening when she finds me standing in the doorway. I smile at her, encouraging her to continue.

As she goes back to reading, I realize that I'm falling in love with Marlow Taylor too. All I can do now is hope that the life Lola and I have to offer is enough for her. Because if she leaves Aspen Grove, I don't think Lola and I will ever recover.

CHAPTER TWENTY-NINE

MARLOW

"Marlow?" Dylan shouts from downstairs.

"I'm in my studio," I yell back.

I'm adding the finishing touch to a red and yellow tulip when he walks through the door with a giant vase of flowers in one hand and a blanket in the other. He looks irresistibly charming in charcoal-gray slacks, a white button-up shirt, and a cobalt-blue tie. His hair is tousled like he's run his hand through it all day, and he's grinning from ear to ear.

I'll never get tired of seeing him smile.

I turn my music off and set my palette knife down on my worktable.

"I missed you today," he says, coming over to kiss me. "I got these for you." He hands me a bouquet that includes pink carnations, purple alstroemeria, white poms, purple statice, lavender and pink spray roses.

The past few weeks with Dylan and Lola have been perfect. Dylan is constantly coming up with thoughtful gestures to show that he cares, and my heart nearly burst when Lola told me that she loved me last week.

"They're beautiful." I take the vase with shaky hands and set it on a nearby shelf. "What's the occasion?"

"Yesterday, you mentioned that your last arrangement wilted, so I stopped by Blooms on my way home to get you a fresh one. I know how important having a bouquet for inspiration means to you."

He remembers me saying that?

I'm overwhelmed with emotions. Of everything Dylan's done for me, this holds the most significance. Throughout the years, I've bought myself countless bouquets, but not once has anyone given me one. It's everything to me that he listened and did something kind simply because he knew it would bring me joy.

"That's incredibly thoughtful of you." My voice trembles as tears well in my eyes.

"Hey, what's the matter?" He frowns as he wraps me in his arms, wiping away a stray tear from my cheek. "I didn't mean to upset you."

I shake my head at his concern. "These are happy tears. No one has ever gotten me flowers before, believe it or not."

"Damn, sunshine." He squeezes me tighter. "I'll buy you flowers every day, if it makes you happy."

I'm falling hard for this man.

"Thank you. How did everything go at your parents' house?" I ask.

"Great. When I left, Lola and Waffles were cuddled on the couch watching *Bluey*."

Johanna and Mike asked if Lola and Waffles could have a sleepover at their place tonight. I'm sure it was Johanna's idea so Dylan and I could have a night alone.

"What if Waffles breaks something or if Lola misses you while she's away?"

"Whoa, there." Dylan pulls me tighter to his chest. "It's only for one night," he reminds me. "Lola's had plenty of sleepovers at my parents' house, and they're smitten with Waffles. I'm sure he will be on his best behavior if he gets as many snacks tonight as I think he will."

I take a deep breath to calm myself down. "Is there any particular reason you brought that with you?" I point at the blanket still tucked under his arm.

"There is," he says cryptically.

I watch as he unfolds the blanket and lays it flat on the ground.

When he's finished, he stands in front of me so we're only inches apart. "See, I have this next-door neighbor who's hot as fuck when she's in her studio painting. It's hypnotizing to watch her hips sway to the beat of the music with each stroke of her palette knife." He gently wipes off a smudge of pink paint from my forehead and rubs it between his fingers as he speaks. "I've had this fantasy lately, involving a palette of paints and her being sprawled naked on the ground."

My breathing quickens, and my cheeks turn red at his declaration. *Lord have mercy.*

"You're serious?"

"Only if you're up for it."

"I am," I rush out. "What exactly did you have in mind?" I'm ready and willing for whatever he has in store, knowing it'll bring me immeasurable gratification.

"Take off your clothes," he says in a low voice.

His all-encompassing presence sends a shiver down my spine, and I desperately want to please him. He's constantly caring for me, and I'm eager to do something that's for him.

Without hesitation, I pull my shirt off and throw it to the floor. As I reach for my bra, Dylan wraps his arms around my waist, placing his hand over mine to stop me.

"Let me help," he states, leaving no room for discussion.

He leans forward to kiss the swells of my breasts, and I inhale deeply at his touch. He effortlessly unclasps my bra, letting it fall to the ground as he greedily wraps his mouth around one of my nipples, sucking hard and pinching my other nipple with his fingers. The sharp pain sends a jolt of pleasure to my core.

"Oh, god," I whine as I rise to my toes.

Foreplay is one of my favorite parts about sex with Dylan. He has a gift for being in tune with my body, and he's learned that I like a little pain with my pleasure.

"I can't wait to see these covered in paint," he says as he keeps toying with my nipples.

A thrill runs through me at his admission. He keeps his gaze pinned on me as he tugs down my yoga pants and hot pink panties.

"So goddamn pretty," he says reverently.

He taps my thigh, signaling for me to step out of my clothes, and I kick them off to the side.

"Lie down on the blanket," he instructs.

I scramble to obey, crawling to the middle and turning to lay on my back. My palms are sweaty, and I'm restless, not knowing what's coming next. I peek at him through my eyelashes with a seductive smile, silently conveying that it's his move.

I watch with rapt attention as he strides across my studio to the wall of shelves, examining my stock of art supplies. When he gets to my vast collection of paints, he grabs a circular artist's palette and squeezes a different color of paint into each well. I bite my lip in anticipation when he chooses a fan brush from a cup filled with paintbrushes.

I wonder what he plans on doing with that.

When he's finished collecting his supplies, he sets them down next to me before standing at his full height, gazing down at me.

"Such a pretty canvas. What am I going to do with you?"

He better intend to do more than look because I'm all keyed up and need his hands on me soon. I'm entranced as he tugs off his tie and unbuttons his dress shirt and takes it off, offering me a front-row seat to his chiseled abs, leading down to his V-line.

I nibble my lip as he pulls his pants down, leaving him standing in a pair of black boxers. I know exactly what he's packing underneath, and I won't lie. I'm ready for it. He smirks at me as he steps out of his underwear, his cock proudly jutting out, pre-cum leaking from the tip.

I'm not the only one affected by this little game of his.

He tosses his clothes out of the way, and takes his glasses off, setting them on the closest shelf. When he faces me, he's holding his tie up for me to see.

"I want to restrain your hands while we play. Is that okay?" he asks.

I nod. "Yes, I trust you."

During our time together, he's stripped me of all my defenses. He's helped to reveal a part of me I never knew existed, and I'm enjoying exploring that side of myself with his help.

He kneels in front of me, bending forward to take hold of my wrists. He lifts them above my head, binding them with his tie. It's loose enough that I can get it off if I want to, but why would I? There's something intoxicating about being at this man's mercy.

Dylan looks at me with an insatiable hunger in his eyes, appreciating his own handiwork.

He sits up to grab the paintbrush and dips it into the red paint. I gasp when the bristles touch my breast, the cold paint sending a shockwave through my system. He draws swirls until he gets to my nipple, stroking back and forth in a teasing motion.

Next, he dips his brush into the yellow paint, disregarding the tinge of red mixed in. He draws wavy lines on my other breast, slowly dragging the brush along the sides. He furrows his brow in concentration as he moves the brush to my chest, writing out words of affirmation as he whispers them one by one.

"Beautiful... kind... strong... courageous..." He glances up at me when he draws out one more word. "Mine."

He tosses the brush to the ground and traces each word with his fingertip before gripping my hip, the paint from his hand smearing on my bare skin.

"You're such a mess," he murmurs. "A beautiful fucking mess."

With his other hand he shoves three fingers inside my cunt, the crude sound of my arousal filling the room as I shamelessly grind against his palm.

"Oh, god." I lift my hooded gaze to meet his heated stare.

"Damn, you're fucking drenched." He lowers his mouth to my ear. "Does getting dirty turn you on, messy girl?"

I whimper, unable to find my voice.

He pumps his fingers in and out in a steady rhythm while massaging my clit in languid circles. My body coils tighter with each thrust, a wave of euphoria washing over me. I beg with my eyes, a silent plea to pick up the pace. I'm frantic for him to move faster. I cry out when he unexpectedly yanks his fingers out of me.

"You're such a greedy little thing," Dylan goads me. "When you come, it'll be around my dick."

He takes hold of his cock, sliding it up and down, coating himself in my arousal. My breath quickens when he lines himself up with my core, impaling me in a single thrust. He doesn't move, taking a moment to gaze down at us joined together, inhaling sharply when he takes in my body covered in his paint. I moan in delight, savoring the fact that I'm stuffed full of him.

I mold my mouth to his, and he grasps my jaw in his hand, deepening our kiss. Time seems to stand still as we're wrapped in our private haven where there are no expectations, requirements, or worries. Just two people driven by a shared passion for each other.

"Dylan, I'm close," I pant.

"Beg for it, sunshine."

When I don't respond fast enough, he slows down his pace, pushing into me in short, shallow strokes. I don't miss his smug smile as I squirm against him, my body desperate for release.

"Beg. For. It."

Another surge of arousal crashes through me at his demanding tone.

"Please let me come, Dylan, please," I whine, urgently needing a reprieve.

"That's my good girl," he croons.

He pounds into me without restraint. All rational thinking is gone as the primal sound of flesh slapping against flesh resonates in the air. I fly higher into oblivion, digging my fingernails into my palms, relishing in the feel of my arms bound above me. I give him a look of lust-filled appreciation, sending my silent words through him with each push.

Thrust.

I'm yours

Thrust.

This is just the beginning.

Thrust.

I'm falling in love with you.

"Come, now." Dylan's command is irrefutable, and after a few strokes of my clit with his thumb, I detonate like a bomb. Tremors pulse through my body as my orgasm rips through me, and his guttural groan is a sign he's found his release.

"You're a fucking masterpiece," Dylan murmurs as he gazes down at me. "*My* masterpiece."

He leans forward to loosen the tie around my wrists and rubs them in a circular motion.

"You okay? Was that too much?"

"It was perfect," I assure him with a sated smile. "I like your idea of painting very much."

"Let's get cleaned up, and then I'll whip up something to eat."

"That sounds nice."

He lifts me into his arms, and I wrap my arms around his neck. As he carries me downstairs, I rest my cheek against his chest, inhaling the scent of mint and cedar, thinking this is what home must smell like.

I've had a silly grin on my face for the past two days. My night with Dylan was, hands down, the most erotic sexual experience I've ever had. There was something exhilarating about being filthy and on display for him as he rutted into me with abandon.

The time we've spent together has offered me a glimpse of what life would be like with him and Lola, leaving me with a sense of peace.

Lola's play is tonight, and I couldn't be more excited to celebrate her big moment on stage. Dylan had to go into the office, so he'll meet us at the school tonight.

As luck would have it, the painting he bought at my exhibition was just delivered to his house. I met the delivery person and had them leave it in Dylan's living room. It'll look so good in here once it's hung up and I know Lola will love it too once she sees what it is.

"Shoot," I mutter to myself.

If I don't leave now, I'm going to be late to pick her up from school. I put my shoes back on and jog over to my place to get Waffles. He's waiting at the door, barking when I grab his leash and clip it to his collar.

"Come on, boy," I usher him outside.

We're halfway down the block when Gavin calls me.

"Hey, Gav. The painting was just delivered to Dylan's house," I inform him. "Thanks so much for shipping it back here."

We've texted almost every day since my exhibition. He mostly wants status updates on Dylan and me and pesters me about doing another show. He was elated by the success of this last one and was disappointed when I told him I wasn't planning on doing another exhibition for a while. I've been painting the last few weeks whenever inspiration strikes, not because of a looming deadline, and it's been rejuvenating.

"That's great, but it's not why I'm calling," he says impatiently.

"It's not?"

"No. I have *the* most fantastic news." Excitement radiates from his voice.

"What is it?"

"I just got off the phone with James Miller, the founder of the Paris Art Collective. His wife attended your art show and purchased the snapdragon piece as a birthday present for James. He's beyond impressed with your artistic ability and wants to offer you a three-month artist residency at the Collective," Gavin practically shouts with excitement. "Starting next month."

"Are you serious?" I dance for joy on the sidewalk, not caring if anyone sees me. "How do you know? Please tell me this isn't a joke."

I've dreamed of doing a residency at the Paris Art Collective ever since I started painting. Some of the best artists in the world teach there, and it would be an incredible opportunity to improve my technique. It's a highly competitive program, so I never thought I'd get an invitation.

"James called The Artist asking about you. His team is sending you an official offer via email next week. Babe, this is the real deal," he assures me.

"This is unbelievable. I'm so—" I stop short when Waffles barks, pulling me out of my daydream. We're near the marquee in front of Lola's school.

Who would take care of Waffles if I accepted the offer? What about Dylan and Lola?

In the past, I always picked up and went somewhere new when an opportunity presented itself. Until now, I've never had people that I care about to consider.

"Marlow? Are you there," Gavin asks.

"I don't think I can go," I whisper.

"What, why?" he asks, his tone frantic. "Wait… does this have something to do with that *GQ* hottie of yours and his darling little girl that you showed Matthew and me pictures of at dinner in New York?"

"I think I'm in love with Dylan," I confess.

"Oh, Marlow. I'm so happy for you but also sad because I don't want you to miss out on this chance. Do you want to talk more about it?"

"No, not right now," I say softly. Dylan and I haven't discussed our future yet, but I don't want to disappoint him by leaving like Maddie did. It doesn't matter that I would only be gone for three months. I worry that he won't see it that way. He trusts me implicitly, and I would never do anything to jeopardize that, not even for an opportunity of a lifetime.

"I appreciate everything you've done for me," I continue. "I would never have gotten an offer from the Collective if it wasn't for you."

"That's not true," Gavin scoffs. "If they hadn't seen your work at The Artist, it would have been online or at another gallery." He lets out a heavy sigh. "Listen, the official offer won't be sent until next week, so why don't you wait a few days before making a final decision? I fully support you trading in a life of travel for small-town living if that makes you happy. I just don't like seeing you put your career and dreams on the back burner."

"Thanks, Gavin."

"Of course, babe, I'll always have your back."

I can't find the right words to express how I'm feeling right now. If I accept the offer, it could jeopardize the chance of building a life with Dylan and Lola. And I can't help but worry how Waffles would adjust to life in Paris after living in a small town like Aspen Grove for so long. This is his home... and it feels like mine too.

The school bell rings, and seconds later, kids spill out of the school's front entrance.

"Gav, I have to pick up Lola from school now. Why don't we talk about this later?"

"Yeah, of course. I'm here if you need me."

I see Lola coming down the steps. Her backpack bounces as she hurries toward me with a toothy grin. I plaster on a smile when she looks my way, not wanting her to think anything is wrong.

I'll tell Dylan about my offer from the Collective after the play. I'm not letting anything get in the way of Lola's big night.

CHAPTER THIRTY

DYLAN

"How's Lola?" Marlow asks as we head to the school auditorium.

"She was practically bouncing off the walls with excitement when I dropped her off. At least we don't have to worry about her getting stage fright," I say with a chuckle.

My team at work has been dealing with several major setbacks with the Vanburen project, and I had to go into the office today to address an urgent issue. Fortunately, I still got to the school early, allowing me to accompany Lola to her classroom, where she'll wait until it's time for her to go onstage.

Marlow smiles warmly. "It seems like we may have a future Alice in Wonderland on our hands."

"I wouldn't be surprised."

And I want you there to share all those moments with us.

In the week since Lola told Marlow she loved her, I've included Marlow in her bedtime routine. We take turns reading to her, and there's something extraordinary about the three of us cuddled on the bed together like we're a family. I never imagined I could be this happy again after Maddie left, but Marlow has changed everything.

She's quickly become integral to our daily routine, and I can't imagine a life without her. I long for the day when I can wake up with her by my side each morning, and she's the last thing I see before I close my eyes at night. She and Lola hold my whole heart, and I want us to be a real family... Waffles too.

I take Marlow's hand in mine as we enter the school's auditorium. Other than the town buzzing with gossip and my mother sharing the news with her friends, we've kept our relationship low profile until now.

"Dylan, are you sure about this?" Marlow murmurs as she looks down at our entwined fingers.

I think back to the night I traced her chest with words of affirmation before fucking her into oblivion. Her body was my canvas to do as I pleased, and if she'd let me, I'd spend the rest of my life worshiping her the way I did that night.

"You're mine, sunshine, and I want everyone to know it," I declare.

"Wait." She grabs ahold of my arm with her free hand. "When we get back to your place tonight, I need to talk to you about something important," she says, chewing on her lip.

"We can talk about whatever you want," I promise. I catch sight of my mom in the second row, motioning for us to come sit with her and Cash. "We better take our seats."

"Yeah, okay," Marlow says hesitantly.

I ignore the onlookers staring in our direction as we make our way to the front of the auditorium. At least now, there isn't any question who Marlow belongs to.

She's mine. Now and always.

"Hi, Marlow. Hey, sweetheart," my mom greets us. "How's our little star doing?" she asks me.

"She's extremely excited. Where's Dad?"

She points to the small section of seats on either side of the stage where my dad's sitting next to Harrison with his camcorder in hand. "He's going to film the play so Presley and Jack can watch it when they come to visit. And he wants Lola to be able to see it later, since she's missing most of it."

"She'll love that," I say.

"I tried to get him to use my phone to record, but you know how he likes that camcorder of his," Cash chimes in. "Marlow, it's good to see you again." He flashes her a big grin.

"You too," she replies sweetly.

Cash snickers as I shoot him a glare and drape my arm around Marlow, drawing her closer to me.

We all settle into our seats as the lights dim and the curtain opens. I smile with satisfaction when Marlow rests her head against my shoulder. While I appreciate my family's unwavering support, having her by my side to share this moment with is more than I could ever ask for.

The first act moves at a glacial pace, while I impatiently wait for the "Garden of Live Flowers" scene in act two. Marlow squeezes my leg when several fifth graders dressed as flowers make their entrance.

"This is it," she whispers with anticipation.

Sure enough, a group of first graders follow the older kids on stage. Lola is the last one to come out. She's dressed in a green leotard and tutu, with a white headpiece shaped like a flower tied under her chin with a green ribbon. She's absolutely adorable.

When the music plays, she sways to the rhythm of the song like we've practiced, but she stops when she notices Marlow waving at her.

"Hi, Marlow. Hi, Daddy," she exclaims, waving enthusiastically with both arms.

"That's my niece," Cash hollers proudly.

The crowd erupts into laughter as Lola's teacher steps out from the stage wing and gently coaxes Lola back into place. Lola goes right back to swaying with a megawatt smile for the rest of the song.

"She's brilliant," Marlow gushes with pride.

"It's all thanks to you." I kiss her forehead. "I'm so glad you're here."

"There's nowhere else I'd rather be," she murmurs.

"Daddy," Lola squeals as she comes barreling toward me, still dressed in her daisy costume.

I catch her in my arms and twirl her around. "I'm so proud of you, ladybug. You were amazing."

"Marlow, did you see me swaying like we practiced?"

"You were perfect." Marlow leans in to kiss her cheek. "I brought you something." She hands Lola a single long-stem white gerbera daisy.

"It's a daisy, just like me," Lola exclaims. "It's so pretty. How did you fit it in your pocket?" she asks with a puzzled expression as she looks Marlow up and down.

Today she's dressed in a hot pink jumper with a light blue shirt underneath and wearing her favorite silver sneakers. Even on a rainy day, she's a ray of sunshine. *My ray of sunshine.*

"It was too big, so I had to carry it," Marlow explains.

She bought it from a booth the owner of Blooms had set up outside the auditorium.

"Oh, that makes sense." Lola gently strokes the petals of her flower.

We move to the side of the hallway that's bustling with families waiting for the rest of the kids to come out from backstage.

When my parents and brothers come to join us, Marlow leans over to me. "I'll be right back. Quinn and Andi are here, and I want to say hi."

I nod. "Sounds good."

"Very impressive, little lady." Harrison ruffles Lola's hair as Marlow walks away.

"Thanks, Uncle Harrison." Lola grins.

"Ladybug, that was killer," Cash exclaims, giving her a high five. "Next time, I want a shout-out too."

"Only if you help me practice," Lola says in a serious tone.

"Pinky promise?"

Lola giggles, extending her pinky as Cash hooks his with hers, sealing their deal.

Next thing I know, she's going to get in the habit of disrupting every play to say hi to someone in our family. I'll definitely need to have a chat with her before the next one.

"Where's my hug?" my dad questions.

"Papa," Lola squeals, rushing over to hug my parents.

"So, brother, how's the dog training coming along?" Cash mocks.

I shoot him a scowl. He knows perfectly well how things are going. Waffles and I have been at it for weeks with nothing to show for it. I've watched countless online tutorial videos and sought advice from several local dog trainers, but nothing has worked. Hell, I'd be content if he would just learn to obey my command to sit.

"You manage a team of a hundred. I'd think you'd be able to train one little dog," Harrison says with mock disappointment. "I may need to reconsider your position at Stafford Holdings."

"You're such an ass," I grumble.

"Daddy said a bad word," Lola shouts.

Great. Of course she heard that.

I shield my face with my hand when the people nearby stare, giving me dirty looks.

My mom shakes her head in dismay.

"Shame on you," Cash mocks.

"I'm going to go find Marlow," I announce. "I'll be right back."

I weave through the crowd to where she's standing with her friends. They're too immersed in their conversation to notice me.

My steps falter when Andi asks Marlow "When did you find out?"

"Gavin called and told me on my way to pick up Lola from school today," Marlow says with a downcast expression.

Why does she look so sad? She was smiling a few minutes ago.

"I can't believe it. *The* Paris Art Collective offered you a residency?" Quinn lets out a low whistle. "Damn girl, that's impressive. I'm sure Gavin was over the moon."

"How long would you be in Paris?" Andi asks.

"Three months," Marlow replies as she anxiously taps her foot.

My stomach drops, and I'm frozen to the spot, unable to move. The hallway is packed with people and I force myself to keep a straight face even though a crippling phantom pain shoots across my sternum.

"That's forever," Quinn complains. "What are Andi and I going to do…"

Unable to listen any longer, I take a step back and walk in the opposite direction toward my family before Marlow and her friends notice me. My ears ring as I run my hand through my hair.

That must be what she wanted to talk about later. Part of me wants to be upset with her for not telling me sooner, but I understand she didn't want to overshadow Lola's special night, and I appreciate it.

We haven't discussed our long-term future, and she hasn't told me she'd stay, but I assumed she would after everything we've been through. I guess I conveniently forgot she's not one to stay in the same place for long, especially when a new opportunity presents itself.

I should have known this was too good to be true. I was always so careful until Marlow came along, and once I finally claimed her as mine, there was no going back for me—consequences be damned. Now, I'll be left to pick up the pieces when she's gone.

I feel like a twenty-pound weight is on my chest, making it difficult to breathe. I know Marlow doesn't want to take away from Lola's big night, but I won't be able to relax until we talk about what I just overheard.

When I get back to where my family is standing around talking, I tap my mom on the shoulder. "Hey, Mom?"

She turns around to face me. "Yeah, sweetheart? Where's Marlow?" She looks behind me.

"She's talking to her friends." I motion in their direction. "Would you and Dad be willing to take Lola out for ice cream? Marlow and I have something we need to talk about in private," I say with a tight smile.

This is one conversation that we should have with just the two of us around—regardless of the outcome.

I don't know what I'll do if I lose her.

"Of course, sweetheart," my mom says with a concerned expression. "Is everything okay?"

No.

"Yeah, everything is fine," I lie.

When Marlow finishes her conversation and strides toward us, my heart aches at how damn beautiful she is. I wish I could throw her over my shoulder and take her somewhere we can talk right now, but I have to keep level-headed for Lola's sake. There will be plenty of time for us to discuss when we get back to my place.

I'll always support Marlow following her dreams, but I'll be damned if I lose her in the process.

CHAPTER THIRTY-ONE

MARLOW

Dylan is unusually quiet on the drive home.

"Is something wrong?" I ask.

"Why don't we wait to talk until we get to my house," he suggests, glancing over at me briefly.

"Yeah, okay," I say with a tentative smile.

Given his death grip on the steering wheel, something is bothering him, although I'm not sure what.

His parents are taking Lola out for ice cream. Although I would have liked to join them to celebrate her special night, I'm thankful for the chance to talk with Dylan alone about my offer from the Collective. But that will have to wait until I figure out what's on his mind.

I was so relieved when I saw Quinn and Andi at the play. I chatted with them afterward and told them about my residency offer. Quinn was overjoyed to hear the great news, but like Gavin, she's disappointed that I'm planning to turn it down. On the other hand, Andi urged me to discuss it with Dylan before making a final choice. She firmly believes he'd be supportive of me going.

I have conflicting thoughts. Despite it being an amazing

opportunity that I may never have again, I can't jeopardize my relationship with Dylan and Lola.

When we get to Dylan's house, he goes inside first, holding the door for me. As I brush past him and step into the entryway, his gaze remains fixed on the floor, like he can't look at me.

"Okay, we're here. Want to tell me what's bothering you?" I ask.

He closes the door, the quiet click sounding louder amongst the tense silence.

There's a mountain of space between us, and Dylan has a blank look on his face.

"I overheard your conversation with Quinn and Andi," he states.

My eyes widen in understanding. "Oh, and what exactly did you hear?" I ask as I tuck my hair behind my hair. Based on his initial reaction, I'm assuming he missed the part of the conversation when I told them I wasn't planning to go to Paris.

"I know you were offered an art residency and will be gone for three months." He maintains a steady tone. "Do you know when you're leaving yet?"

He's so quick to conclude that I won't stay. I don't blame him after what he went through with Maddie, but I wish he would trust that I have him and Lola's best interests at heart.

I take a calming breath, understanding that he must be hurting right now.

"Did you hear me say that I was going to Paris?" I ask gently.

"No, but why wouldn't you? It sounds like an amazing opportunity—"

I hold out my hand to stop him. "The head of the program called Gavin this afternoon to get my information. His team is extending me an offer for a three-month artist residency in Paris. I've always wanted to do it, but I never thought I'd get the chance." I nervously wring my hands as I explain. "I was going to talk to you about it tonight after the play so as not to ruin

Lola's big night. Plus, I didn't want you to worry for no reason, since I don't plan on accepting the offer."

"You've already told them no?"

I shake my head. "I will once they send the official offer next week."

"Why?" He appears perplexed by my answer. "If it's something you've always wanted to do, why would you turn it down?"

"Because I know how much this would affect you and Lola. After everything you've been through, I don't want to be another person who leaves you behind. You're both incredibility important to me." The words spill freely from my mouth.

I think I'm in love with you.

He moves closer, a downcast expression on his face. "Honestly, I figured you'd move on when you found something better."

I wish he could see things from my perspective. The time I've spent with him and Lola has made me feel loved, cherished, and content. After years of wandering like a lost soul, being with them feels like the home I've been searching for my whole life.

He closes the distance between us to stand in front of me, and I gaze up at him.

"Don't you get it? No one else can make me feel the way you and Lola do. Believe me when I tell you there is nothing better." A blush creeps across my cheeks at my admission.

From the moment I met them, I recognized the unique bond they shared. I've always longed to be a part of something so extraordinary, and now that I've found it, I'm never letting go.

"Marlow, I—" Dylan pauses mid-sentence, glancing over my shoulder into the dimly lit living room. "What is that?" He gestures toward the painting, leaning against the wall. Striding past me, he switches on the overhead light for a better look.

"The painting you bought at my art show," I say softly as I follow behind.

"It's perfect," he says in awe.

The piece he purchased is of two daisies—one red, one white.

It's the last piece I painted for my collection a few days after I went with Dylan and Lola to the Family Craft Corner class and had dinner at their house for the first time. The white daisy represents Lola's innocence and purity, and the red daisy was inspired by my romantic feelings for Dylan. It's even more special because of Lola's role as a daisy in her school play.

"What's it called?"

"*Love's Beginning,*" I say softly. "I never intended to sell this one."

"Why did you then?"

"Because Gavin advertised that there would be seven pieces in the collection. I figured if I set the price high enough, no one would buy it, and I could keep it."

"How much?"

"You should know. You bought it," I remind him.

"I had my assistant take care of the payment," he says.

"Oh, I see." I'm a little nervous to tell him now. "It was ninety grand," I admit with a sympathetic look.

He places my hands in his. "I would have paid a million dollars for a Marlow Taylor original. But for this particular piece, I'd give up everything. It's priceless because I'll think of you and Lola every time I see it. You've brought color into our lives both literally and figuratively, and there isn't a version of our future without you."

Dylan's declaration leaves me blinking up at him in shock, taking a moment to realize I'm not dreaming. The intensity of his gaze is proof that he means every single word.

"You and Lola are my entire world," he says as he clasps my hands tighter. "Whatever happens, we'll get through it together because—" Dylan's phone goes off in his pocket. He ignores it, but it goes off again as soon as it stops.

"Dammit," he mutters when he checks it. "I'm so sorry, it's Harrison."

"You should answer it," I encourage him.

"Hello?" He listens intently, his face scrunching up into a scowl. "You've got to be kidding me. Yeah, I'm joining now."

He hangs up and gives me an apprehensive look.

"Is everything okay?" I question.

"There's a time-sensitive issue with the Vanburen project. I have to get on a call with our team to figure out the best course of action." He motions toward his office upstairs.

I cup his cheek with my hand. "Go take care of your work emergency. When you've finished, come over to my place and we'll continue our conversation. I'm not going anywhere," I promise him.

"Marlow, you mean everything to me." He places a kiss on my temple before jogging up the stairs to his office.

As Dylan climbs the stairs, I'm left feeling uncertain about my future. Part of me is questioning my initial decision about the residency, and I'm wondering if there's a possibility for us to make this work.

The only thing I can say for certain is that I have no doubt that Dylan will be by my side for whatever comes next.

CHAPTER THIRTY-TWO

DYLAN

"Thanks for your hard work, everyone," I say with a weary expression. "Take the day off, and I'll see you all in the office tomorrow morning."

I had to pull an all-nighter, collaborating with Harrison and my team over a conference call. We're set to break ground on the Vanburen development next month but encountered a particular roadblock that required an overwhelming volume of financial paperwork. We had to submit it by 8:00 a.m. to prevent further delays.

Lola spent the night at my parents' house, and they dropped her off at school this morning.

I shut off my computer and lean back in my office chair. It's unusually quiet over at Marlow's house, and she never went into her studio last night.

Yeah, I checked countless times.

When I realized I'd be working well into the night, I texted her, and she told me to come over to her place this morning so we could finish our conversation. I regret ending our discussion abruptly, especially after jumping to conclusions I shouldn't have. I never want her to feel like what's happening with me takes precedence over her.

I stand up and stretch my arms above my head, anxious to go over to her place. I'm debating whether I should shower first when there's a knock on my front door. Half-expecting it to be Marlow, I'm slightly disappointed to find my mother standing on my porch with two cups of coffee in hand.

"Mom?"

"Hey, sweetheart." She gives me a kiss on the cheek as she pushes her way past me into the house.

"What are you doing here?"

"I stopped by Brew Haven after dropping Lola off at school." She holds out one of the cups she has in her hand. "Your father mentioned you and Harrison were up all night, so I figured you could use the caffeine. Good thing I did because you sure look like you could use it."

What's that supposed to mean?

I steal a glance at my reflection in the mirror hanging on the nearby wall.

My hair sticks out in every direction, and I have a five o'clock shadow. My shirt is a rumpled mess. There's also an ink stain across the front from a pen that exploded earlier.

"Uh, thanks?" I cautiously take the cup of coffee from my mom as she looks around the house, not even being discreet. "Mom, what are you doing?" When she doesn't respond, I wave to get her attention.

"Yeah, sweetheart?" she says, finally looking at me.

"Why did you really stop by? We both know it wasn't to bring me coffee," I call her out.

She wouldn't drop in unannounced without an ulterior motive, especially when Lola isn't here.

"I was worried," she admits with a heavy sigh. "You and Marlow left abruptly last night. I ran into her friend Quinn in the parking lot, and she told me Marlow was offered an artist residency in Paris. I assumed that's what the two of you came home to talk about last night. Please tell me you sorted things out." She sounds hopeful.

"Not quite," I say, raking my fingers through my hair.

"Why not?" She sounds alarmed.

"Marlow and I were in the middle of discussing it when Harrison called," I explain. "She told me to come over this morning when I finished work so we could talk more."

"What are you waiting for?" my mom urges. "Go to her house right now and tell her to accept that offer." She tries to shove me out the door.

"Whoa, slow down," I hold my hand out to stop her. "What do you mean?"

My mom lets out an exasperated sigh. "Sweetheart, I looked up the Paris Art Collective online, and it's one of the most coveted opportunities for an artist. If Marlow goes, she'll be working with some of the most successful artists in the world. If she doesn't take this opportunity, I think she'll regret it."

I blink rapidly. Marlow didn't mention that it was such a prestigious offer, and I regret not asking her more about it when I had the chance. Now I'm even more confused about why she is planning to turn it down.

"If it's that important, why didn't she just tell me she was going to take it?"

"If Marlow had told you she was leaving, can you honestly tell me you wouldn't have assumed the worst?" my mom responds.

No, I can't. I did that last night. When I heard her talking with her friends, I was quick to come to an assumption without getting the facts first.

It occurs to me that I never even asked Marlow if she was interested in the residency. I was so swept away by her declaration about how much Lola and I meant to her that I wasn't thinking of much else.

I move away from Mom and sit on the bottom step of the stairs, setting my coffee on the floor next to me.

"You really think I should encourage her to go, don't you?" I ask.

"Yes, I do," my mom says matter-of-factly. "If you love Marlow like I think you do, you'll support her every step of the way while she's gone, and when she returns to Aspen Grove, you and Lola will be here to welcome her back with open arms."

"What if she decides she loves Paris more and doesn't come back? Or what if she isn't content with life in Aspen Grove with Lola and me?

My mom offers me a sympathetic look as she takes a seat next to me on the stairs. She places her hand on my knee, offering her support. "Sweetheart, Marlow isn't Maddie," she says earnestly. "She knew from the start that you and Lola came as a package deal, and she still grew to love you both, regardless."

Although I rarely let it show, it almost destroyed me when Maddie left. Lola wasn't the only one she left behind. At first, I carried the weight of blame on my shoulders. I used to believe that if I had been a more attentive partner or had accommodated her wishes, she would have stayed. It took a long time for me to come to terms with the fact that nothing I could have done would have changed the outcome.

My mom is right. Marlow is nothing like Maddie. She's compassionate, selfless, and nurturing. Instead of celebrating her once-in-a-lifetime opportunity, her immediate reaction was to worry about its effect on Lola and me.

"Have I told you the story about how I met your father?" my mom asks.

I shake my head. My parents rarely share details about their lives before my siblings and I were born, so I'm intrigued.

"When we met, he lived in New York, learning the ropes at Stafford Holdings. I was a sophomore in college in California. I worked part time as an assistant at a law firm that did business with Stafford Holdings regarding their properties on the west coast, and your father occasionally flew in for in-person meetings.

He asked me out for dinner the day we met, and I was

instantly smitten. I thought we had an incredible time and was sorely disappointed when he didn't contact me again before he left for New York."

I pick up my coffee and take a sip as I listen intently.

"After that, like clockwork, he flew in every three months. He'd invite me to dinner while he was in town, we'd have a wonderful time, and then he'd go back home." She shakes her head as if still disappointed by my dad's decision all these years later.

"A month before I graduated college, your father came into town for one of his business trips. He was furious when I declined his invitation to dinner," she says with a twinkle in her eye. "I told him I was seeing someone else and had no intention of waiting around for him if he was only going to string me along."

I let out a low whistle. "Damn, Mom, I'm impressed."

"Watch your language," she scolds me before continuing her story. "Your father confessed that he knew that he was going to marry me the first time he saw me. When he found out how important it was to me that I got my college degree, he waited to pursue anything serious until I graduated. Sure, he could have gone about it differently. But in the end, what impressed me most was his willingness to sacrifice his immediate gratification so I could achieve my dreams."

"What happened to the other guy?" I can't help but ask.

"What other guy?" she says, seeming genuinely confused.

"The one you told Dad you were dating."

"There wasn't anyone else." She gives me a mischievous grin. "I couldn't wait around forever, so I had to give your father a little push in the right direction."

Why does it not surprise me that my mom played a crucial role in orchestrating her own relationship?

Now that I've heard the story, I understand why my dad made the decision he did. He must have cared for my mom deeply and wanted her to be happy, regardless of the sacrifices he had to make.

I want the same for Marlow. She should be with someone who champions her ambitions, not restrains them.

"Marlow's worth waiting for," I say, more to myself than anything.

She's like the sun, and we're all lucky enough to be in her orbit, basking in her warmth. She deserves nothing less than unwavering support as she chases her dreams, and I'm committed to making sure she has it.

"How did you know?" I ask my mom.

"Know what, sweetheart?"

"You were very persistent in getting Marlow and me together. How did you know it would pay off?"

She shoots me a bewildered glance. "What on earth are you talking about?"

"Come on, Mom," I challenge her. "You set us up on multiple occasions. There's no way you can tell me that wasn't planned."

"Sweetheart, you're giving me too much credit." She dismisses me with a wave of her hand. "I merely mentioned certain events to multiple people. I couldn't have known you'd both show up." She shrugs casually.

Unbelievable.

I suspect she'll never admit to her involvement in getting Marrow and me together. At least I know the truth, and I'll always be grateful for what she did.

"Regardless, thank you." I wrap my arm around her shoulders in a side hug.

She smiles. "You better get going, sweetheart. Marlow's waiting."

———

Ten minutes later, I'm on Marlow's doorstep in a clean pair of clothes, my hair is brushed, and I'm armed with a cappuccino with three pumps of coconut creamer, courtesy of my mother.

I grow impatient when I knock twice, and there's no answer. I turn the knob, grumbling when I find it unlocked.

Marlow is halfway down the stairs when I step inside. She's wearing mint green sleep shorts and an oversized hot pink sweater, her hair tossed into a messy bun.

She's absolutely gorgeous.

"For the love of god, woman, will you please start locking your door?"

I'm not opposed to the idea of getting her an automated lock that I can manage with my phone.

"Dylan?" Marlow rubs the sleep from her eyes. "Is everything okay?"

I set her coffee on the console table near the entryway so my hands are free and advance toward her, wrapping her in my arms. I bury my nose into her hair, breathing in the comforting scent of citrus and rose.

In this moment, I realize that there's nothing I wouldn't do for Marlow. I'm in love with her, and no matter how long she asks me to wait, I'll do it. I will do whatever it takes to have her by my side for the rest of my life.

I gently lift her chin, meeting her mesmerizing blue-green gaze. "I love you, Marlow Taylor. I love you so damn much, and I'm sorry it took me so long to tell you."

She places her hand over mine as tears stream down her face. "I love you too, Dylan Stafford."

"Thank god," I sigh in relief. "I'm not sure what I would have done if you didn't say it back," I tease as I wipe away her tears with my thumbs.

She smiles. "Lucky for you, that wasn't the case."

Since the day we met, her smile has had an inexplicable effect on me, and I'll never tire of seeing it.

"You should go to Paris," I blurt out.

"What?" Marlow seems confused. "You just told me you loved me."

"You're right. I love you so damn much." I press a kiss to her lips. "But this is a once-in-a-lifetime opportunity. You've spent your whole life worried about pleasing others and sacrificing your happiness. It's time someone prioritizes you first." I give her a comforting glance of reassurance. "If this is something you truly want, I'll support you in every way that I can, and when you get back to Aspen Grove, Lola and I will be here waiting for you."

"You mean it?"

"I do."

"What about Waffles?" she asks hesitantly. "I don't think he'd be much of a city dog, and I wouldn't be comfortable leaving him with a sitter that long."

"He'll stay with Lola and me," I declare.

She raises a brow. "You want Waffles to stay in *your* house? A couple of months ago, he wasn't even allowed inside, and now you're giving him free rein?"

"He's your family, sunshine, which makes him part of my family. The only place he's not welcome is on my memory foam pillow," I say half-teasingly. He really isn't allowed on my pillow.

I can see the wheels turning in Marlow's head as she considers if this could be a possibility.

"What about Lola? Won't she be upset if I go?"

"No offense, but she'll be so overjoyed that Waffles is moving in she won't even notice that you're gone."

Marlow playfully swats my chest. "Dylan, I'm serious. Who's going to watch her in the mornings? What if you find a nanny that she likes better than me?" She nervously chews her lip.

"That's never going to happen. Besides, my parents have already offered to help out while you're away." I hold my hand out to stop her from arguing. "You should know that my mother insisted. She wants to do this for us. You're family now."

I must have said the right thing because Marlow's features soften.

She leans her head against my chest. "It's such a long time. What if we can't make a long-distance relationship work?"

"It's only three months," I remind her. "That's twelve weeks, a fourth of a year, or approximately ninety days. It pales in comparison to spending forever with you."

She tilts her head, blinking up at me with shock. We might not be ready for a proposal, wedding, or more kids, but that doesn't stop me from conveying my desire for those things to her. She's my end game, and whatever challenges we face, we'll navigate them together.

"Wait. What about this house? My lease is up in two months."

I chuckle softly. "You can do whatever you want with it. It's yours."

"What do you mean?"

"Rick owned several properties in Aspen Grove and wasn't maintaining any of them. As of last week, Stafford Holdings owns them all. Except for this one." I motion around us. "I bought this one for you, because I know how much you like it."

"Wait. What do you mean Rick wasn't maintaining the properties?"

"He never hired anyone to shovel your sidewalk," I tell her honestly.

"So, let me get this straight. Even though you weren't particularly fond of me when we first met, you took it upon yourself to shovel my driveway and mow my lawn without being asked?" She appears genuinely perplexed.

"I liked you from the beginning, sunshine." I drop a kiss to her sweet lips. "I just wasn't ready to admit it to myself."

It took me a while to come around, but now that Marlow is mine, I'll do whatever it takes to ensure she stays that way.

CHAPTER THIRTY-THREE

MARLOW

"Hey, Marlow."

"Hey, lolabug."

"Don't worry, I'll take good care of Daddy and Waffles while you're gone." She pats my hand with a big smile on her face.

My lip trembles, and I fight tears at her thoughtfulness.

It's my last time putting her to bed before I go to Paris and I'm an emotional wreck.

The past three weeks seemed to have flown by.

Dylan, Lola and I have spent every moment we can together. Making popcorn, and watching movies, huddled on the sofa. Eating dinner together. Going to the Family Craft Corner class and taking long walks through the neighborhood with Waffles. Like a real family.

I'm going to miss them all so much.

My flight leaves early in the morning. Dylan is taking me to a hotel in the city tonight, so we're closer to the airport and can have some alone time before I go. His parents are staying with Lola and Waffles while he's gone.

When we broke the news to Lola about me going to Paris, she was unfazed. Her first question was if she could come with me so she could see the Eiffel tower like Madeline. Her second question was to ask if Waffles could move into her room while I was away.

The jury is still out on that last one. Dylan's adamant that Waffles will be sleeping in the living room. I give that arrangement one night before he gives in and lets Waffles stay in Lola's room.

"I appreciate it, lolabug. They're lucky to have you," I say.

"Why are you going to Paris again?" Every few days, she asks the same question.

"I'm going to school to become a better painter," I explain.

"Will they teach you to paint pictures that are pink?" Her eyes light up with excitement.

When I showed Lola the daisy painting that's now hanging in her living room, she thought it was pretty but was disappointed that the flowers weren't pink. However, she was beyond excited when I told her I'd paint a giant pink daisy on one of the walls in her room when I got back.

"Of course," I promise. "I love you, lolabug."

"I love you too, Marlow." Lola jumps up from under the covers, wraps her little arms around my neck and presses a kiss to my cheek.

I cling to her tightly, committing this moment to memory. Saying goodbye to her is one of the hardest things I've ever had to do, and I'll be counting down the days until I have her back in my arms.

———

The drive to the hotel is quiet. Dylan booked a suite, wanting us to have an uninterrupted night together, free from any distractions.

When we finally get to our room, he drops our bags in the entryway and takes hold of my hand. He leads me past a lavish sitting area and through the master bedroom, bypassing the king-sized bed, heading straight for the door leading to the bathroom. Once he turns on the light, he lifts me onto the white marble countertop and leans in to gently kiss the tip of my nose.

"Dylan, what are you doing?"

"You've had a stressful day, so we're going to take a relaxing bath."

I nod. As long as I get to spend the rest of the night with him, that's all that matters.

"That's my girl," he commends. "Stay right there while I fill up the tub."

This moment reminds me of when he took care of me when I was sick. His selfless act opened my heart to the possibility that we could be something more. It's incredible to look back and see how far we've come since then.

Dylan might think of me as the color in his life, but he's the brush-stroke and the canvas in mine.

He goes to the freestanding tub and turns on the faucet. As the water rises, he drops in a lavender bath bomb.

When he redirects his attention to me, I crook my finger, motioning for him to come closer. I let out a shuddered exhale as he advances toward me, his determination clear. This is the last night we'll have together until I get back from Paris, and neither of us are going to take it for granted.

He positions himself between my legs, firmly gripping my hip with one hand, tilting my chin with the other. His chocolate brown eyes mirror the longing in mine, conveying our deep-seated desire.

"I love you, sunshine." The declaration spills freely from his lips. "You own my heart and soul, and I'll spend the rest of my life showing you how much you mean to me. No matter the distance between us, you're mine. Now and forever," he vows.

This might not be the first time he's said those three little words, but they hold a new meaning. I'm with a man who loves me unconditionally. A man who is giving me the chance to spread my wings and will be there waiting when I'm ready to fly home to him.

"I love you too, Dylan," I whisper. "Always."

"You going to miss my cock, sweetheart?" He leans in to nibble the shell of my ear.

"Yes," I groan. My panties are wet just thinking about it.

He plants a sensual kiss on my lips before stepping back, and I grumble in protest.

"Don't worry. I'll be fucking you until you're begging me to stop." He stands up straight, a sly smirk plastered on his face.

I'll never get enough of this man.

"Let's get you out of these clothes," he says.

He lifts my right arm, pulling it through the sleeve of my shirt before repeating the same process with my left. He drags the shirt over my head, tossing it into the corner. His hands are back on me within seconds as he unclasps my bra. I'm sorely disappointed when he doesn't pay my breasts any attention.

Instead, he gently grabs my wrists, tugging me to a standing position, and effortlessly unbuttons my jeans. He pulls them down and traces his fingers up my thigh until he gets to my panties, dragging them down my legs.

"I'm keeping these," he states, setting them on the counter.

I can't stand the clinical way he's undressing me when what I want is for him to tear my clothes off and fuck me into oblivion. I'll lose my mind if he doesn't give me more—and fast.

"Dylan, I *need* you, please."

"Be my good girl and take what I give you."

I'm practically drooling when he takes his shirt off, revealing his toned rock-solid chest. His breath hitches when I lean forward, tracing every definition of his abs. As I trail my finger toward his V-line, he moves back, stripping out of the rest of his clothes.

"Dylan?" I moan in frustration.

"Patience, sunshine."

He works his hand up and down his thick shaft. I'm mesmerized as he strokes, starting at the bottom and reaching the tip, smearing the drop of pre-cum over the crown of his dick.

"Watch what you fucking do to me, sunshine." He glances down at his erect cock as he moves his hand faster up and down his shaft. His eyes are sinfully dark, his jaw tense, his nostrils flaring. He looks wild, uninhibited and all mine.

His dark brown eyes sear into me, like he's marking me in more ways than one, only leaving my face long enough to look down to where his cock is aimed. He groans as he angles himself at my entrance, ropes of cum spurting onto my bare skin as he finds his release. One hand coaxes every last drop from the head of his cock, the other smearing it along my exposed thighs and pussy. Like he's the artist, and I'm now the painting.

A glorious and depraved masterpiece.

"You're my messy girl," he murmurs before he crashes his mouth to mine, pressing a passionate kiss to my lips.

His cock is still hard as he wipes the tip around in his cum on my skin, before pushing inside me in a single, deep thrust, his patience long gone.

Oh. My. God.

"I'm going to miss this perfect pussy of yours," he says in a guttural tone.

I wind my hands around his neck, tangling my fingers in his hair as he pushes in and out in deep, steady thrusts, savoring the moment. I moan in delight, relishing the fact that I'm stuffed full of his big dick.

"More, Dylan. Please, give me more," I beg.

He grips my chin with his hand while he relentlessly pounds into me. "Who do you belong to?"

"You," I mewl.

"That's right. You're mine."

"Always." I caress his cheek.

"Damn straight. Now ask me if you can come."

"Please let me come, Dylan," I cry out, desperate for relief.

"Show me how you play with your clit," he orders.

His eyes blaze with lust as he watches me roll my clit between my fingers, pinching it when I need something more to send me over the edge. Soon we're both barreling toward our release.

"Oh god, I'm going to…"

I throw my head back as my orgasm crashes over me, riding the euphoric wave for as long as I can. Dylan holds me close as we both come down from our heightened state.

"That's my girl." He presses a kiss to my lips. "Damn, I forgot that I promised you a bath," he mutters before he slowly pulls out of me.

Once he's refilled the bathtub, he helps me into the piping hot water and settles behind me. I welcome the accompanying sting, letting the heat soak through my tense muscles. The smell of lavender envelops the room with a sense of tranquility.

I lean back against Dylan's chest as he wraps his arms around me.

Every muscle in my body relaxes as his lips graze my shoulder. He presses featherlight kisses against each freckle as he whispers in my ear, "Don't forget, sunshine, you're mine."

"And you're mine," I vow.

———

"Maybe this is a mistake." I adjust the strap of my backpack over my shoulder.

"Whoa, hold on a minute." Dylan guides me to a quieter spot off the walkway of the airport, out of the way of other travelers heading to the security checkpoint.

"It hasn't even been twenty-four hours and I already miss Lola and Waffles. How am I going to go three months without seeing them?" I ask with a hint of vulnerability.

"Trust me." He tucks a piece of hair behind my ear. "You're going to have an incredible time in Paris and you'll be so busy you won't have time to miss us. Plus, we're going to video chat every day and before you know it, you'll be back home where you belong."

I love the sound of calling Aspen Grove my home.

"Before I forget, I packed you this yesterday." He holds up a unicorn lunch bag.

I burst out laughing as I take it from him. "I'm flying first class, remember? I'm sure they'll have plenty of snacks."

Dylan wanted me to take the Stafford Holdings jet to Paris, but I declined. He said the next best thing was flying first class and wouldn't back down until I agreed.

"Do they have Cheez-Its and Frosted Strawberry Pop-Tarts?" He smirks.

I point at the bag. "Please tell me that's what you put in here."

"You'll have to wait and find out," he says playfully. "God, I'm going to miss you so damn much."

He leans forward, molding his mouth to mine, his tongue passing my lips. He grasps my jaw in his hand, deepening our kiss. Time seems to stand still as we stay wrapped in our private bubble, not caring about passersby or our surroundings. We're just two people head over heels in love, finding it hard to say goodbye, even if it's a temporary separation.

When he finally pulls back, he rests his forehead against mine. "I love you, sunshine."

"I love you."

"You better go or you're going to miss your flight." He motions toward the security checkpoint.

I throw my arms around his neck for one last hug, choking back tears when I have to step away. Glancing back, I laugh when I find him blowing me kisses.

God, I love him so much it hurts.

As I'm waiting in line for security, I take out the unicorn bag to see what's inside and find a yellow sticky note on top.

Morning, sunshine,

I love you & am so proud of you. I can't wait until you're back in my arms.
-Dylan

Tears trickle down my cheeks. I can only hope that I've made the right decision and that even though it won't be easy, Dylan and I will grow closer because of this experience.

CHAPTER THIRTY-FOUR

DYLAN

It's only been a week since Marlow left, and I miss her so much.

Saying goodbye to her at the airport was one of the hardest things I've ever done. I cried on the way home, unable to control my emotions—however, I'll never admit that to anyone.

In the days leading up to Marlow's departure, her face lit up whenever she spoke about the residency program and how excited she was about this opportunity. Seeing her enthusiasm makes all the difficulties that come with it worth it.

For the most part, Lola and Waffles are holding up better than I expected. Granted, it's only been a week, and Lola asks me every day when Marlow's coming back, and Waffles whines at the front door, confused why she hasn't come to take him home to their pink house.

The first night, I attempted to get Waffles to sleep in his dog bed in the living room, but after hours of his whining, I eventually caved. Now he sleeps with Lola. I have to admit, they're damn cute when they're snuggled up together in Lola's bed.

The most challenging part of our situation is navigating the six-hour time difference and finding windows in our busy schedules to connect.

I check my watch to see that it's 5:15 a.m., which means 11:15

a.m. in Paris. Marlow should be on a break right now, according to the schedule she sent me. I try calling her twice, but she doesn't answer. A few minutes later, she sends me a text.

MARLOW

I'm sorry I missed your call. I had to go back to my apartment in between classes to grab some paint supplies, and now I'm running late.

Did you eat breakfast?

MARLOW

Do Cheez-Its and a croissant count?

Please tell me that's not all you've had to eat today.

MARLOW

I plead the fifth.

Did you lock your front door?

MARLOW

I did. 😊 I'm walking into class now. I'll talk to you later. I love you! 🥰

Love you too, sunshine. 🩶

———

It's been over twenty-four hours since I've talked to Marlow, and I'm feeling irritable.

I'm working from home today, and it's depressing whenever I glance at her house and see her empty studio. The silence is suffocating, making me miss the sound of her playlist as I watch her hips sway to the beat of the music. I'm hard just thinking about her in those tight yoga pants and what I wouldn't give to watch her fall apart beneath me right now.

My phone rings, and I immediately answer the video chat when I see who it is.

"Hey, sunshine."

Marlow's smiling face greets me. She's styled her hair in a halo braid, and she's wearing her floral overalls with a pastel tie-dye shirt underneath. Next to her is an easel displaying a canvas with a partially painted flower.

God, I miss her so much.

"Hi," she sighs in relief. "I'm so glad I caught you."

This time of day is a gamble, depending on my meeting schedule and if I'm working from home or flying to and from the city. Tonight Lola's with my parents since I had to work late.

I glance at my watch to see that it's 12:30 a.m. in Paris.

"What are you doing up so late?"

"I was practicing a new technique I learned in class today and lost track of time. I figured I'd try to call you before I went to bed."

She has a smudge of red paint on her nose, and I'd give anything to be there in person to wipe it off and re-create the scene from her studio.

"How are your classes going?"

"Oh, Dylan, they're incredible," Marlow gushes. "It's only been a week, and I've already learned so much. It's a dream come true." She pauses as a guilty expression crosses her face.

I hold my finger up to the camera. "None of that," I warn. "You're where you're supposed to be, and I'm so damn proud of you. Now tell me, did you remember to eat dinner tonight?"

"I had the most incredible Boeuf Bourguignon tonight, thanks to you," she says.

After she told me she was eating Cheez-Its for breakfast, I reached out to a client of Stafford Holdings who owns multiple restaurants in Paris. I arranged for regular meal deliveries to Marlow's apartment, complete with handwritten sticky notes I overnighted so they could include them in the delivery.

While I can't be there in person to care for Marlow, I'm committed to showing her she is cherished and loved, even when I'm thousands of miles away.

"Anything for you, sweetheart." I watch as she chews on her lower lip, a sign that she's usually nervous or has something she wants to talk about. "What are you thinking?"

"About how much I miss you."

"Why don't you show me?" I suggest with a smirk.

Since she's been gone, we haven't had a private moment, and I think we're both desperate for each other.

Her cheeks flush before she hurries to the other side of the room to get another easel. She places it at the foot of her bed and sets the phone on it, giving me the perfect view as she unfastens the buttons of her overalls. I watch as she slowly tugs them down over her hips. They fall to the floor and she steps out of them.

My cock twitches as she lifts her shirt over her head and tosses it to the ground.

"Fuck, you're a goddamn vision," I groan, taking in her lacy blue bra and green panties.

"I wish you were here in person," she murmurs.

"Me too, sunshine, more than anything." *So much that it hurts.* "Why don't you show me what I'm missing?" I coax her.

She smirks at the camera as she unfastens her bra, revealing her luscious breasts for me. I wish I were there to put one of her pert nipples in my mouth, tugging and biting as she cries out from the overload of sensations.

"Did you get your present that I packed for you?"

"Uh-huh," she nods. "It's right here."

She gives me an obscene view of her ass as she bends over to retrieve the pink vibrator I put in her suitcase before she left. When she turns around, she's holding the device up with a smile.

"Lie down on the bed so I can see that pretty pussy of yours," I order.

Marlow crawls onto the mattress and lies down on her back. She takes a pillow, tucks it under her hips, and spreads her legs so I can see her pussy is already wet for me.

"Damn, you're sexy. Play with your nipples."

She grabs a breast with each hand, cupping them tightly. She tugs and pinches on her nipples like I would if I were there, except she's not giving them enough pressure.

"Pinch harder," I command.

She squeezes her nipple firmer between her fingers, and her mouth parts open in a surprised gasp.

"Oh god, that feels so good," she cries.

While she plays with her breasts, I yank open my desk drawer and take out the pair of panties I kept from our night at the hotel before she left. I unbutton my pants and take my cock out with a sense of urgency.

"Take the vibrator and slide it into that dripping wet cunt of yours."

As she pushes the device inside herself, I wrap the panties around my shaft and stroke it in slow, steady pumps. I let out a sharp hiss when the lace rubs against my skin, sending a shock of arousal through my veins.

"Close your eyes, sweetheart." I pause, as I watch her pleasure herself with the vibrator. "Imagine I'm there, kneeling in front of you, my hands gripping your thighs." The pace of her breathing picks up as she turns up the speed on the device. "I'm licking your pussy with my tongue as I play with those pretty little nipples of yours." I squeeze my cock harder as I watch her push the vibrator in and out of her cunt in even strokes. "When you're writhing beneath me, begging for me to let you come, I pinch your clit between my fingers until you fall over the edge."

"Oh, Dylan," she pants out.

"Harder. Fuck yourself harder."

I'm mesmerized as she quickens her pace, and with her other hand she pinches her clit just as I described. Her back arches off the bed as she cries out in ecstasy, chasing her release. I let out a low groan, placing my hand against my desk, jerking off like a horny teenager. My own release hits me like a freight train, cum shooting onto my stomach.

Marlow pulls the vibrator out of herself and tosses it aside. Her head falls back on her pillow as she murmurs incoherently.

"My beautiful, messy girl," I murmur. "I love you so damn much, sunshine."

"I love you too, Dylan," she whispers.

Only eighty-three days until Marlow comes home, but who's counting?

CHAPTER THIRTY-FIVE

MARLOW

I roll out my shoulders and stretch my arms. It's been a long day of painting, and I haven't taken a break in hours.

Most days, I'm in class from 8:00 a.m. until 6:00 p.m. on weekdays, and I spend the weekends locked in my small apartment practicing the techniques I've learned. The other artists in the program explore the city or nearby countries during their free time. They're world travelers, never settling in one place.

I used to share a similar view, but my perspective has shifted. Now, my heart longs to be back in Aspen Grove, where a particularly grumpy single dad and his little girl are waiting for me to come home. And while this has been a truly remarkable experience, once it's over, I don't plan on ever leaving them again.

I pick up my phone to video chat with Dylan. It's 7:00 p.m. there, and he should be home from the office and making dinner.

"Hey, sunshine," he answers. "How come you're up so late?"

He leans his phone against something so I can see him while he chops vegetables at the kitchen counter.

"Inspiration struck before I could go to bed, and I had to start this new Dahlia painting that I haven't been able to stop thinking about."

"I'm glad you called," he says with a smile.

Dylan pushes his glasses up his nose, and I'm captivated by his sexiness. His disheveled hair makes me long to be in the same room with him, so I can run my hands through it as I pull him in for a searing kiss. The first two buttons of his dress shirt are undone, giving me a glimpse of his chest. We have phone sex almost every day, but it's nothing compared to the real deal.

"Daddy, Waffles did something bad," I hear Lola shout, accompanied by Waffles barking.

"What now," Dylan grumbles, running his hand across his face.

He places the knife he was using to chop vegetables on the counter, grabs his phone, and rushes up to Lola's room, stopping abruptly in her doorway. When he turns the phone around to show the craft corner I set up for Lola before I left, I have to cover my mouth to stifle a laugh.

Lola, Waffles, and everything around them is completely covered in shimmering pink and purple glitter.

"Fu—dge," Dylan corrects himself. "Ladybug, what happened?"

"Waffles wanted to make Marlow a picture because he misses her so much, and when I opened the jar of glitter, it exploded." She throws her hands up in the air for emphasis.

"I see," he says calmly. "And where exactly did you find glitter?"

"It was in my new arts and crafts cabinet that Marlow got me," Lola chirps.

Oops.

Before I left, I wanted to do something special for her, so I set up a complete craft station in her room so she could color and make art without having to go downstairs. I may have gotten carried away and bought her a variety of glitter since she loves it so much. It didn't occur to me she might use it without supervision.

Dylan turns the phone to face me with a raised brow.

"I'm so sorry." I chew anxiously on my lower lip. "I can see now that the glitter might not have been the best idea I've ever had."

"It's oka—"

"Is that Marlow?" Lola squeals, interrupting Dylan.

I can hear her scrambling off her chair and running toward him. Dylan's abrupt movement with the phone suggests she's trying to grab it with glitter-covered hands.

"Whoa, ladybug," he says gently. "You can say hello, but I'm going to keep the phone, okay?"

He crouches down and holds his phone out so Lola and I can see each other.

"Marlow, hi." She gives me a toothless grin. "I miss you so much. Has it been three months yet?"

I'm overwhelmed by a wave of emotion, and I don't have the heart to tell her it's only been one month. She lost both her front teeth, and Johanna took her for a haircut yesterday. I hate missing all these important milestones, making me feel guilty for being across the world when I should be home with my little girl. I may not be her biological mother, but in all the ways that count, I consider her mine.

"I'll be home before you know it, lolabug." I muster a smile.

Waffles lets out a bark, and I can hear his panting, followed by his nose pressing against the camera.

"Hey, boy. I miss you too," I croon.

We've been inseparable since the day I brought him home from the shelter, and being apart for so long has been incredibly challenging. Despite the guilt I have for leaving him behind, there's no one else I'd rather him be with than Lola and Dylan.

"Lola, why don't you and Waffles head into the bathroom?" Dylan suggests. "I'll be there in a minute to help get you washed up."

"Okay, Daddy. I love you, Marlow." Lola waves goodbye.

"I love you too, lolabug," I call out after her with misty eyes.

Once she and Waffles have left the room, Dylan turns the

camera back to himself, his face etched with concern as if he can read my mind.

"Should I come home early?" I blurt out. "I shouldn't have left you alone with Lola and Waffles, especially considering how busy work is for you."

Stafford Holdings began construction on the Vanburen development, so Dylan has been putting in long hours.

He's been working from home more frequently, and his parents have been watching Lola in the mornings and afternoons until I get back. They've been equally supportive as Dylan, and I couldn't be more grateful.

"Sweetheart, I'm fine," he reassures me. "I will hold the fort down until you're back. I promise."

"But what about the mess?" I point to the glitter-covered portion of Lola's room.

"It's just glitter. I've had plenty of experience cleaning up messes. I'll survive this one," he says with a chuckle. "You need to stay and learn as much as you can, because when you get back, I can't promise that I'll ever let you go again."

I hope he never does.

How did I get so lucky to find someone so remarkable? His caring nature, thoughtfulness, and unwavering support for my dreams is beyond compare.

"Daddy, Waffles got soap all over his head," Lola cries from the bathroom.

"Oh dear, you better go," I hurry out. "I love you, Dylan."

"I love you too, sunshine."

After he ends the call, I'm hit with a wave of nostalgia. I want to be there to help clean up all the messes, to watch Waffles and Lola chase each other around the kitchen before dinner, and curl up next to Dylan as he reads to Lola before bed. It's the little moments that I miss the most, and I can't wait for the day I'm able to be a part of them again.

CHAPTER THIRTY-SIX

MARLOW

"Hey, Dylan, it's me again. Please call me back as soon as you can." I hang up, anxiously tapping my finger against my lips as I walk down the street toward my apartment.

I've been a nervous wreck all day. Dylan sends me a text when he wakes up every morning, and we usually squeeze in a video chat before he starts work. However, he hasn't reached out today, and I'm worried something happened to him or Lola.

I tried checking in with Johanna, but she hasn't responded to my messages either.

If anyone in Aspen Grove has any information, it would be Quinn.

"Hey, stranger," she answers in a singsong voice. "Only one more week. God, it feels like you've been gone for ages. Andi and I can't wait until you're back. Brunch isn't the same without you."

"Have you seen Dylan or Lola?" I cut right to the chase, tightening my grip on my floral tote.

"Marlow, what's wrong? You sound upset."

"I haven't been able to reach Dylan or his mom, and I'm worried something is wrong." I dodge a passerby who's jogging past me, barely missing hitting him with the canvas tucked under my arm. "Have you heard any news?"

"Johanna stopped by Brush & Palette on her way to Brew Haven this morning, but everything seemed fine."

My shoulders slump forward, and I let out a sigh.

"Okay, well if you—" I stop when I hear a child's voice calling my name. When I hear it again, I turn around, and sure enough, Lola's bounding down the street toward me. Pigtails flying. She's a ray of sunshine in a bright yellow jumper with a short-sleeved white shirt underneath and silver sneakers that match mine.

"Marlow, are you there? Please tell me your surprise finally arrived," Quinn says, full of excitement.

"You knew about this?"

"Yeah. Dylan and I needed something to talk about at the Family Craft Corner class, considering gossip has been pretty scarce since you've been gone," she teases. "Now, enough chitchat. Go spend time with your family." She doesn't wait for my response before hanging up.

My family. I love the sound of that.

Dylan and I may have taken an unconventional path and hit road bumps along the way. Still, our relationship has flourished over the past three months, and I'm genuinely excited for what the future holds.

My heart nearly bursts with joy when I lay my eyes on Dylan, his arms loaded with backpacks and suitcases. He's jogging alongside Lola but stops briefly to push his glasses up on his nose. He's positively mouthwatering in his black crewneck T-shirt, light wash jeans, and gray sneakers. *And he's all mine.*

"What are you doing here?" I shout as they get closer.

I drop all my art supplies on the sidewalk when Lola sprints toward me, opening my arms wide as she throws her arms around my neck. I lift her off the ground and twirl her around in a circle.

"Marlow," she exclaims.

Tears threaten to spill as I hold *my* little girl in my arms after three months of separation. I'm never letting her out of my sight again.

"I'm so glad you're here, lolabug," I say as I stroke her hair.

Dylan drops their bags next to my art supplies before enveloping us in a warm embrace. He presses his nose into my hair, inhaling deeply. "I missed you so damn much," he murmurs.

"I missed you too. Why didn't you tell me you were coming?" My voice trembles with shock. "Is the rest of your family here?"

He shakes his head. "No. I wanted to spend quality time alone with my girls." He presses a tender kiss on my forehead. "Waffles is in Aspen Grove, staying with my parents."

"I was concerned when I couldn't reach you or your mom."

"I'm sorry for making you worry. My dad probably wouldn't let my mom answer. She's terrible at keeping secrets and would have spilled the beans if she talked to you." He chuckles.

"That's alright." I nuzzle closer to his chest to make sure he's really here. "I'm so glad you're here.

"Me too, sunshine. Me too."

———

"Come on, Marlow. We have to hurry." Lola tugs on my arm, practically pulling me up the stairs.

"Slow down, lolabug," I urge her. "We have plenty of time, I promise."

Dylan planned their trip to make sure they arrived in Paris on a Friday, giving us the full weekend to explore the city.

When we reach the top of the steps, Lola lets go of my hand, weaving between other tourists to get to the scenic overlook. She grasps the chain-link fence, and her eyes fill with wonder as she

271

takes in the scenery. I step up behind her, gasping at the stunning view of Paris below.

From here, we can see the Seine gracefully winding its way through the heart of Paris, with the Arc de Triomphe and the Notre Dame Cathedral off in the distance.

"Wow," Lola says with disbelief. "I can't believe I'm at the Eiffel Tower just like Madeline." Clutched to her chest is the copy of her favorite book she insisted on bringing with her.

On the way here, she asked Dylan to take a photo of her in the street near the Eiffel Tower so she had a picture similar to the one on the cover of *Madeline*. This is a trip she's going to remember for years to come. So will I.

There's nothing better than sharing these priceless moments of happiness with the two people I love most, and this is only the beginning.

While Dylan gave Lola a bath last night, I tried calling my parents. We haven't talked since before my art exhibition in New York. They didn't pick up, but I left a voicemail. I told them about Dylan and Lola, and how we'd love for them to come visit us in Aspen Grove. There's no guarantee they'll ever take me up on my offer, but I'll always hold out hope that someday they'll come around.

Regardless, I'll be okay. I'm incredibly fortunate to have found family and friends who will brave any storm by my side and who love me unconditionally.

As Lola and I take in the view, Dylan wraps himself around me, pressing his nose against my neck. Goosebumps travel up my arms at his touch, and I lean back, inhaling his heady scent of mint and cedar. He plants soft kisses along the column of my neck, slowly making his way up to the shell of my ear.

"What do you think?" he whispers, motioning to our surroundings.

"It's absolutely beautiful." I tilt my head to look him in the eyes. "But I much prefer Aspen Grove."

His eyes widen in surprise. "Really?"

"Really," I say confidently.

I'm looking forward to getting back and starting the next chapter of our lives together.

CHAPTER THIRTY-SEVEN

DYLAN

Lola holds my hand as we climb down the steps of the private jet, letting go as soon as her feet touch the tarmac.

"Gigi, Papa," she exclaims as she runs towards my parents.

I turn around and reach out my hand to help Marlow down the last couple of stairs, clasping her hand tightly in mine. She seems surprised to see my family here to welcome us home. The only people missing are Jack and Presley. They're visiting next month for family pictures, and my mom is thrilled at the prospect of having everyone gathered under one roof for a few days.

It's hard to believe that Marlow is really back in Aspen Grove. I've been counting down to this moment for the last three months.

We spent the past week soaking up every minute we had in Paris. The weekend was spent sightseeing, and on the days Marlow had class, Lola and I explored.

In the evenings, after Lola went to bed, Marlow and I stayed up well into the early morning hours. She's been fucking insatiable since we reunited, and I've thoroughly enjoyed worshiping every inch of her body, making up for lost time.

Thank god, she agreed to move in with me because I need her in my bed every night from now on, no exceptions.

The next time she wants to go to Paris or anywhere else, we can go as a family because I can't bear the idea of being apart from her again.

"Oh, Marlow, we're so happy you're home," my mom gushes, pulling her in for a hug.

"It's so good to be back," she says, grinning from ear to ear.

"Welcome home." My dad gives her a side hug as he holds Lola in his arms.

"You've got to be kidding me," I mutter when I see Cash holding up a sign that reads World's Best Dog Trainer. Harrison stands beside him with a smirk on his lips as he holds back Waffles from darting toward Marlow.

What are they up to?

"Oh my gosh, did you finally train Waffles?" Marlow asks me when she sees the sign.

It's a topic of conversation I avoided while she was in Paris.

"Sure, if you count teaching him to sit," Cash playfully mocks. "Why don't you show her, Dylan?"

Harrison gives me an amused look as he walks towards us with Waffles leading the way. When they get closer, I block Waffles' view of Marlow, so I have his undivided attention.

"Waffles, sit," I command, raising my hand like we've practiced.

After the third try, I'm relieved when he actually stops. However, instead of sitting down like I've taught him, he sniffs the air and spins in a circle, chasing his tail.

What the hell?

"Um, Dylan, I think you broke my dog," Marlow says as she peeks over my shoulder.

When Cash and Harrison erupt into laughter, my suspicions are confirmed that they're up to something. Sure enough, when I look closer, I spot a piece of a dog treat loosely tied to the end of Waffles' tail.

I crouch beside him, placing my hand on his back to settle him down as I untie the treat from his tail and bring it up to his nose.

"Waffles sit," I order again with my hand held out.

He tilts his head as if contemplating whether it's worth complying before sitting on his haunches.

Marlow rushes over to kneel down next to me and Waffles jumps in her lap, yipping with excitement.

"I'm so proud of you, boy," she croons as she scratches him behind the ears.

I clear my throat. "What about me?"

"You want a good scratch behind the ear too?" she taunts, sending both my brothers into another round of laughter.

God, it's so good to have her home.

I squeeze Marlow's hand as we pull into my driveway.

"Dylan, wow." She gestures to the daisies, lilies, and dahlias I planted in the front yard. "They're all so beautiful," she gushes.

"I know how much you like to have real flowers around when you paint. I figured having a variety right outside your window would make for good inspiration."

"Thank you." She leans across the console to hug me.

"Daddy, can Waffles and I go play in the backyard?" Lola asks.

"Yeah, sure, ladybug."

"Oh goodie. Come on, Waffles." Lola scrambles out of the car, and Waffles chases after her.

Lola walks right past the gate leading to the backyard toward a particular section of the wooden fence.

"What is she doing?" Marlow asks.

"I'm not sure, but we're about to find out," I say.

Waffles nudges against the wooden panels, and three of them

swing upward like a doggy door, allowing Lola to follow behind him.

Marlow bursts out laughing and looks over at me. "That explains how Waffles was getting into your backyard."

I rub my hand across my face, realizing that I never checked the fence panels to see if any were loose. I don't think I've ever shown Lola how to open the gate; I just assumed she knew. We usually go through the garage or the backdoor.

"Why don't we go inside?" I suggest to Marlow.

"I'd like that." She smiles.

I go around to her side and open her car door for her. She squeals when I lift her into my arms and carry her to the house.

"Welcome home, sunshine," I say as I carry her over the threshold.

Never before have I spoke words that sound sweeter.

"There's nowhere else I'd rather be," she says as she cups my cheek with her hand, kissing me fervently on the lips.

I used to view the world in black and white. I prided myself on maintaining a strict schedule and followed a carefully planned regimen. Now, shoes are scattered across the floor, there's a giant fort in the living room, and a dozen small canvases featuring brightly colored flowers hanging on the wall in the entryway. Marlow mailed us one each week she was away, and Lola was excited every time we put a new one on the wall.

When Marlow fell into my life—quite literally—she brought with her a new perspective. She taught me how to step outside of my comfort zone and to live in the moment. Because of her, I now see the world around me in technicolor, and it's a beautiful thing.

Getting a new neighbor didn't turn out anything as I expected, but now I know what happens when a single dad gets a nanny for his daughter...

She becomes their whole universe.

EPILOGUE
DYLAN

It's been a month since Marlow got back from Paris, and every day has been better than the last. Things get chaotic with two adults, a kid, and an energetic dog in the house, but I wouldn't trade this life of mine for anything.

Marlow decided to keep her pink house for now, not ready to part ways with it just yet. She still uses her studio when she paints, and I rather enjoy having a front-row view of her from my office when she does.

Gavin was ecstatic when Marlow told him she was working on a new art exhibition. It will be a collection of ten pieces inspired by the flowers in our front yard. However, she's waiting to set a date until she's completed most of the pieces.

Her main priority right now is making the most of Lola's summer vacation.

She tossed a shoe at me when I suggested we hire a part-time nanny for the next couple of months, so she's not overwhelmed. Marlow told me that we weren't having anyone else take care of *our* daughter when she was more than capable. It means everything that she considers Lola her own, and I worshiped every inch of her body that night to show her just how much.

I did convince her to let my parents watch Lola one day a week, so she has free time to paint and visit her friends.

The Vanburen development is well underway, and I recently hired another senior analyst to take over some of my day-to-day job responsibilities. I needed more time with my family.

Like tonight. We were watching *Frozen*—Lola's latest obsession—as a family. However, it seems I'm the only one who stayed awake during the entire film.

I'm on the edge of the bed with Marlow and Lola taking up most of the space. Lola is snuggled against Marlow, one hand draped across her stomach and the other tucked against her chest. Waffles has made himself at home on my memory foam pillow. He raises his head like he can sense me staring, and I swear he gives me a smug expression.

He's rarely allowed in our room, but I can be persuaded when my girls give me *that* look. Besides, I admit during Marlow's absence that I developed a soft spot for him, and it helps that he's learned to roll over *and* shake in the last month.

Careful not to wake anyone, I quietly get out of bed and go around to the other side to scoop Lola into my arms. She nuzzles into my chest as I carry her to her room, with Waffles following close behind.

Her room looks like a rainbow exploded. The newest additions are paintings on two of her walls—a rainbow with a unicorn sitting on top and a giant pink daisy.

I gently place Lola in her bed and pull the covers up around her. Waffles hops onto the mattress and settles in next to her.

"I love you, lolabug." I press a kiss to her temple.

"Goodnight, Waffles," I say, giving him a pat on the head.

When I get back to our bedroom, Marlow is still in the middle of the mattress, her mouth slightly parted as she sleeps.

She's so damn beautiful.

I lie down next to her and pull her close. She gives a little stretch before draping her arm across my chest, tangling her leg with mine and resting her head on my shoulder.

"Is everything okay?" she murmurs, still half asleep.

Everything is perfect.

———

"Where is your brother?" My mom anxiously paces the entryway. "He knows better than to be late."

"I'm sure he'll be here soon," I assure her.

I pull out my phone and send another text message to Cash. He was in London this past week but was supposed to fly back yesterday. Presley and Harrison are standing nearby, both trying to reach him too.

My mom has been eagerly anticipating having new family photos taken to include Jack, Marlow, and Waffles. If Cash doesn't show up, we'll all pay the price.

I'm about to text him again when he comes barreling through the front door, all out of breath, like he just sprinted a marathon.

"Where have you been?" Presley demands, pointing at the clock on the wall. "We've tried calling you a dozen times, but it goes straight to voicemail."

"You're late," my mom echoes. "You know how important this is to me."

"Sorry. Our flight was delayed, and I came straight here from the airfield," he rushes out.

"You were supposed to fly back from London yesterday," Harrison says, studying him suspiciously.

"Yeah, well, something held me up… or should I say, someone." His tone is cryptic.

"What are you talking—" Presley cuts herself off as she points to the ring on Cash's finger. "What is that?" she asks with a gasp.

"My wedding ring."

"I'm sorry, your what?" she screeches.

"I got married." Cash shrugs casually. "My wife is on a

conference call, but she will come inside as soon as she's finished. You don't mind if we wait for her, do you, Mom?"

She gapes at him in shock.

"Your *wife?*" Presley laughs. "Very funny, Cash. Who put you up to this?" She turns her glacier stare on Jack. "Was it you?"

He holds his hands up in defense. "I know better than to play practical jokes on you, little vixen."

"What about you two?" She glares at Harrison and me. "Because this joke is even less funny than the time you had Jack arrested."

I hold my hands up in defense. "It wasn't me."

Harrison shakes his head. "I had nothing to do with this."

Cash places his hand on Presley's shoulder. "I'm serious, sis. We flew to Vegas last night and got hitched. We came straight to Aspen Grove after, so we could share the good news with our families."

"Are you out of your mind?" my mom interjects, smacking him upside the head. "You got married and didn't invite your own mother? Shame on you," she scolds him.

You've got to be kidding me.

I pinch the bridge of my nose, trying to maintain my patience. Of course Mom doesn't see the problem with Cash getting married, even though just last week he wasn't dating anyone.

"Oh, here she is now," Cash says enthusiastically.

Harrison and I exchange confused glances when Everly Townstead walks through my parents' front door with a giant diamond on her ring finger.

"Oh, Everly," my mother exclaims. "Welcome to the family, sweetheart."

She pulls her into a big hug, and I don't miss the glare Everly shoots Cash as he smirks back at her.

Things just got interesting.

———

Want to see what happens when Dylan's proposal to Marlow takes an unexpected turn? Find out how she reacts to another very important question Dylan and Lola have for her! Type this link into your browser to read the extended epilogue for *If You Give a Single Dad a Nanny*: https://bookhip.com/KHVTCCN

———

Thank you for taking the time to read *If You Give a Single Dad a Nanny*. If you enjoyed this book, please consider leaving a review on your preferred platform(s) of choice. It's the best compliment I can receive as an author, and it makes it easier for other readers to find my books.

ACKNOWLEDGMENTS

There are so many people who made this book possible, and I can't thank you all enough for your love, kindness, and support. *If You Give a Single Dad a Nanny* wouldn't have been possible without each and every one of you.

To my readers—For rooting for me from the very beginning and motivating me to keep writing even on the days I think this might be all for nothing.

To my ARC team—Even before you saw the cover, read the book, or fell in love with Dylan and Marlow's love story, you gave *If You Give a Single Dad a Nanny* a chance. Thank you for all your thoughtful messages, posts, stories, reviews, and comments. Your endless love and support never ceases to amaze me.

To Bryanna, Tabitha, and Becca—Words cannot adequately express my gratitude for you. Thanks for putting up with my endless DMs, questions, and concerns. This story would never have made it down on paper without you cheering me on from the sidelines.

To Paula, Nicole and Victoria—I couldn't have asked for a better editing team. I'm grateful for your expertise and for pushing me to write a story worth reading.

To Ashleigh, Emily, Jess, and Madison—For being wonderful friends and collaborators. You make the day-to-day of being a writer so much more fun and far less lonely.

To Sarah—For designing the most adorable cover for this

book. It was love at first sight and it makes my heart so happy that my readers love it just as much as I do.

To Isabella, Salma, Caitlin, Wren, Alexia, Hunter, Izabela, Zae, Caroline, Lauren Brooke, Diana, Amy, Meghan, Jenna Lynn, and Claire—Your honest, detailed, and candid feedback drove me to create the best possible version of this book. Thank you!

To Sandea, Roxan, and Randy—You taught me to believe in myself and to chase my dreams, no matter the cost. I love you always.

To Kyler—Thank you for supporting my insane work schedule, for tolerating the endless amounts of takeout and piles of laundry that accrued in the months leading up to this book's launch, and for helping to make my dream of becoming a full-time author come true.

ALSO BY ANN EINERSON

ASPEN GROVE SERIES

If You Give a Grump a Holiday Wishlist - Holiday Novella

Cash & Everly's Book – Coming June 2024

THE SOVEREIGN KINGS SERIES

The Spotlight

STANDALONES

Forgive or Forget Me

ABOUT THE AUTHOR

Ann Einerson is the author of imperfect love stories that will keep you invested until the very last page.

Ann writes stubborn heroines who aren't afraid to put their moody men in their place. Each of Ann's books features a found family, an ode to her love of travel, and serves plenty of banter and spice. Her novels are inspired by the ample supply of sticky notes she always has on hand to jot down the stories that live rent-free in her mind.

When she's not writing, Ann enjoys spoiling her chatty pet chickens, listening to her dysfunctional playlists, and going for late-night runs on the treadmill. She lives in Michigan with her husband.

KEEP IN TOUCH WITH ANN EINERSON

Website:
www.anneinerson.com
Newsletter:
www.anneinerson.com/newsletter-signup
Instagram:
www.instagram.com/authoranneinerson
TikTok:
www.tiktok.com/@authoranneinerson
Amazon:
www.amazon.com/author/anneinerson
Goodreads:
www.goodreads.com/author/show/29752171.Ann_Einerson